HAPPILY EVER AMISH

Read more Shelley Shepard Gray in

Amish Christmas Twins

An Amish Second Christmas

Christmas at the Amish Bakeshop

NEW YORK TIMES AND
USA TODAY BESTSELLING AUTHOR

SHELLEY SHEPARD GRAY

HAPPILY EVER AMISH

www.kensingtonbooks.com

This book is a work of fiction. Names, characters, businesses, organizations, places, events, and incidents either are the product of the author's imagination or are used fictitiously. Any resemblance to actual persons, living or dead, events, or locales is entirely coincidental.

To the extent that the image or images on the cover of this book depict a person or persons, such person or persons are merely models, and are not intended to portray any character or characters featured in the book.

KENSINGTON BOOKS are published by

Kensington Publishing Corp.
119 West 40th Street
New York, NY 10018

All Kensington titles, imprints, and distributed lines are available at special quantity discounts for bulk purchases for sales promotion, premiums, fund-raising, educational, or institutional use. Special book excerpts or customized printings can also be created to fit specific needs. For details, write or phone the office of the Kensington Special Sales Manager: Attn. Special Sales Department. Kensington Publishing Corp, 119 West 40th Street, New York, NY 10018. Phone: 1-800-221-2647.

Library of Congress Card Catalogue Number: 2022939857

The K with book logo Reg. US Pat & TM Off.

ISBN: 978-1-4967-3982-7
First Kensington Hardcover Edition: November 2022

ISBN: 978-1-4967-3985-8 (trade)

ISBN: 978-1-4967-3988-9 (ebook)

10 9 8 7 6 5 4 3 2

Printed in the United States of America

Don't worry about tomorrow, for tomorrow will bring its own worries. Today's trouble is enough for today.

Matthew 6:34

Everything has its beauty—but not everyone sees it.

Amish proverb

Chapter 1

Daniel Miller was bored. It made no sense. Not really. It was Saturday night, there was no church in the morning, and he was standing with a group of longtime friends in the Troyers' backyard. Furthermore, he was holding a mug of hot chocolate, there was a bonfire keeping everyone warm and comfortable, and the sky was clear.

So, it was a good night. A nearly perfect one, really. However, he'd recently learned that valid reasons didn't always matter when feelings were involved. When all was said and done, strong emotions overruled most everything.

Or, in his case, the nagging sense of restlessness he couldn't seem to banish.

Looking around at the almost one hundred people listening to the laughter and stories that were being told, Daniel knew he should be entertained.

He wasn't, though. Not by a long shot. The fact of the matter was that Aaron and June's engagement party was a carbon copy of practically every other engagement party he'd been to before.

And Daniel had been to a lot of them in his twenty years of living.

As his best friend Roman started telling everyone a complicated story of mishaps that had happened during the last corn harvest, Daniel tuned him out. While the story was amusing, he'd heard it before. Instead, he scanned the crowd, looking for familiar faces.

Scanning crowds was an unfortunate habit he'd developed of late, an attempt to ease his restlessness and corral his interest. Oftentimes it was a rather successful activity. He'd usually spy someone new or a friend he hadn't seen in years. Or he'd catch sight of an acquaintance who looked in need of attention. When that was the case, he'd jump at the chance to visit with him or her.

Unfortunately, at the moment, even with a hundred people surrounding him, he wasn't finding anyone of interest.

As Roman's voice rose, nearing his punch line, Daniel bit back a sigh. If he couldn't find anyone else to chat with for a spell—well, then he wasn't going to stay much longer. There was no reason to stand around with the same group of people and listen to the same stories that he'd already heard many, many times.

He liked his friends, but he could only take so much.

The winter evening might be mild, the multitude of lit candles might be very pretty, and the occasion might be joyous . . . but he'd rather be home. If he were, he could be sitting on the couch with his feet propped up on the coffee table. He could be eating a grilled cheese sandwich next to his dog Bob. Bob was a mighty easy companion to be around.

His faithful dog was also probably watching out the window for him to return. Bob was a creature of habit and liked the house to be shut tight by nine, ten at the latest.

He really ought to be relieving Bob's anxiety soon.

When everyone laughed and a couple of folks slapped Roman on the back, it was obvious the story was over.

Everyone began to move away, heading toward the hot chocolate. Daniel sighed in relief. He could go now without causing a fuss.

"Who are you staring at, Daniel?"

He blinked, identifying the speaker. It was Bradley Park, their Mennonite buddy who not only drove a car but also worked at an RV factory near Kidron. "Hmm? Oh, no one."

"Come on. You were staring at something across the yard. What was it? Better yet, who was it?"

"I don't know." That was the truth. He might have been staring, but he'd been thinking about cheese sandwiches and Bob.

Still looking amused, Bradley grinned. "If you aren't gonna tell me, I'm going to figure it out myself."

"Bradley, there ain't nothing to see. Actually, I think I'm gonna head out. . . ."

"Hold on." Obviously his friend was feeling at loose ends, too, because he wouldn't give up his silly search. His voice rose. "Let's see now . . . I'm fairly sure you weren't scowling at old Lester and his cronies or the half dozen *kinner* playing hopscotch next to the lanterns. Nooo . . . I'm thinking something more interesting caught your eye."

Daniel felt like rolling his eyes. "Nothing caught my eye."

"Sure it did. I've known you all my life, remember? You and I sat next to each other in sixth grade."

"I haven't forgotten that." Or that Bradley never could name all the states and their capitals. Charleston, West Virginia, had always messed him up.

"Knowing you forever means I know when you're thinking hard about something." He waggled his eyebrows. "Or someone." Grinning, Bradley said, "I'm guessing you found someone you haven't seen in a while. You always do that, you know . . . look for people who are unfamiliar or different."

Daniel was flummoxed. Had he really been that obvious? Did people truly watch him watch crowds? "I wasn't doing that." Of course, that was a lie.

"Sure you were. No worries, though. We're all used to it."

"What are we used to?" asked Roman, another of his good friends. "What's going on?"

"I'm trying to guess who Daniel was looking at tonight," Bradley answered. "You know how he likes to watch people."

"Bradley's talking crazy. I wasn't doing that."

No one paid his words any mind. "If it's a guessing game, I'll play along," redheaded Ruthie said. Sounding amused, she added, "Let's see. I'm pretty sure Daniel wasn't scowling at Aaron and June—he's never that rude."

Rude? "I'm not—"

She continued. "Hmm. The couple sitting next to the fire pit doesn't look all that interesting either. What were their names again?"

"Eddie and Sylvia," Roman supplied as he scanned the crowd. "And I don't think Daniel was paying them any mind either." He folded his arms over his chest. "My guess is that our *gut* friend here was staring at a woman."

This conversation had gone from bad to worse to . . . to . . . he didn't even know. "Everyone, *halt*. All I was doing was gazing off into the distance. That's it. You know how I get tired at night. Speaking of which, I think Bob is looking for me."

His protest was ignored. Ruthie scanned the area again, then smiled. "Ah ha. Daniel, I know exactly who you were looking at, and who can blame you? You were staring at Addie Holmes, weren't ya?"

He had noticed Addie but wasn't going to admit that. Addie was a sweet girl who had the unfortunate reputation of being something of an odd person. It was too bad.

She *was* odd, but there was nothing wrong with that—at least not in his book. At least she wasn't boring.

Unfortunately, a lot of other people didn't see things the same way. Mild panic began to form inside him. The last thing he wanted was for everyone to start talking about her. Addie had enough problems without being the focus of stupid conversations. "I was not looking at Addie Holmes."

"Of course he wasn't," Bradley said. "I mean, does anyone really look at her anymore?"

"Don't be mean," Ruthie chided.

"I'm not being mean. All I did was state a fact. No one takes a second glance at a woman who'd rather speak to her donkey than any of us."

Daniel reckoned he'd rather be speaking to a donkey instead of them as well. "Let's talk about something else."

Ruthie and her friend Mary Jo, who'd just joined them, exchanged glances. "That's probably for the best, though I do feel sorry for her."

"Why is that?" Daniel blurted.

"She's had such a hard life already."

Mary Jo nodded. "She's the only person I've ever heard of whose parents didn't want her."

"I heard that rumor isn't true."

"Come on, Daniel," Mary Jo chided. "Of course it's true. Addie Holmes lives with her grandmother, and she hasn't seen her parents in years. Not since they dropped her off in Apple Creek when she was four." She lowered her voice. "Why, I bet if her parents came knocking on her door tomorrow, she probably wouldn't even recognize them."

"How do you know this?"

Ruthie shrugged. "We asked her about her parents when we were little."

"You mean, back when you were her friend?" Daniel asked. When Ruthie's eyes got big, he knew he should regret his pointed remark, but for the life of him, he could not. "You shouldn't be sharing things like that."

"It's not gossip if it's the truth, you know," Mary Jo pointed out.

"It is, and you're being hateful."

"My word, Daniel. You don't need to sound so judgmental." Ruthie lifted her chin. "All we're saying is that she's had a number of tough breaks, and they began when her parents chose not to raise her."

"Have her tough breaks ever ended?" Bradley asked. His voice was full of mirth.

"It's doubtful. I've never heard of any man who took an interest in her," Roman said. "Though that might be as much to do with her *mommi* as anything. Lovina Stutzman is formidable."

"I really do feel sorry for Addie," Mary Jo said. "After all, she's the only girl I know who's never had any boy show interest in her. Why, even back when we were in school and passing notes to each other, she never received a single one."

"Maybe Addie did but she didn't tell you," Daniel said. Why he was continuing this conversation he didn't know.

Mary Jo shook her head. "No, she didn't. I know because we girls used to walk home together and share news about our secret admirers." She lifted her chin. "We all used to get notes. Some of us even got them from you, Daniel."

Remembering those days, those awkward, hormonal days when he was likely to be more fascinated by a girl's smile than he was by a new chapter in their history books, his cheeks flushed.

Daniel crossed his arms in front of his chest. "That doesn't mean much."

"Daniel, not to correct you again, but I think you're wrong," Roman said. He rocked back on his heels. "Now, *I* personally don't care if Addie has a suitor or not. All I'm saying is that even back when we were fifteen and sixteen and all went to Singings on Sundays, no boy ever showed interest in Addie." He shrugged. "And who can blame them, really? She's a foundling, she wears glasses, is too thin, and talks to donkeys. None of those are traits I want in a wife."

"Roman does have a point," Bradley said quietly. "Not to be mean, but it's a fact that not everyone finds a match, right? You're a good man, Daniel, but this is the first time I've ever heard you say much about her at all."

"I never mentioned her in the first place!"

"See? Don't you think that would be different if she'd ever, ever caught your eye?"

Daniel's mouth went dry. As much as he hated to admit it, Bradley did have a point. He might not like everyone talking unkindly about Addie, but not everything they were saying was false.

The truth of the matter was that Addie simply didn't fit in. Whether it was her looks or her circumstances or her odd interests, he didn't know. But it certainly was sad.

Gazing across the way at her again, he realized that she was staring at his group. He was too far away to guess if she was looking at him and his friends with irritation, longing, or if she felt nothing at all. And maybe it didn't even matter.

What did matter was that something needed to change.

Thinking of one of the men at work who'd only turned into a good worker after he'd been praised and then befriended by one of the other men, Daniel wondered if a bit of interest and kindness was what Addie needed. Maybe she simply needed someone to care enough about her to boost her confidence?

If that was the case, he knew he should walk right over and chat with her for a spell. But as soon as he imagined doing so, he froze. First of all, he doubted they'd have much to say to each other.

Secondly, if he did such a thing publicly, it would only cause more talk. That would be bad for her and him.

No, he needed to do something better. Something thoughtful but secret. Something that girls seemed to like but would not backfire on him . . . Something secret, but in a good way.

And that was when he knew what to do.

"I'm heading home," he said.

Roman frowned. "Already? June and Aaron haven't made their speech yet."

"Let me know if they say something out of the ordinary. Bob's waiting. Plus, I just realized that I've got something important to do."

Daniel had a letter to write.

Chapter 2

Looking out the kitchen window, Addie Holmes frowned. It might be Sunday morning and the start of the second week in March, but it sure looked the same as it had back in February. The sky was gray and overcast, and there was a blustery chill in the air. Snow flurries seemed likely.

March was such a tease. Everyone loved to talk about the approaching spring and their planned gardens, but sunny, warm days were weeks away yet.

Still exhausted from Aaron and June's party, Addie took the time to enjoy two cups of coffee on her grandmother's ancient couch in front of the fireplace. Yes, she did have a lot to do, but all those chores would have to wait. She needed a few moments to simply sit. It was a no-church Sunday. Their church district, like most every other Old Order Amish community, only gathered every other Sunday to worship.

Clad in her thick woolen tights and gray wool dress, she sipped her coffee, said her prayers, and tried to think more positively.

Unfortunately, all she seemed to be able to do was relive the awkward feelings she'd experienced during the party.

Yet again.

Not for the first time, Addie wished things were different. No, she wished *she* was different. For some reason she seemed to lack whatever was necessary to fit in with everyone her age in Apple Creek.

She'd certainly tried—but no matter what she said or did, it was met with derision. She was one of those square pegs attempting to fit into a round hole. No matter how hard she tried, her rough edges were never going to smooth out or go away. She might be nineteen years old, slim, and blond . . . but she was also a bit too thin and her facial features a bit too bold. Her glasses didn't help, either.

Neither did her family history.

Most days Addie didn't let it bother her, but this morning, remembering just how happy June and Aaron had looked together, she couldn't ignore how far she was from their engaged bliss.

"You need to stop feeling so sorry for yourself, Addie," she said out loud. "There's nothing you can do about your eyesight—or your parents. You have a great many blessings. It's time you started appreciating them."

Taking another sip of coffee, she promised to do just that. Then, she threw an old blanket over her shoulders and headed outside to say hello to Snickers and gather eggs.

Heading into the warm barn, she found Snickers still half asleep. "Good morning, donkey," she whispered.

Snickers opened one eye, then two . . . then seemed to yawn. Addie giggled as it took him a moment to get his bearings; at last the little donkey trotted to the front of the stall and stuck his head out.

She rubbed the dark forelock on the top of his head before

kissing his nose lightly. "I'll come back later to chat and give you breakfast."

The snow she'd been dreading had just begun, and the fresh flakes dotted her glasses and chilled her cheeks as she left the barn. She picked up her pace and pulled open the door to the henhouse. "*Gut matin!*" she called out to the hens.

Unfortunately, the six hens seemed to realize she wasn't at her best. They warily watched her every move with dark, beady eyes, clucking their annoyance when she moved each aside to gather eggs. "Sorry, ladies. I fear it is a hen's lot in life to give up her eggs to the one who puts food in her stomach."

Betty, the oldest hen, squawked.

It almost made Addie smile. After tossing out their corn and grain, she hurried back to the house, her old blanket doing little to shield her from the spitting snow or frigid temperature.

She'd just finished washing off the eggs, making biscuits, and frying bacon when her grandmother woke up, at eight o'clock.

Mentally preparing herself for the questions that were sure to come, Addie summoned a smile. "*Gut matin, Mommi,*" she called out when she heard her grandmother slowly begin making her way to the kitchen. Two years ago, the doctor had insisted that she get a walker. At first, she'd protested, but now the metal contraption seemed like a part of her. Addie had become used to listening as the muted *thunk* of the tennis-ball-covered legs on the wood floor announced her presence.

"Good morning to you, child. How was the party last evening?" Mommi asked as she continued to slowly make her way into the kitchen.

Ack! Mommi sounded so hopeful. Again and again, her grandmother imagined that Addie would suddenly fit in and be the belle of the ball. Just like a fairy princess in the children's tales she used to get from the bookmobile.

Addie knew better. Of course, that was never going to happen, but relaying the news made her feel terrible. She hated to disappoint the woman who'd done so much for her.

A half dozen answers swirled in Addie's head, all of them only half-truths. After weighing the pros and cons of various replies, she settled on the vaguest one. "It was all right."

After treating Addie to a long, measured look, her grandmother carefully maneuvered her walker to the percolator on the stove. She steadied herself on the counter with one hand while she pulled down a coffee cup, added sugar, then poured milk into the cup with the other.

Addie watched with misgiving. After attempting to prepare her grandmother's coffee several times, Mommi had told Addie to leave her be.

Addie understood her grandmother's need for independence, but she was biding her time until Mommi missed the carafe and hot coffee spilled all over the counter.

This wasn't the morning to take over, however.

After giving the brew two stirs, Mommi carried the cup to the table with one hand.

Only when she sat down did she speak again. "Ah," she said.

Thankful that they weren't going to have to discuss the engagement party any further, Addie said, "You were sound asleep when I got home. I'm glad I didn't wake you."

"I'm glad, too, but I wouldn't have minded. Especially if you were singing because you were so happy."

Addie hid a smile. There was a reason that she'd loved those children's fairy tales so much—Lovina Stutzman did, too. "Oh, Gram. No one does things like that except in books."

Faded brown eyes met her own. "Young ladies do sing, and you would too if you were happier."

"I am happy. I'm just not happy at parties like that."

"I see. You're not happy to attend engagement parties that include all of your friends in Apple Creek?"

"You know what I mean." Especially since most of her friends were not people her own age.

Her grandmother took a long sip of coffee. "Things are still not better." It was a statement. Not a question.

Addie could lie, but there were some things one couldn't lie about. There was no way she could hide the hurt in her voice. "*Nee* they are not."

Her grandmother sighed. "Addie, I truly don't know what is wrong with everyone. I keep waiting for all the young men to finally see you."

Remembering the way she'd spied Roman, Bradley, and Daniel staring at her the evening before, her cheeks heated. "Oh, they do." The problem was that they didn't like what they saw.

"*Nee,* child. I mean, *really* see you. If they did, they would realize that you are a lovely girl. So full of life and so much fun, too. And you have the best heart, caring for your old grandmother the way you do."

Addie loved her grandmother and was happy to care for her . . . but caring for the elderly wasn't exactly something that would bring men flocking to her side. "Can we not discuss this anymore?"

"All right. We don't have to. I mean, we don't have to talk about this if *you* don't want to." Which meant, of course, that her grandmother did.

"I do not."

"You sound so sure."

"I am. And that's because there isn't anything to discuss."

When her grandmother's chin lifted, Addie explained. "Mommi, I know you care about me, and I love you, too. But discussing why I don't fit in doesn't help my situation. I am what I am, ain't so?"

"I suppose."

Glad that the topic was put to rest at long last, she stood up. "What would you like for breakfast now? Bacon, eggs, and biscuits?"

At her grandmother's nod, she walked to the refrigerator and pulled out some cream and the plastic holder for the eggs.

"What are your plans for today?"

Relieved they were no longer discussing her faults, Addie smiled. "I'm going to clean Miss Tina's house."

"On Sunday?"

"I canna clean it tomorrow. I'm going to the Beaumonts' *haus* to babysit, and then I need to do a little bit of grocery shopping."

"It's still a shame for you to be working on a Sunday. The Lord prefers you to rest, you know."

"Miss Tina likes the company. Besides, she offered me a fresh chicken in exchange for my help. We can have roast chicken for supper. What do you think of that?"

"It sounds fine."

Feeling a little disappointed that her grandmother wasn't more pleased, Addie whisked the eggs with the cream, added salt and pepper, then poured them into the hot skillet. "We have lots of potatoes, so I'll mash them for supper. And the last of the beans we put up this past summer."

"Are you working too much?"

"Of course not, Mommi."

"Sundays should be a day of rest. Instead of settling in on this snowy day with a good book, you'll be cleaning a house and then coming home to do more chores." Looking agitated, she added, "I can do more around here, you know."

Addie brought over the percolator, refilled both of their coffee cups, then returned to the range. "*Nee, Mommi.* You've already done more than enough for me. It's my turn to take care of you. It isn't a burden, either. It's a blessing." She divided the eggs between the two plates and added bacon and biscuits.

"It is still a lot for your slim shoulders."

"It isn't anything I can't handle," she replied as she set the plates in front of them. "Don't you remember telling me the same thing years ago?"

"I do."

After they silently gave thanks, a sweet, wistful smile lit Mommi's expression. "I surely remember the day you arrived in this house. You were four years old, so tiny and shy. So pretty, too."

"I remember thinking that your *haus* was warm and cozy." And that her grandparents looked like people who could give good hugs.

Mommi speared a forkful of scrambled eggs. "Dawdi and I were so shocked to see you, we could hardly put two sentences together."

"Because you hadn't seen my *mamm* in years." Biting into a warm biscuit, Addie frowned. Her mother's behavior had been so outlandish, it was still talked about to this day. She'd left this house when she was sixteen with a wild Englischer she'd met during her *rumspringa*.

Or at least that's what was rumored. Addie didn't recall much about her parents except that they had hardly been around when she was little. All she really remembered was always being cold, hungry, and told to keep quiet.

"I still don't know how you carried on after my mother

left the house. She was only a child herself. You must have been so worried about her."

"Those were dark days, for sure and for certain." Mommi sighed. "I didn't think I'd ever be able to breathe again. The way Kate took off upset me too much. Your grandfather, too." She ate another bite. "But then I realized that tears couldn't solve my problems. All they did was make my face wet."

"Then, five years later, Kate returned with me." Addie's father had been long gone.

"*Jah,* she did." Mommi's smile widened. "You were a beautiful child. So bright and shiny. Like a new penny!" Her voice lowered. "Your grandfather fell in love that very second. Boy, he was smitten."

"And you?"

"And I was right behind him." She nodded as if she'd just analyzed the memory and was satisfied with it. "Even your mother knew you were something special. That's why she gave you to your *dawdi* and me. She kissed the top of your head, then told me that she'd taken as good care of you as she was able. But you were too precious to be raised by a single mother."

Her grandmother loved to retell the story, but Addie was fairly certain that her mother had never said anything like that. The mother she remembered had never been one for sweet words. "I think you're adding shiny details again," she teased.

"I am not. Kate said you were precious, Addie. And when she went back on her way, I knew in my heart what she meant. My Kate was a lot of things. Smart and willful and pretty. But she was never delicate or bright like you were on that day." Much of the enthusiasm in her voice faded. "Even a mother's love ain't that blind."

"Oh, Mommi."

"That's why I knew the Lord understood what Kate was doing and also how much I had suffered. He gave you to us to mend our hearts and He made sure we'd love you instantly so Kate wouldn't take you into harm's way."

"How did you know that my mother was in harm's way? Mommi, what exactly happened to her?"

"I don't know for certain. It was just a hunch."

"Uh huh." Mommi might be slow on her feet, but her brain worked just fine. She was also stubborn. It was frustrating, especially when Addie wanted—no needed—some answers about her parents. But she'd learned over time to pick her battles. Her grandmother had a fierce need to protect both Addie and Kate. Long ago Addie had come to terms with that.

"Dear, all that matters is that I'm glad you came here. Your grandfather said the same thing until he died, true?"

Addie nodded.

"Child, all that is why you shouldn't feel obligated to spend so much time taking care of me that you never live your own life, too. Money might be tight, but we have enough. The Lord always provides."

"I know." She also knew that He was providing her with opportunities to earn the money to pay their bills.

"Then maybe you should think about kicking up your heels more often. No one is going to admire your light if you never let them see it."

Addie laughed. Because what else could she say? Her grandmother's hope sprang eternal. "I'll try, Mommi."

"I hope so."

At the end of the day, she knew her grandmother was right. Addie had been loved; she'd never suffered because she'd been raised by her grandparents.

She never wanted to think about her parents. For some

reason it had never made her all that happy to think that her parents had felt they'd be better off without her.

As she had always done, Addie pushed the hurt to one side.

Dwelling on something like that was simply too painful. She picked up a biscuit. "I think these turned out very well today, don't you?"

"*Jah*. They are good biscuits, indeed."

Both of them tried not to notice that neither of them cared all that much about biscuits.

Chapter 3

Writing a thoughtful secret admirer note to a person one didn't actually admire secretly was harder than Daniel had thought it would be. Actually, it was next to impossible.

Feeling vaguely foolish about the whole thing, he was tempted to shove aside his good intentions. He had no experience writing love letters. In fact, even in school, he'd never been especially good at putting thoughts to paper.

Now, looking over his various drafts, he feared that instead of boosting Addie Holmes's mood, his awkward letter would lower it instead. Maybe even send her a couple of chills because a strange man was writing her a mediocre note. He was pretty sure that the only thing worse than not ever receiving a secret admirer note was receiving one that was stilted, stupid-sounding, or less than effusive.

However, there was something inside him that wasn't willing to give up. Every time he recalled the expression on Addie's face as she stared at his group across the lawn, he knew she deserved to learn that she was admired. Everyone needed to feel that way sometime in their lives.

Maybe even more than that.

So that was why, after giving himself a dozen reasons why he should give up this campaign, Daniel picked up his pencil and tried again.

Dear Addie, I am your secret admirer.

After reading it twice through, he read it again out loud. "Dear Addie, I am your secret admirer."

That would be a firm *no*.

During his *rumspringa*, he'd once spent a weekend watching movies with Roman and Bradley. One of them had heard that *Star Wars* was something every boy should see. The three of them had camped out in Bradley's basement, consumed tons of junk food, and watched three of the movies in a row. He'd been mesmerized and enjoyed them very much. So much that some of the lines had stuck with him to this day.

Which was why there was no way on earth he was going to be able to begin his love letter like that. No, no, no.

After mulling over a couple of new lines, he tried again.

Roses are red, violets are blue.
You are mighty . . .

She was mighty what? He had no idea.

Irritated, he crumpled up his latest effort and tossed it on the floor. It landed with a tiny crunch, then rolled in with the other seven attempts on his small living room floor.

Bob, half asleep on the couch, opened one eye, gazed at the pile with a baleful expression, then closed his eyes with a sigh. No doubt even his beagle realized that poetry was not his forte.

"I'm in agreement with ya, *hund*. I'm a sorry poet, and that is for sure and for certain."

Confused by both his inability to write a simple letter—and the mere fact that he was writing pretend love notes in the first place—Daniel stood up and walked to the kitchen. He poured himself a tall glass of water and drank the contents in one gulp.

Perhaps it was time to face some hard truths. First, he didn't have a good reason for deciding to write Addie Holmes a secret admirer note.

It wasn't as if he had a crush on her. In actuality, Addie wasn't anything to him at all—nothing more than a woman he felt guilty about not talking to more often. The truth was that he hadn't spoken more than a few words to her in years. Not since they were in school together, in fact. That was too bad . . . but was it a reason to start spouting poetry? He thought not.

He was beginning to be confused about why he thought he was qualified to write her notes. No one had ever said that he had a way with words. Most had said the opposite, in fact.

So, he really didn't need to write Addie a note. He wasn't good at it, and he had no burning desire to become close friends with her, let alone her boyfriend.

Why then, Daniel?

He felt chill bumps appear on his arms. He wasn't sure if the Lord had just spoken to him—or if it was his conscience. But whatever it was—he was thankful for the pointed question. Perhaps he needed to know the answer before he continued his writing crusade.

"Why do you want to write a secret note to Addie, Daniel?" he asked himself out loud. "Why, out of all the things you could be doing, or even out of all the women in Apple Creek, why have you picked Addie to write?"

He tried several answers on for size. "Because Bradley, Mary Jo, and Ruthie were speaking dismissively of her and that wasn't right."

Their gossip had been rude, even bordering on cruel.

Of course, the counterpoint to that would be the question of why he hadn't simply said something to his friends. He could've stood up for Addie right then and there. If he had, he wouldn't feel guilty, and he wouldn't be going through sheets and sheets of paper while pretending to be a romantic poet.

Though it made him uncomfortable, Daniel forced himself to seek a reason. He wasn't perfect, but he considered himself an honest, upright man. Letter-writing subterfuge wasn't his norm.

Not even close.

"All right, how about this. . . ." He pushed himself to admit the truth. "I want to write Addie a few notes because she seems so alone, and no one should be that lonely." He almost smiled—until he thought about how he'd seen her volunteering to help quite a few other folks around Apple Creek. She might not be his particular friends' cup of tea, but Addie certainly wasn't a recluse. Not by a long shot.

"Is it because you're bored?" It was not that. He might get bored at engagement parties, but otherwise he felt engaged in his life. He had a busy job, many friends, and Bob. Not to mention a half dozen assorted family members living in the vicinity.

Growing even more confused, he sat down next to Bob and ran a hand down his soft ears. "Why am I doing this, Bob?"

Bob stretched his neck so Daniel wouldn't miss his favorite spot. When Daniel complied, he wagged his tail. Bob's usual response, but not exactly helpful.

Standing up again, Daniel opened the front door of his house and contemplated going for a walk. Maybe what he needed was to clear his head.

But then the buds on the sycamore tree caught his eye. At last, new leaves were starting to form. New, bright green leaves would appear by the end of the month. By June, the green would deepen and provide welcome shade for his front walkway. Then, come October, they'd turn yellow and gold and brighten the fall sky.

He'd always been so fond of fall leaves. He loved the colors, loved the scent of fallen leaves on the trails, loved their symbolism of death and renewal. Loved that he'd always found so much pleasure in their beauty. A small memory came to him then. One afternoon last November, he'd caught sight of the tree's last, lone leaf as it fell off its branch. It was bright yellow, almost blinding in its brilliance, and it floated in the air. It had taken forever to reach the ground. For over a minute—maybe even two, it was buffeted by the wind, floating this way and that.

Transfixed, he'd watched it meander through the air. When it landed on the ground at long last, it lay on a patch of bright green grass. One of the last spaces of his lawn that hadn't gone dormant. That one, single leaf had been perfect and different. Memorable.

"It was like Addie," he murmured.

That was it. Sure, it was just one little leaf. It was exactly like the others on the sycamore tree. Really not worth a second look. But because he'd taken the time to focus on it, he'd seen its unique beauty.

"That is what I'm seeing in Addie." Yes. He didn't need to become her best friend. He did, however, want her to know that she wasn't invisible. People did see her, and she was worthy.

"You admire her because she's admirable," he said. Yes, she was one of the Lord's children, which was enough in itself. But it was more than that. He also admired her because she was different. She could travel her own trail. Didn't need to be part of the pack.

"I have a plan, Bob."

Of course, the beagle continued to be unimpressed, but that no longer mattered. What did, however, was his new goal. Just to write Addie a simple letter, relaying that he'd seen her—and that she was worth seeing in his eyes.

Sitting down at his kitchen table again, he picked up his pen and wrote a simple note. It wasn't flowery and didn't try to be anything that it wasn't. Instead, all he'd done was try to explain why he was writing.

After he was done, he looked it over and figured it would do. He didn't sign it. Just folded it, slipped it into a plain, business-sized envelope, and wrote down her address. After putting a stamp on it, he was ready.

Already craving anonymity, he knew he needed to post the letter at the post office. He put on his boots and coat, fastened Bob's leash on his collar, and then headed off. He had an important errand to run.

As luck would have it, he practically ran into Addie right outside the post office. It was Bob's doing. When he spied Addie, he tugged his lead with a happy bark.

"Bob, hang on now!"

Bob barked again and scampered closer, stopping mere inches from Addie.

"Oh!" she said. Looking down at Bob, she smiled. "Hello there, beagle."

"Addie, are you all right?"

"I'm fine." She stared at him curiously. "I didn't think you knew my name."

"Of course I do. I mean, we went to school together. I'm Daniel," he said.

"I know who you are. Of course I know."

Well, they'd now introduced themselves, even though they'd known each other since the first day they'd walked through the doors at the Amish schoolhouse. Feeling foolish, he added, “This is Bob.” But of course, she already knew that, too.

Bob lifted his big brown eyes to Addie and wagged his tail.

“Indeed you are,” she said with a smile. Looking far more at ease than he felt, she knelt down on the sidewalk and rubbed Bob behind the ears. “You are a mighty handsome *hund*, Bob.”

Bob lifted his head so she could rub his neck. “Aren’t you a charmer?” she murmured.

“My dog greets everyone like they’re a long-lost friend.” Feeling a little left out, Daniel said, “I really am sorry that we nearly knocked you over.”

“You didn’t.” She stood up and brushed off a speck of dirt from her skirt. “See, I am fine.”

“Yes. Of course. Ah, how are you?”

She blinked behind her glasses. “I am fine.”

“I am on my way to the post office.” Because he seemed to be determined to be completely awkward, Daniel pointed to the building with the letter he was holding.

Looking amused, Addie nodded. “Most folks do like to post their letters there.”

“I do.” He looked at the letter, realized that her name was boldly written across the front, and stuffed it in his coat’s front pocket.

Addie raised her eyebrows. “Well, I had better let you mail it.” She smiled tightly. “Good day.”

Just as she started walking away, he blurted, “Hey, Addie, why did you think I didn’t know your name?”

Her cheeks turned pink. “I guess it’s the same reason you told me your name—because even though we know each other, we never speak.”

Unable to help himself, Daniel watched Addie walk away. Next to him, Bob seemed to be staring after her, too. Addie had been wearing a bright blue dress. The color made her hair seem a little less brassy and a little more golden. It fit her well, too. Why, she didn't look too skinny at all. When she was out of sight, the beagle sat down, looked up at him, and tilted his head to one side.

"I agree, *hund*. I'm not sure why the Lord decided that she and I needed to run into each other at this point, but it was a close call."

They crossed the street, stopped in front of the mailbox just outside the post office, and he pulled out the envelope. It looked a little bent from being gripped in his hand and then stuffed in his pocket, but nothing too terrible.

Feeling as if he was making a big change in his life, he deposited it into the mailbox. There. It was out of his hands and into the world. In a day or two, it would arrive at Addie's house, and she would read it. Maybe smile.

If that happened, all his efforts would be worthwhile.

All he had to do was figure out what he should do next.

Chapter 4

"Here you go, Addie," Gretchen Beaumont said as she handed over an envelope. "Thank you so much for watching Tabby last night. You were a lifesaver."

Gretchen's husband Howard had knocked on her door yesterday morning in a panic. His mother had been admitted to the hospital in Erie. He'd wanted to bring his wife with him, since she was as worried as he was, but they also needed someone to watch their nine-month-old baby.

Addie had babysat little Tabitha multiple times, though never overnight. She didn't like to leave her grandmother in the evenings, especially since there were still moments when Mommi would try to cross a room without her walker. However, Addie knew she would enjoy the job. Tabby was a sweet baby who liked to crawl, be read to, and cuddled in the evenings.

After receiving both her grandmother's blessing as well as a promise not to do anything foolhardy, Addie had accepted the job and arrived at the Beaumonts' house shortly after lunch.

Tabitha had been just as delightful as ever. She'd smiled brightly when Addie had arrived and had hardly made a fuss when her parents had left.

For herself, Addie had enjoyed the stay at the Englischers' home. Though it might not be exactly encouraged in her district, she enjoyed watching their television, eating a microwave dinner, and snuggling under the electric blanket that covered the guest bedroom bed.

Now it was near three o'clock the following day and time to head back home. "Thank you for asking me to sit for ya. I love playing with Tabitha."

Gretchen beamed. "You're the only babysitter that she always looks happy to see. You have a way with babies."

"Thank you."

"I guess you were meant to be a babysitter, hmm?" she teased.

Addie kept her smile in place, but some of the joy she'd been feeling faded. It wasn't that Gretchen had meant anything mean; it was simply hard to take the comment in a good way. All she'd ever wanted was to have a husband, a home of her own, and a houseful of children calling her Mamm.

She'd wanted to be the one to provide the stable, nurturing home she'd always wished she'd had when she was small. While her grandparents had been wonderful, they'd been older and sometimes too old-fashioned and strict compared with the other kids' parents.

Then, too, there had also been the sense that something wasn't quite right. Almost like something intangible had been missing from her childhood.

Or maybe it was the opposite. Maybe her grandparents and Addie always carried had an extra burden within their hearts. For her grandparents, Mommi especially, it was that she'd raised a daughter who didn't want to keep her child.

Addie, on the other hand, had grown up sure that she'd been missing something her mother had wanted. Even though she'd been just a child and therefore not at fault, Addie had always felt that she'd never been enough.

Shaking off those melancholy thoughts, Addie pulled on her red cardigan over her long-sleeved, rose-colored dress. "Well, I had better get on my way. I am glad your mother-in-law is doing better."

"Me too. While I have to admit that I wish she hadn't caused quite so much commotion for a mild stomach ailment, I guess it's better to be safe than sorry."

"Indeed." She smiled at Gretchen.

Howard followed her to the door. "Addie, I know you like to walk, but it's a little chilly out. Are you sure I can't drive you home?"

She slipped on her backpack. "Thank you for the offer, but I really do enjoy walking. When I get home, I'll be busy with chores and such. It's nice to have a bit of time to relax."

"I hear what you're saying. Well, let us know about next weekend, okay?"

"Of course." They'd come up with a system in which the Beaumonts asked her for several babysitting dates in advance, and then Addie would use the phone shanty to call and tell them which dates were best for her.

Even though the temperature was only in the fifties, Addie was glad she'd refused Howard's offer. The sun was out, and the road was dry. It wasn't unpleasant at all. Besides, she needed a few minutes of silence, probably because Gretchen's comment had hit her hard. She wasn't old, not even close to that.

She was not destined to be an old maid.

Thinking of her appearance, Addie decided it was good enough. She might have glasses and bold features, but she wasn't too plain. Especially not since she'd grown up.

Oh, she might not be the beauty that Mary Jo was, but she had a lot of pleasing things about her. It might be prideful to admit that she had analyzed herself in the mirror more than once, but it was the truth. She had pretty green eyes and really lovely hair.

Addie was also fairly sure she was in good company. As far as she was concerned, there was nothing wrong with taking a good long look at what the Lord had given her and wondering if she needed to try to improve on His work by keeping in shape or smoothing her hair in a better way.

Addie knew she was reasonably attractive, not too old, and self-sufficient. She was also, at least according to the Beaumonts, good with small children.

If all of that was true, then why did no man see her as worthy of his notice?

As a buggy passed, she waved to the couple inside. They were strangers to her but smiled back and waved.

When they were out of sight, she sighed again. Was it something else entirely? Was it her personality that wasn't pleasing? Was she boring? Rude? Unpleasant?

Or was the problem not with herself at all, but rather her circumstances? She still felt a stab of pain when she remembered what a few girls had said to her back when they were all fourteen and almost out of school.

She'd been sitting with them, so glad to be included for once. But she'd soon learned that they'd only included her out of spite. Ruthie had asked Addie about her parents and if the rumor was true that she hadn't been wanted.

Addie had been so shocked that she hadn't known how to reply. Which, of course, had been the other girls' intention. She'd giggled while she tried not to cry.

Though she usually did a good job of pushing that painful memory down, it returned in a flash, almost taking her breath away.

"You need to get a handle on yourself, Addie Holmes," she told herself sternly. "These self-doubts are not good and will only cause you pain." Those were good words to remember. She knew that.

It was just too bad that sometimes even the best intentions failed terribly when one was human.

All of that was on her mind as she walked in the front door. Her backpack felt heavy, almost as heavy as her heart.

"Mommi, I'm home," she called out.

"Hello, child," Mommi called out from the living room. "Did you have a good time with Tabitha?"

"I did." Addie grinned. Noticing that her grandmother was sitting on the sofa with her walker within reaching distance, she breathed a sigh of relief. "I'm glad you're using your walker."

Mommi waved a dismissive hand. "Ack. I told you I would."

"How was your night?"

"It was *gut*. A far sight better than yours, I'm guessing." Her grandmother studied her intently. "Your eyes look tired, even behind your glasses. Did Tabby keep you up all night?"

"Not at all." Tabby had slept like an angel, but the excuse was tempting. She set her backpack on the floor. "Now, what can I help you do?"

"You may pick up that pack and take it to your room, just like I taught you to do. You might now be my caregiver, but I still like a clean *haus*."

"I haven't forgotten." Picking up the pack, she said, "I'll be right back."

"Take your time. I'm fine."

"Yes, Mommi."

"Oh, Addie, I almost forgot. You received a letter today. I put it on the stairs."

"Who is it from?"

"There was no return address, and I didn't open it up. I guess it's a surprise, *jah*?"

"*Jah.*" Holding her pack with one hand, she walked to the stairs. Sure enough, there was a small letter addressed to her resting on the first step. She picked it up and carried it to her room. She was curious about what was inside, but she supposed it could be anything. No doubt it was simply an ad for medicine or some such.

Curious, she tossed her pack on the floor and sat down on her bed. She picked up the envelope again, glanced at the back for an address. As her grandmother had mentioned, there was none.

It seemed she had a little mystery.

Since there was only one way to solve it, Addie carefully opened the seal and looked inside.

Chapter 5

Dear Addie,

I reckon this letter is something of a surprise to you, but if you've read this far, I hope you'll continue.

See, I decided it was past time I wrote you a note. We've known each other for a long time, but we've never had much of a conversation. I don't know why.

No, actually I do. It was because I wasn't sure what to say to you. I don't know if that makes me sound foolish or not.

Maybe it's really just that I wasn't sure what to say first. I mean, how do you tell a woman she is pretty special when you've hardly done anything but say hello from time to time?

I guess that's why I'm writing. I think that there is a lot about you that's worth getting to know, and I'm hoping you'll give me a chance to get to know you better—at least through letters. Of course, this might be a really bad way to get to know each other. If it is, then I apologize.

Feel free to toss this paper in the trash can and forget about it.

If, however, you'd like to maybe get to know each other better, you could write me back. Since I don't want to give you my address, here's an idea: Put your note in the old oak tree down near Blossom Lane. Do you know which one I mean? It's got a hole in it that's big enough to put a letter in but small enough so no one will know there's something hidden inside if they happen by.

What do you think of my idea?

I'll go by there on Friday afternoon. If you decide to write to me, I'll write you back and put my letter in the same place by the following Friday.

Addie, if you decide to throw this note away and forget about it, well, I can't say that I blame ya much. No one writes letters like this anymore, do they? Actually, who even knows if anyone ever did?

On the other hand, if you do decide to take a chance and write me back, I have to admit that would make me real happy.

Your Secret Admirer

Addie dropped the letter onto the quilt covering her bed as if it was on fire.

Still stunned, she stood up and backed away from it. The

letter felt toxic. Surely no honest man would write a letter like that. It had to be a joke at her expense. And what kind of man would do such a thing? If she could trust his words, it was someone she'd known for quite some time, too. They'd known each other but they'd never said much more than hello to each other.

Who could it be?

Against her will, she thought of all the men she knew. Some of them she'd known since she'd started school. Maybe it was one of the boys who'd been in the schoolhouse with her. Of course, the author could also be English. She'd known quite a few English boys over the years. But that didn't seem like a good fit. After all, why would an English man write an Amish girl and suggest a hollowed-out oak tree as their makeshift delivery system?

She couldn't imagine an Englischer doing that.

So, it was likely an Amish man whom she'd known for a while. And now, instead of merely speaking to her, he'd decided to mail her a secretive note. Which made no sense.

This letter had to be a joke. It had to be. Tears pricked her eyes as she imagined the awful game the author was playing. Suggesting she was so pitiful, she'd actually consider writing back to a complete stranger.

She hurried over to the note, crumpled it in her hands, and threw it on the floor. It landed just a couple of inches from her feet.

Teasing her.

"Addie? Addie, are you gonna come back out?"

"*Jah,* Mommi!"

Hastily, she picked up the paper and put both it and the envelope in the drawer in her bedside table. She needed to keep it safe so there was no way it could accidentally fall into her grandmother's hands.

After splashing cold water on her eyes, she hurried back down the hall. "Mommi, are you still in the living room?"

"*Jah.* All I've done is move closer to the fire. It's a little chilly out, don't you think?"

Walking into the room, she discovered her grandmother had relocated. She was now sitting in her rocker with a crocheted afghan covering her legs. And, thankfully, the walker was nearby. "I'd better go get the eggs before those silly hens decide they don't want to give them up."

"They'll be in a state, anyway. I forgot all about feeding them."

Her heart sank. Even just a few months ago her grandmother had enjoyed walking to the henhouse and throwing grain out for the hens. "I'd best do that now," she said as she hurried toward the back door. "Do you want some hot tea when I get back?"

"I do." Sounding hesitant, Mommi added, "And maybe an egg and some toast, too?"

That meant she hadn't eaten either. Forcing a smile when all she felt like doing was crying, she replied, "Of course, Mommi."

"*Danke*, child."

Hurrying out the back door, she said a quick hello to Snickers, gave him oats, then focused on the hens. She cleaned the ladies' water container and tossed out a generous portion of grain. With some affronted-sounding squawks, three of the hens left their eggs in order to eat. Addie gathered those eggs, then carefully claimed the other three from the roosting birds. The last bird, whom she'd privately named Jezebel, pecked at her thumb.

"I know you're not pleased with my delay, Jez, but it couldn't be helped. I couldn't very well be here and at the Beaumonts' at the same time, now could I?" When the hen turned her head away, Addie groaned. Only her hens could have such attitudes.

After she carried the eggs back to the kitchen and rinsed them off, she started the kettle.

"Addie?"

"I'm working on your eggs and toast, Mommi."

"I want strawberry jam, too."

"I'll get it out."

As she pulled out a loaf of bread and carefully sliced it, she let her mind drift back to her letter.

Thought back to the words that were written in it.

Thought back to the comment Gretchen had made.

Reflected on how she seemed to be constantly doing things for everyone else. Even grouchy hens named Jezebel.

What if she took a chance and did decide to write this person back? What if it wasn't a cruel joke but something entirely different? What if this secret admirer of hers was actually something real?

She cracked the eggs, whipped them with cream, and poured them in the pan. Made tea and set it on a tray. Toasted the bread and slathered it with butter and jam. Finally she carried the whole thing out to her grandmother.

Who'd fallen asleep.

Sighing, Addie went back to the kitchen and ate the simple meal, then carried the tea to her room. She pulled out the crumpled piece of paper and read it once more. This time with an open mind.

And—dare she admit it?—she was intrigued.

So she read the letter again. Then folded it, put it back in the envelope, and stuck the envelope under her pillow. As if she was in danger of getting caught with such a thing.

What if this letter was something good, after all? What if this man was actually hoping she would write him back?

What might happen if she actually did write him a note . . . just to see what could happen?

"The possibilities are endless," she said out loud.

Just like the scent of freshly baked chocolate chip cookies, the thought of something wonderful happening was too tantalizing to ignore.

Chapter 6

Addie had written back to him. Standing in front of the oak tree that he'd described in his letter, Daniel held the plain white envelope in his hands and stared at it in wonder.

He could scarcely believe that she'd done it. Oh, he'd hoped she would, but he hadn't counted on it. Part of him figured that she would be creeped out by her anonymous correspondent and throw the note away. He wouldn't blame her if she did. Receiving a letter at one's house from a stranger who asked to continue an anonymous correspondence was fishy. Especially in this day and age. He might be Amish, but he read enough of the news to know that odd, and yes, dangerous people lurked everywhere.

As much as Daniel wanted to sit down, rip open the envelope, and read what Addie had to say, he stuffed the paper in his pocket and headed toward the post office. He only had ten minutes to get to work on time.

They were short-handed at the hospital where he was a janitor. Last night Stefan, his boss, had left a message on the phone he shared with his neighbors. He'd sounded panicked and had practically begged Daniel to come in the following afternoon.

Daniel had replied that he'd be there. Working an extra shift would cut into the chores he'd planned to do around the house, but other than that, he had no reason to refuse. He'd started working for Stefan as a janitor about four years ago and trusted the man. Stefan wasn't the type of person to beg Daniel to come in on his day off unless it was really necessary.

More than once his parents had asked why he hadn't moved on to a different occupation. Each time he'd only shrugged, knowing that no reason would be good enough for them. He could see their point. To be sure, janitorial work wasn't something a lot of people aspired to do, but he liked it well enough. The pay was good, most of the staff were pleasant and easy to work with, and he liked to think he helped people in a small way, even if it was just making the rooms clean and safe.

He also liked that he knew enough folks who worked at the hospital so he didn't have to hire a driver. He'd heard of some Amish workers being taken advantage of by their drivers—or even their company's shuttle service.

Checking his timepiece, Daniel picked up his pace. His friend Kristen, one of the receptionists in the main lobby, was picking him up today.

Hurrying to the parking lot of the post office, their designated meeting spot, he scanned the area. Kristen was parked near the front. She was sipping coffee in her car. She smiled and waved him in when he approached.

"Hi, Daniel, how are you?"

"I'm grateful that you're driving me to work today," he said as he buckled up. "I hope you weren't waiting too long."

"Not at all. I stopped over by the bakery and got a coffee

and two donuts." Handing him a small sack, she smiled. "One for me and one for you."

"You didn't have to do that."

"I know, which is why I'm glad I did. You're an easy person to do something nice for every now and then."

Opening up the paper sack, he saw one perfect buttermilk cake donut inside. "You got me my favorite."

She laughed as she pulled out onto the highway. "It wasn't hard to do. You never make a secret about your preference."

Taking his first bite, he smiled. "Tell me about your family. How are Jeff and the kids?"

"Jeff's fine and the kids are good. Jake and Biancha had spring break and are back in school."

"How's the homework?" Kristen had confided more than once that she dreaded all the homework her kids came home with, mainly because her husband worked late, and she was tired when she got home from work.

"So far, so good. Maybe Mrs. Cartwright is going to take pity on us this month. Biancha's only had about an hour every night."

"And Jake?"

She smiled. "His teacher told her class that they weren't allowed to get help from their parents anymore! She's trying to teach them some responsibility."

"Good for you."

"I agree. Well, I say that until I find out that he's goofing off or something. Jeff doesn't trust Jake's newfound responsibility much and I can't blame him. Eight-year-olds are squirrely." Turning onto the hospital's street, she said, "How are you? Anything new?"

"No. Same old, same old."

"I want to be you when I grow up, Daniel. You're always so steady."

Thinking of his recent journey into letter writing, he grimaced. "I don't think that's true, but I'm glad you think so."

Pulling into the hospital parking lot, she said, "How long is your shift today?"

"Eight hours. Noon until eight. You?"

"Just six today. How are you going to get home?"

"I don't know yet," he admitted as they got out of her vehicle. "I'll ask around, though." He wasn't too worried; a lot of people got off at eight. The Lord always seemed to look out for him by putting someone in his path who was driving near his house in Apple Creek.

"I'll do the same," she said as she buttoned her coat. "I'll let you know when I find someone."

"That ain't necessary."

"Of course it is. Daniel, it's not just that everyone thinks you're a nice person. We love how well you clean. In this day and age, with all sorts of stuff floating around, we don't want to lose you. Plus, dropping you off at your house only adds another ten or fifteen minutes to most people's commute."

"Thank you, then. I don't have so much pride that I'd refuse."

"You're welcome."

They walked in the employee doors together, then branched off, each going to their respective area to check in and stow their items.

The custodial staff had their area in the basement of the building. It wasn't half as fancy as the stations for the doctors and nurses, but it wasn't half bad. It was also comfortable and always warm, thanks to the close proximity to the furnace.

When he arrived, Stefan looked up from his desk. "Ah, you're here. Thanks again for coming in."

"It wasn't a problem. How are you doing?"

"Well enough." Stefan shrugged. "It's been a day around here. Any chance there's a full moon?"

He smiled. "Not a one. What's been going on?"

"We had a pipe burst near the maternity ward. It's been a real mess." He frowned. "And Catalina didn't show up again."

"I'm sorry about that. Are you worried about her?" Cat was in her early fifties and a favorite of Stefan's. She also had kind of a tough home life, which led her to call in sick at the last minute at least twice a month.

"I called but she didn't pick up." He shrugged. "So, yes, I'm worried, but it could be nothing. One never knows, right?"

"Right." He pulled out a cart and stocked it with supplies. "Where would you like me today?"

"Sabrina asked if you could clean over in radiology this afternoon. They're expecting a light afternoon."

"I can do that."

"If there's time, I'm going to send you over to the ER, too."

Daniel controlled his grimace, but just barely. The emergency room was the polar opposite of radiology. Every custodian dreaded working that area since it was always crowded, the bathrooms were usually dirty, and the waiting rooms were hard to keep sanitized. The staff was often flustered and out of patience, too.

But what could he do? "Sounds good." Realizing that he still had Addie's note in his pocket, he peeked at Stefan, noticed he was on the phone, and decided to finally take a minute to read the note before getting to work.

Feeling nervous, he carefully opened the seal, pulled out a half sheet of lined loose-leaf paper, and read the note.

Dear Secret Admirer,

Well, I did it. I wrote you back. I don't mind sharing that I feel silly about it, though. Part of me is worried that you're playing me for a fool, but the other part of me feels that it would be rude not to respond. So, I decided to write you back, and then blame my eternal optimism if this experiment (or whatever it is) goes wrong.

Something happened today that got me thinking maybe I've been playing it safe for far too long. Perhaps I've gotten in a rut.

So, I guess that's the real reason I decided to write you back. You're my risk.

I don't know if I'm special or not. Maybe, instead, it's that each of us is special. We're taught that the Lord believes it, you know. Sometimes I'm not sure if I believe that as much as I should.

You'll have to tell me the rules of this type of correspondence. Do we share information about our lives? Our families?

I'm curious about what you'd like to happen. And no, I'm not being judgmental—it's just the way my mind goes.

If you get this note, I hope you understand what I mean and you write back.

Sorry if I seem hesitant and wary, but if our places were reversed, I believe you'd be suspicious, too.

Addie

After scanning the paper again, Daniel folded it and returned it to its envelope, then put it back securely in his coat pocket and closed his locker door.

All the while, he wondered how to answer Addie. What did he want to happen? That was a legitimate question. A fair one.

Why had it never occurred to him to think about that? Had he really been so stuck in his own world that he hadn't thought of anything besides trying to be a ray of light in poor Addie's life?

Daniel felt his cheeks heat as he realized that just about summed it up.

What did he want, anyway? Nothing more from her? That felt harsh, but maybe like the cold winter wind, he needed that burst of reality.

Stunned by her words and the thoughts that were spinning in his head, Daniel clipped on his badge and pushed his cart out of the room.

He had a lot to think about—and a response to prepare. At least this time he was determined to be a lot less self-serving and a whole lot more thoughtful.

Perhaps he needed to be a little more worthy of her regard.

Chapter 7

After placing her secret admirer's note in the tree on Friday, Addie had been a bundle of nerves. Not only could she not believe that she'd actually written back to a stranger and stuck the note in a tree . . . she kept fretting about the letter she'd written!

When her grandmother had approached her on Friday night and asked what in the world had gotten her into such a state, Addie knew she had to calm down. She pushed that letter from her mind as best as she could for the rest of the weekend. She spent the majority of Monday washing clothes and hanging them on the line in the basement.

Now it was Tuesday—one of her favorite days of the week. She grocery shopped on Tuesdays, which meant she spent several hours with Brooke, her best friend and English driver.

Brooke was eighteen, still living at home, and was taking a few courses at the community college. About a year ago, when she was still a senior in high school, a mutual friend had connected them. Brooke needed a small job to help pay for her classes, and Addie needed someone to drive her around on Tuesdays.

Addie was sure she'd never forget the first time they met. They'd both been expecting someone middle-aged. When Brooke had pulled up and knocked on the door, Addie had even asked if she was delivering something. Brooke had replied that no, she was there to drive an old Amish lady around.

Boy, that had made them both burst out laughing.

That first, awkward meeting soon turned into a wonderful friendship. Addie liked how young and easygoing Brooke was. She liked the fact that the girl didn't seem to judge her. She even liked how Brooke would sometimes wander around Walmart's aisles with her, discussing her favorite shampoos, conditioners, and face moisturizers.

Brooke had once revealed that she liked being with Addie because Addie didn't judge her for not going away to school. She also really liked the fact that Addie wasn't in her circle of friends, so she wasn't catty about either girlfriends or even the guys she went out with.

Addie was standing by the door, double-checking her list again, when her grandmother's walker made its familiar *thunk, thunk, swish* noise.

"Are you getting ready to leave, Addie?"

Turning to her, she nodded. "I am, but I thought you were settled on the couch."

"I was, but I thought a bit of exercise would do me good." Looking almost girlish, Mommi kicked out one of her black-stocking-covered legs. "I need to give these knees a little bit of a spin every now and then, you know."

"I'm glad, but you know I worry about you falling when I'm not here. Try not to do too much exercise while I'm gone, okay?"

"*Psh*. Addie, you worry too much. When was the last time I fell?"

"I don't know. Maybe three months ago?"

Obviously irritated that she'd had a ready reply, Mommi scowled. "I was sick, girl. That wasn't what I was getting at."

"Maybe not, but I spoke the truth, *jah*?"

"Perhaps."

Addie chuckled. Putting her purse down, she wrapped an arm around her grandmother's waist. "Come on, Mommi, don't be difficult. Let me help you."

Her grandmother didn't argue, but Addie knew she was irritated. She didn't blame Mommi for feeling frustrated. She was probably justified. However, the fact remained that Addie lived in fear of her grandmother falling and lying on the ground for hours until Addie returned home.

"Brooke and I are going to go to the Dollar Store, Walmart, and the market. Is there anything besides what's on the list for me to get?"

"*Nee,* dear. You go right ahead. I'll be just fine sitting here on the couch. All day long."

Uh oh. Her grandmother really was in a snit. "If I see something interesting that you'd like, I'll bring it home," she said lightly as she helped her grandmother sit back down.

"Addie, perhaps we should start thinking of other places for me to live one day."

"What are you talking about?"

"All you do is run around helping other people or stay here helping me. The only day you do something for yourself is on Tuesdays, and it's to go grocery shopping with a driver. That ain't exactly a day off, you know."

"Brooke isn't just my driver. She's my friend."

"I'm sure she is your friend, but it's not the same as being around other women like you, ain't so?"

They'd had this conversation before. Her grandmother

wanted Addie to have a close circle of Amish girlfriends and never seemed to be able to come to terms with the fact that it wasn't going to happen. "There's nothing wrong with Brooke."

"Of course there isn't. I know she helps you a lot, but she's not Amish, Addie. She doesn't believe the things we do, and she doesn't know the other men and women in our church community."

"So?"

"Addie, if you don't do more with the young'uns in our community, you won't meet any eligible men. If you don't meet them, you aren't gonna be able to get married. It's that simple."

Nothing like her grandmother skipping from point A to point Z. "I'm not in a hurry to get married, Mommi. I'm only nineteen, remember? I've got plenty of time for that."

"If you keep thinking that way, you're going to turn into an old maid." She waggled a finger. "Mark my words."

"Most people already think I am." She smiled to take the sting out of the words, but her grandmother didn't smile back.

"You think about it, okay? If I was in a retirement home, you would have more free time for yourself. It would be better for you."

"*Nee.*"

"What did you say?"

"I said *nee,* Mommi. I like how things are. I don't want them to change." Besides, it wasn't like they could afford fancy retirement digs, anyway. It was better to be content with what they had.

Hearing a beep outside, Addie silently praised the Lord. "That's Brooke. I'll be back in four hours."

"Stay for five. Go out to lunch or something."

"Fine."

"*Gut*. Now go."

Feeling as if she'd just had a sparring match with a teenager, Addie hurried down the front steps of the house to Brooke's navy SUV. "Hi!" she said as she climbed into the vehicle. "I am so happy to see you."

"Well, I'm so excited to see you. Guess what?"

"What?" she asked as she buckled her seat belt.

"Cameron Phillips asked me out."

"No way."

"Way! It was magical, Addie. Just magical. I've been dying to tell you all about it."

Brooke's enthusiasm was already making Addie's spirits lift. "I canna wait to hear about it. What happened?"

"Hold on. Where to first?" Brooke asked as she backed out of the driveway.

"Dollar Store?"

"Sounds good." She turned left onto the main road.

"Now that that's settled, don't keep me in suspense. What happened?"

"Well, I was studying in the community college commons. Remember how I told you they have a coffee shop there now?"

"Yep."

"Well, I was sitting there, trying to figure out why I thought Psych 101 was going to be easy when he walked over and said that he took that class last semester." Brooke smiled as she turned right at the stop sign. "Then he sat down and started telling me about the professor's tests and gave me some advice."

"That was mighty kind of him."

"I thought so, too." Brooke grinned. "Anyway, after I thanked him for the tips, we started talking about high school and how we both are living here instead of going away. Addie, he's practically the first person besides you who doesn't act like I'm making a big mistake."

"I like him better and better."

"Me too! Next thing I know, he asked if I'd like to go out to eat over in Medina on Thursday, and I said yes."

"Good for you! He must really like you."

"Maybe." She bit her bottom lip. "Though, you don't think he's only asking me out because there isn't anyone else?"

"Last I heard, you aren't the only female going to community college, Brooke. There's likely another reason he asked you out besides the fact that you two went to high school together."

Pulling into the parking lot, Brooke smiled at her. "Thanks for saying that."

"I'm not just saying that. It's the truth." Pulling out her list, Addie said, "Do you want to come in or wait?"

"I need to study, so I'm going to wait here when you shop here and at the market. I'll go into Walmart with you, though."

"Sounds like a plan. I won't be too long."

Turning off the ignition, Brooke shrugged. "Take your time. I've got a ton of terms to learn."

Walking into the Dollar Store, Addie wandered through the aisles, but she couldn't find any of her usual enjoyment in it. She kept thinking back to her grandmother's words—and to the note that she'd written to her secret admirer. She'd had as many second thoughts about both her letter and the fact that she'd responded as Brooke seemed to have about the elusive Cameron. She wondered what Brooke would think.

After they'd gone to all three stores—and even stopped for a quick bite to eat at their favorite sandwich shop, Brooke headed back to Addie's.

"So, same time next week?"

"Yes, if that's okay with you?"

"Of course. All my classes are on Mondays, Wednesdays, and Fridays, so I can keep this day free."

"I appreciate you doing that."

"Don't be silly. I look forward to our Tuesdays together. I mean, we're friends, right?"

Addie smiled. Brooke would likely never understand how sweet those words were to her ears. "Right."

"And no offense, but you always calm me down."

"Why would I be offended by that?"

"I don't know." She waved a hand in the air as if she was hoping to grasp her words. "It's just that your life is so calm and constant. It's nothing like mine—I'm always running around and worrying about my future."

Addie couldn't help but chuckle at that. "I don't run around quite as much as you do, but it doesn't always feel so calm and constant." Making a decision, she added, "As a matter of fact, something really unusual happened the other day."

"What?"

"I got a note from a secret admirer."

"Get out! Really?"

"Really. When I got home from babysitting on Friday, my grandmother told me that I'd received a letter and she'd placed it on my bed. All that was on the envelope was my name and address. No return address."

Brooke's eyes were wide. "What did it say?"

Addie wasn't sure how much to share but figured she might as well keep going. "It was kind of long. The person said that he'd been wanting to talk to me for a long time, but since he'd waited so long, he was going to write me a note instead. Then he added that I was pretty special."

"Pretty special?" Brooke didn't look too impressed.

"Is that bad?"

"Of course not, it's just not too exciting, you know?" It was obvious Brooke was trying to sound more encouraging than she felt.

"I thought it was exciting." Which, of course, was part of her problem. She didn't have much in her life to be excited about.

"Well, what did you do?"

"Since he invited me to write back, I did."

"How did you know where to send it?"

"You're going to laugh. He told me to place it in a hole in a tree."

Brooke reached for her hand. "You have got to be kidding me."

"Nope. There's an oak tree that's been around for a hundred years. Everyone knows about it."

"Did you really stick it in there?"

Feeling her cheeks heat, she nodded. "I really did."

"Addie! You're so brave."

"I'm not. I've regretted it a hundred times, but I'm tired of always being so safe."

"I hope he's not a creepy person."

"Me too. But if he was the dangerous type, don't you think he'd talk to me in person instead of writing me a note?"

"You've got a point there." She slowed as they approached the light. "So what did you write?"

"Not all that much . . . but I did mention that I needed to know what he wanted. Like, what was his goal."

"Has this mysterious man answered you yet?"

Addie giggled. "You and your texting, Brooke. You've gotten used to everyone responding at lightning speed. I have to wait until he gets the letter and responds. We're supposed to give each other a week to write back. I have to wait until Friday."

"You have to wait three more days to see what he says?" Brooke asked as the light turned green and she approached Addie's street. "Or if he even got your letter?"

Put so bluntly, it did seem like a rather big leap of faith. "I don't have to wait that long to see if he got my note. I could go to the tree to see if it's been picked up."

"All while hoping and praying that a squirrel or some kid didn't take off with your note first."

"That's not making me feel very optimistic."

Pulling into her driveway, Brooke said, "I'm sorry, but I think some guy sending you a note like that is odd."

"Maybe he's shy and didn't know what to say to me in person."

"That's what text . . . Addie, you're right."

"See, making friends and dating in different ways isn't all that easy when one is Amish."

"You can say that again. Well, you'd better promise to let me take you shopping next week even if you don't need anything. I can't wait to hear what happens."

"Don't worry. I always need to go shopping," she teased as she handed over Brooke's payment. "Though, I'm going to want to see you, too. After all, you've got a real date with Cameron. You're going to have to tell me all about it."

"Wish me luck and I'll do the same for you," Brooke said as she helped Addie carry her bags to the front door.

"Good luck," Addie said. "And may God bless you, too."

"Same to you," Brooke said as she hugged her tight. "Have a good week."

"Yes, have a good week, too!" she called out as Brooke trotted back to her car. They surely led different lives, but it was moments like this that reminded Addie they were, perhaps, not so different.

Maybe not so different at all.

Chapter 8

Almost seven days had passed since Daniel had first read Addie's letter in the basement of the hospital. He'd been so relieved that she'd responded, and had been so consumed with how to respond, that his eight-hour shift had passed in a flash.

Unfortunately for him, every day since then had felt twice as long. First, he'd gone over to his parents' house. He got along with his parents just fine, but since he was the eldest of ten children, he always felt like he was entering a carnival when he got there.

Sure enough, things were just as chaotic as they'd been the previous week. After saying hello to Emily and Beth, his thirteen-year-old twin sisters, he found his mother in the kitchen chatting with two of his siblings.

A huge bag of potatoes sat on the counter. Potato peels covered a plate beside her. On the commercial-sized range sat two big stew pots. One of them was boiling.

"Hey, Mamm."

"Hi, Daniel. I'm glad you're here." She tilted her head so he could kiss her cheek.

"Why is that?" he asked. "Do you want some help peeling potatoes?"

"*Nee*. I need your help with Brodie and Anna." She pointed to the huge table on the far side of the kitchen. Years ago, their father had taken out the dining room wall. The dining room table was massive and now served as the homework station, craft area, laundry folding facility, catch-all, and dining room table.

Wondering what his two youngest siblings needed, he turned to Anna and Brodie. "Hi, you two."

"Hey, Daniel," Brodie replied. He looked around the kitchen. "Did you bring Bob over with you?"

"Not today, sorry."

"I wish you did."

"Bob probably wishes he was here, too," he teased.

"Hiya, Daniel," Anna said with a sunny smile.

"Hi, sweetpea." Sitting on the long bench beside her, he wrapped an arm around her shoulders and gave her a gentle hug. "How's my best girl?"

"Busy, 'cause I've got a lot of homework."

"How come you two are working in here? Where's everyone else?"

"Everyone else already finished," Brodie replied.

"Uh oh."

Brodie, always serious, frowned. "Mamm ain't happy about that either, 'cause I was supposed to help her peel potatoes."

"I guess I'd better help you then. What are you working on?"

"This." Brodie glared at his open notebook. "*Mei* teacher said I'm doing poorly with my report. Come help me, wouldya?"

"I'll do what I can. What is it on?"

"Types of bees." The twelve-year-old wrinkled his nose.

"Hmm." Other than the fact that they made honey and could sting a person, Daniel knew next to nothing about bees.

His little brother pointed to a half-filled page. "This is what I have so far."

Scanning the page, Daniel frowned. It looked like a lot of chicken scratch. "This ain't *gut,* Brodie. In fact, it looks pretty bad."

"*Jah.*" He sighed. "That's what Miss Hannah said."

"Where are you getting all your information?"

When Brodie shrugged, Daniel looked up at their mother. She had a potato in one of her hands and a paring knife in the other. She was also shaking her head at Brodie. "Do you see why I needed your help, Daniel? That boy needs a fire lit under him."

Noticing that Brodie looked a little embarrassed, he sent his little brother a sympathetic look. "I'll do my best."

"*Danke.*"

Anna tugged on his shirt. "What about me, Daniel? Are you gonna help me, too?"

"Maybe," he teased. "What do you need help with?"

"Subtracting big numbers and my spelling words."

"That's it?"

"*Nee.*" Looking guilty, she added, "And my reading homework."

"Anna, how come you have so much to do?"

After peeking to make sure their mother was back in the kitchen, Anna whispered, "Because I've been playing after school instead of working."

"Anna, you know better."

"Emily was going to help me do homework in her room, but she said I liked to play too much. She sent me back downstairs. Now I've got to sit here. Mamm ain't happy."

"I'm starting to see why."

Anna stared up at him with her big blue eyes. "You can help me, right? If I don't get all this done, Miss Hannah won't let me go out for the extra recess."

"It doesn't sound like you deserve it."

She shrugged. "Please?"

It was moments like this when Daniel prayed that he would never be blessed with ten kinner. He didn't know how his mother ever kept her patience. "You got any *kaffi*, Mamm?" he called out.

"I do. It's fresh, too. Come on over and I'll pour you a cup."

"Brodie, go find one of the encyclopedias that Autumn and Henry and I used to use. Bring down the *B*. Anna, you start doing that math."

Whether it was his tone of voice or because they knew they were out of choices, both of them did what he asked.

Handing him a cup of coffee, his mother said, "*Danke* for your help, son. I swear, I don't understand how I can have eight children who do what they're supposed to but two who don't do anything I ask. They're maddening enough to drive a mother to throw her hands up in the air!"

Daniel chuckled at the image. "Mamm, you have to admit that eight out of ten is pretty good odds."

"Your father says the same thing. Of course, he doesn't try to make them do their homework every afternoon."

"I don't blame him," he joked. "It's maddening."

She sipped her coffee. "Me neither, since these two are going to be the death of me."

Noticing that Brodie still hadn't returned from fetching the encyclopedia, he murmured, "They might be the death of me, too."

She smiled. "At least we'll go to Heaven together, hmm?"

"I reckon so." He kissed his mother's cheek. Then, after refilling his cup, he sat down and did homework with his two siblings for three hours. By the time he got home, he was almost too tired to walk Bob.

The next day, he worked a double shift. The number of people in the emergency room increased, and the number of absences among the hospital staff increased, too. Even folks who seemed to have a Teflon coating were affected. Every day two new people called in sick.

Everyone who remained was feeling run-down either from all the extra hours of work they were putting in or because they were coming down or recovering from illness.

Daniel had so far been blessed with good health, but he was surely becoming one of the many who was feeling overworked. He was all for doing his part in a crisis, but he wasn't ready to start living in the big three-story building. If he worked much more, he was pretty sure he might as well bring his bed there, too.

All he wanted to do was shower, put on fresh clothes, and relax in his easy chair. He wanted to hang out with Bob, too. The more he was gone, the more resentful the dog seemed to get. Just last night the beagle wouldn't even run to his side with a happy tail wag or spin.

Daniel felt so guilty.

Now, he was counting the minutes until he could leave the hospital and breathe some fresh, clean air. He wouldn't be opposed to eating a big plate of chicken and noodles, either.

But first he had to get home.

Stefan had been kind enough to drive him home, though he didn't seem very happy about it.

"Thank you again for the ride," Daniel said when they were just a few minutes from his house.

"Hmm? Oh, it's not a problem, Daniel. Besides, it's the least I can do since you've been taking on so many extra shifts."

"I'm grateful for the work." It wasn't exactly how he was feeling, but he was thankful to have such a good job.

"We're grateful to have you." He frowned. "I wish everyone in my life was as dependable."

Daniel noticed that he'd said "my life" and not "my team." Even though they weren't very close, he'd worked for Stefan long enough to ask a personal question or two.

"Is something at home troubling you?"

Stefan stiffened, then sighed. "You could say that. My brothers and sisters and I are having a tough time taking care of our parents. A couple of my siblings have forgotten to either help pay for the nurse or help out around the house. I learned a couple of hours ago that my sister forgot to spend time with my parents today."

"I'm sorry. That must be hard."

"Yeah." He rubbed a hand over his beard. "So, that's what's been on my mind. I've been debating with myself. Do I go over there and do what's right? Or, do I go home, take a shower, and finally sleep?" He chuckled. "I bet you're sorry you asked."

"Since all I want to do is shower and sleep, I think you should do that as well."

"Really?"

"Really. We all have to sleep sometime. You aren't gonna be much good if you show up grumpy and tired."

"I'm starting to get the sense that you're as tired as I am right now."

"Let's just say that I understand how you're feeling."

Stefan smiled. "Thanks for that." Turning left, he said, "I always forget where to turn to get to your house."

Realizing where they were—by the tree with the hole inside it—Daniel made a sudden decision. "If you wouldn't mind stopping up here at this park, I'd appreciate it."

Stefan pulled off where Daniel pointed. "Where's your house?"

"It's close by."

"What's going on? Dan, if you thought I was complaining about taking you home, I wasn't. I'm not going to make you walk."

"It's not that. It's . . . well, I've been exchanging notes with a woman." Feeling his cheeks heat, he added, "This tree is the place where we leave them."

"Are you serious?"

"I'm afraid so."

For the first time in days, some of the stress around Stefan's eyes eased. "Is this some kind of secret Amish postal service or something?"

"Not at all. It's, well, it's something I started myself."

"Are you pleased about that?"

"You know, I think I am. This woman, well, I'm beginning to realize that there's more to her than meets the eye."

He studied the tree. "How do you know if she's left you a note? Do you have a secret sign?"

Daniel grinned. Stefan was letting his imagination get the best of him, but he didn't blame him. The whole situation did seem like something out of a storybook. "We agreed to do pickups on Fridays. Unfortunately, I didn't get here yesterday. I'm afraid if she stops by and sees that I didn't pick up the note, she'll be upset."

"You can, ah, check the tree, and then I'll take you home if you'd like."

"That's kind of you, but I think a walk home would do me good."

"Understood." As Daniel got out, Stefan added, "Hey, Daniel?"

"Yes?"

"Would you mind if I stayed here a sec to see if you got a

note?" He held up a hand. "I'm not being creepy, I promise. It's just that, well . . . I could use some good news, even if it isn't good news for me."

Daniel grinned as he got out. "I don't mind. But, ah, I'd appreciate it if you wouldn't tell anyone at work about this."

"I think we both shared some secrets we're not anxious for the rest of the hospital staff to know."

"Thanks. And thanks for the ride. I meant what I said—I think you should get some sleep and see your parents in the morning."

"Even though my sister blew them off?"

"No offense, but if you keep filling in for her, she has no reason to worry, *jah*? Besides, sleep is needed for both of us."

"You're right about that."

After closing his door, Daniel walked over to the tree and stuck his hand inside. At first, he didn't find anything, but then he touched the envelope. Feeling a little triumphant, he pulled it out and held it up to Stefan.

Stefan gave him a thumbs-up sign through the window, then turned around.

When he was completely alone, Daniel smiled. At long last, the best part of his week had arrived.

Dear Secret Admirer,

I decided to write you back again, though I'm still skeptical about your motives. Or, maybe I'm second-guessing my motives, too. I keep thinking that I must be rather desperate to encourage such a correspondence. My English girlfriend says so.

That said, since I decided to write to you, and our intention is to get to know each other better, I thought I'd share a bit more about myself. I know you know that I don't do a lot with the other Amish girls my age. But I do spend time on other things. I keep busy taking care of my grandmother, babysitting, and helping a woman who needs an extra hand.

Something that you might or might not know about me is that I have a pet donkey. He was abused by his previous owner. When I heard that he was so withdrawn that he was going to be put down, I adopted him. He was given to me for free. I figured that everyone—even a lowly donkey—needs someone to believe in them. His previous owner had never even given him a name, which I thought was very sad. I decided to call him Snickers because I happened to have that candy bar in my pocket when I got him. It was the first thing that he showed any interest in.

Now, Snickers is a wonderful pet and very smart. He even works as a therapy donkey from time to time. That little donkey does so much good for so many. I really think he deserved to finally have someone believe in him. I hate that others in his life were so cruel. No one deserves that.

So that's my note. I'll look forward to reading your response.

Addie

Daniel felt his face heat. It was something of a joke around town that Addie had a pet donkey. But now that he'd read her note, he would never joke about Snickers again.

Obviously, he was the one who had been in the wrong.

Who was he to decide that saving a donkey who had survived a lifetime of abuse was a foolish thing?

No, the real question was why no one who gossiped about her pet had simply asked Addie how Snickers had come to live at her house. Why had no one ever cared enough to do that?

Another uncomfortable feeling nestled inside him, reminding Daniel that he had a lot to make up for.

Chapter 9

"So, that's what I wrote, Snickers," Addie concluded as she continued to curry comb his dark brown mane on Saturday afternoon. "I tried to explain how you came to live here—and how glad I am that you did. It makes a lot of sense to me. But who really cares about that?"

The donkey wiggled his ears as if to signal that he cared. Very much so.

His sweet expression looked so hopeful, she chuckled. "You are right. Your opinion does count. It counts a lot, for sure and for certain." As she leaned forward, attempting to gently loosen a particularly bad tangle in his mane, Addie murmured, "I just hope my letter didn't sound like a lecture. I have a tendency to do that when it comes to you, I'm afraid. . . ." She sighed. "What do you think? Did I just scare off my pen pal?"

Snickers brayed, then lifted his head. A car was approaching.

Curious as to who it could be, Addie left the comfort of the barn to see who had arrived. As soon as she saw the blue SUV she grinned. "Brooke? Is that you?"

"Of course, it's me, silly!" Brooke called out as she rushed across the gravel drive toward the barn. "I came over here as soon as I got out of class. Addie, I couldn't wait to talk to you!"

After giving Brooke a brief hug, Addie quickly looked her over. "What's wrong? Are you okay? Did something happen?"

"I'm so better than just okay." She motioned with her hand. "Come meet Cameron."

"Now?"

"Of course, silly."

Only then did she notice a tall man in a black hoodie leaning against Brooke's car. He wasn't smiling until he caught sight of Brooke. Then his expression warmed.

Pushing off from his position against the car, he walked over, his dark eyes seeming to take in every inch of Addie. "Hi. I'm Cameron."

"I'm Addie." She felt a glimmer of unease. She didn't like that a strange man knew where she lived, and she couldn't shake the feeling that Brooke had made a bad mistake.

"I figured. I would've recognized you anywhere." He grinned. "Brooke talks about you all the time."

Feeling even more self-conscious, she pushed her glasses up on the bridge of her nose. "I see."

Brooke reached for her hand and squeezed it. "I haven't been saying anything bad, Addie. I've just been telling Cameron about how I drive you around on Tuesdays."

What could she say? "*Jah,* she does, at that."

"She said it's good money."

Addie didn't like their Tuesdays reduced to being just a good source of income for Brooke, though she figured that it wasn't wrong that her friend had told him about her job. "She is mighty helpful to me. That is true."

Cameron grinned. "She's cute, babe."

Feeling a bit like Brooke's show-and-tell project, Addie

folded her hands together. "Did you stop by for any other reason, Brooke?"

Her friend looked embarrassed. "No. We were out for a drive, and I thought stopping by was a good idea." She lowered her voice. "Cameron, I said she was a friend, not just a client."

"Whatev. Are you ready to go?"

"Sure." Turning to Addie, she mouthed, "Sorry," before walking to her car. "I'll see you on Tuesday."

"Yes."

"Good to meet you, Addie," Cameron called out as he got in Brooke's passenger seat.

"It was good to meet you, too," she replied, though that wasn't exactly true. Brooke's crush hadn't seemed very nice or caring. Addie was having a hard time imagining the two of them together. But, maybe she was the one in the wrong? She'd begun to look at Brooke as a friend, but maybe they were nothing like that. Maybe Addie was nothing more than an Amish client to the Englischer.

And now, here she was, trusting someone who said he was an admirer. What if she was being played for a fool with him as well?

Hating these new doubts but unable to shake them, Addie returned to the barn to check on Snickers. The donkey seemed to be dozing in his stall. After double-checking that he had water and food, she went into the house.

The warmth of the living room, combined with the scent of the balsam candles burning on the coffee table, was welcoming. She wished they could lift her spirits, too. She pulled off her cloak, the black bonnet that covered her white *kapp,* and the blue scarf that she'd wrapped around her neck.

"Addie," her grandmother called out from the cozy hearth room right behind the kitchen. "Who was here?"

Walking over, she replied, "My driver friend, Brooke. She,

uh, brought her new boyfriend over here to meet me." She knew her response sounded halfhearted, but she couldn't summon anything more enthusiastic.

"Did she now? That is exciting." She moved to stand up. "Where are they? Should I make some fresh *kaffi*?"

"*Nee,* Mommi. They've already left."

Some of the light faded from her grandmother's eyes. "You didn't care to bring them inside? I would have enjoyed meeting Brooke's young man."

"There wasn't time. I, uh, don't believe they planned to stay very long. They only stopped by so I could say hello."

"That says a lot about your friendship, ain't so?"

"*Jah.*" Bless her grandmother's heart. Here she was, once again attempting to put a positive spin on things.

"Well, if it's a new romance, their only wanting to stay for a short while makes sense." Mommi smiled. "They probably only have eyes for each other."

"I dare say you're right."

"Don't feel bad, child. Next time you see them together, I'm sure they'll want to come inside for a good spell."

"I don't know about that, Mommi. Cameron didn't seem like the type to want to come in for coffee and conversation." Deciding to share her thoughts, she added, "Actually, he didn't seem very nice."

"Oh?"

"He acted like I was Brooke's unusual job. You know, because I'm Amish."

Mommi brushed off her comment with a wave of her hand. "Don't be so judgmental. Even if he did think that, he wouldn't be the first." She looked hard at Addie over the rims of her glasses. "Nor, I'm afraid, will he be the last."

"I guess not."

Her grandmother peered up at her. "Ach. Sit down, Addie, and talk to me. You look so blue. What has upset you so?"

Addie sat. "It's nothing."

"We both know it ain't nothing."

"Fine, it isn't."

"Now, the question is, are you saying that to protect me or you?"

"You, of course," she blurted before she thought better of it.

"Addie, I have trouble walking, and sometimes my body doesn't feel like working all that well. But that doesn't mean I've forgotten everything about living. Or even being nineteen. If you'd care to trust me, I'd love to listen to what is worrying you."

Her grandmother was right. She'd gotten in the bad habit of treating her grandmother as if she was fragile in both heart and body, when that wasn't the case at all. "Mommi, you know how I feel about Brooke. Even though she drives me around on Tuesdays, I've felt that she and I have become good friends."

"I know."

"I thought Brooke felt the same way about me. When she dropped me off on Tuesday, she even said that she couldn't wait to see me next Tuesday so we could catch up."

"But . . ."

"But when she was standing with Cameron, all I could see was how different the two of us are. I started to doubt myself. I started to think that maybe I was the one looking for friendship, but she was merely looking forward to another day of work."

"Do you really think that?"

Just as she started to nod, she shrugged. "I don't know. Maybe I'm simply a little jealous. Now even Brooke has found a boyfriend, while I am still waiting for someone to notice me." Someone beyond an anonymous writer.

"I've told you this many a time. The Lord is watching and

waiting. When He feels your time is right, He'll help you find the right man. You must be patient."

"I'll try."

"That's all you can do, yes. Be patient and try not to think the worst all the time."

"I don't do that."

"I know that there are a great many people who think you are a very sunny girl. But I also know that sometimes you let insecurity take hold of you. You have to let it go."

"Letting go isn't easy."

Mommi chuckled. "Of course it ain't! That's why the Lord is your anchor. You can't do it on your own. You don't have to."

Addie gave her a hug. "*Danke*. I'm so glad I have you."

"You are my greatest blessing. I promise that you have a long future ahead of you. Be patient and true."

"I'll do my best."

"That's all one can do, *jah*?"

Addie thought about those words long into the day. They were a soothing balm to the hurt feelings she'd experienced after Brooke's visit.

Those thoughts were also a nice break from wondering if her admirer had picked up her note—and if he intended to deliver another note on Friday.

"Yet another exercise in patience!" she griped to herself.

Then, of course, she had to laugh. It seemed that the Lord was determined to help her with that.

When Brooke picked her up on Tuesday, conversation between them was strained. Brooke wasn't her usual chatty self and Addie was feeling self-conscious.

When Brooke had said she'd simply wait in the car while Addie went into Walmart, Addie knew they needed to clear the air.

"Did you get everything you needed?" Brooke asked after Addie put her bags in the trunk.

"Yes."

"So, where to now? Or are you ready to go home?" Hardly looking at Addie, she moved to shift the vehicle into drive.

"Home, but wait for a moment, wouldya? I think we need to talk."

"What about?"

"You and me." She swallowed. "And your boyfriend."

Brooke put the car in park but didn't turn to face Addie. "What about him?"

Addie said a quick prayer for the right words. She didn't want to hurt Brooke's feelings, but she needed to be honest. "Come on. You heard how he talked to me. I didn't think he was very nice."

"I know Cameron acted like a jerk, but he'd never seen an Amish person before. You should give him a break."

"Brooke, every Amish person I know has been confronted with curious Englischers. We're used to being stared at, listened to, and even questioned about our ways. He wasn't acting curious. He was rude to me."

"I'll make sure I don't bring him by again. Is that all?"

Addie felt like crying. She'd known their conversation would feel awkward, but she'd actually hoped that Brooke would be more apologetic. Sad that things were likely going to get even worse, she added, "No. Um, Cameron said some things that made me wonder if you only think of me as a client."

"What? You heard what I said, Addie. I told him that we were friends."

"It just kind of sounded like you might have told him that we weren't really friends."

Brooke sighed. When she turned to face Addie, she had

tears in her eyes. "I'm sorry. I was so embarrassed by him that I didn't handle things all that well. Please don't think I'm horrible. We *are* friends. I promise you that."

"All right. I'm sorry I doubted you."

"No, you were right to bring it up." She chuckled. "I guess I'm starting to realize that dating isn't all that easy."

Addie smiled at her sympathetically. "I have a feeling you aren't the only person who feels that way. Not by a long shot."

Brooke chuckled. "So, home? Or would you like to go out to this new bakery I found? They serve three kinds of cupcakes every day."

"Cupcakes, of course."

Putting the car back in drive, Brooke pulled out of the parking lot. "I was hoping you'd say that."

Chapter 10

The day was a brisk fifty degrees—almost warm. The sun was shining, too—which was still a rarity in March. Daniel was sure that spring came later and later every year.

However, it likely didn't matter what month in the year it was. What did matter to Daniel was that it was a mighty fine day, and he wasn't working in the basement of a hospital. Instead, he was outside, breathing fresh air, and he even had his best friend by his side.

For his part, Bob was acting as if they were on the beach in Florida, he was so pleased to be outside. He was sniffing and prancing and wagging his tail. Glad he had the day off, Daniel tossed his coat on a bench and picked up Bob's squeaker toy, which he'd carried in his mouth during their walk. "Okay, boy. Let's play fetch." He'd barely tossed the toy into the air when the beagle ran after it with a happy bark.

A minute later, Bob had dropped the toy at his feet and was wagging his tail in anticipation. "Here you go now." When Daniel threw the toy again, Bob tore off after it. The game was repeated again and again. Usually, he would've put a stop to it, but Bob looked so jubilant, he didn't have the heart to end it early. Besides, he surely owed the hound a longer than normal excursion. The poor dog had been alone in the house far too many hours of late. Though one of his siblings often came over to check on Bob when Daniel worked a double, few of them took time to let the dog run and play.

Only when Bob's happy run had turned into a determined stride did he call it quits. "This is your last run, Bob. Don't forget, we've got to walk back home."

"I don't know who's going to be happier to sit on the couch. You or the dog," a merry voice called out behind him.

Startled, he turned around—and just about lost his voice. "Addie. Hello."

"Hi. Sorry. I was walking by and couldn't help but watch you toss that pink pig for your dog. He looked like he was the happiest *hund* in Apple Creek."

"I wish I'd known you were nearby. You could've tossed it a few times as well," he joked. "My arm is gonna be sore."

As he'd hoped, she grinned. "I fear Bob would've been disappointed in my efforts. I doubt I could throw it half as far."

He couldn't help but stare at her for a long moment. Addie wore a royal blue dress, black stockings, and tennis shoes, and the shawl she'd obviously been wrapped in earlier had been tossed over an arm. He realized then that Addie, with her curly blond hair, full cheeks, and green eyes, was striking. Her features seemed to go together perfectly, and he now thought her glasses were rather fetching.

But what drew his attention was her smile. For once, she wasn't trying to temper it or hide it. Instead, it was all white teeth and sunshine. She truly radiated happiness. It was infectious.

"Come over and give it a try," he invited.

That fetching smile vanished. "Truly?"

The longing in her eyes made a lump form in his chest. The more he got to know her, the more he realized that Addie didn't expect much from anyone at all.

Especially not him, since he'd spent most of his life ignoring her. "Of course," he said in a gentle tone.

Daniel thought she might refuse, but she seemed to pull courage from deep within herself instead. After tossing her shawl on the ground, she stepped closer and held out her hand.

"Be warned, it's wet and slimy."

"It's a pink rubber pig." She laughed. "I wouldn't expect it to feel like anything else."

"Here you go, then." Bob, his eyes on his toy, sat down at her feet. Every muscle in his body seemed to be ready to spring into action.

Addie squeezed the pig. When it squawked, Bob barked joyfully. Which brought forth another giggle. "I've tossed things, of course, but never far. Do you have any hints? I'd hate for Bob to be disappointed."

Bob, of course, wasn't picky, as long as whoever had his pig released it. But Daniel couldn't help playing along. "How about you toss it first? You might not even need my advice."

"All right." She pursed her lips, took a deep breath, then tossed the pink pig four feet away. "Oh, dear."

Bob watched it, tilted his head to one side, then trotted over, picked it up, and brought it back to her side.

"I think your beagle is a bit unimpressed with my toss."

"You might be right." He grinned.

Squeezing the pig again, she said, "I think I'm going to need that advice, now."

Taking the wet pig from her, he held it in his right hand. Realizing that it had been a long time since he'd even thought about throwing a ball correctly, he paused to think about it a moment. "All right. First thing you do is lift your right elbow a bit, then step forward with your right leg and toss with a bit of power." He demonstrated. Pleased to see the pig sail across the grass, he smiled as Bob barked happily and ran full speed toward it.

"You make it look easy."

"It is easy—at least for someone who first learned to throw at the age of five or so."

"Here he comes." She still looked wary. "What do you think? Should I give it another try?"

"I'd be disappointed if you didn't."

That seemed to be the right thing to say. She took the pig from Bob's mouth, carefully lifted her elbow a few inches, and then glanced his way. "Is this right?"

"Almost." He reached out and pressed her elbow up a bit more. "Like that."

She smiled. "I feel like I have a chicken wing."

"If you do, then you're holding it correctly. Now, step forward and as soon as you transfer your weight, let the pig fly."

She stepped forward, shifted, then froze. Bob, who'd been eyeing that pig with an eagle eye, whined when it remained in her hand.

"What happened?" he asked.

"I'm worried I'm going to mess up." She shook her head. "Sorry. I'll try again."

Unable to help himself, he placed his hand on her shoulder. "Hey."

"Jah?"

"Addie, there is no right or wrong. Not really. At the end

of the day, all we're doing is playing fetch with my dog. I promise, Bob will be happy with anything. Me too."

Her eyes widened; then she seemed to catch her breath. "*Jah*. I mean, you're right. I don't know why I'm overthinking this." Looking more determined, she lifted that elbow again, stepped forward, and threw.

The pig went about six feet.

As Bob ran to fetch it, she sighed. "I still have a way to go."

"You do, but it went further. And look, Bob seems happy enough."

As he trotted back, the beagle's tail was wagging and his ears were perked up. Daniel could almost feel Bob warming to Addie.

"This time, push your arm all the way forward." He demonstrated without the pig. "Like that."

"All right." Leaning down, she said, "Bob, may I have your pig now?" The dog dropped the toy at her feet. After she picked it up, she threw it again. This time it went almost twice as far.

Addie's eyes grew wide as Bob raced out to get the pig, barking happily. "I did it!"

Her smile was beautiful. "You sure did. I knew you could, too. Good job."

"*Danke!*"

When Bob raced back, she said, "May I throw it again? Do you mind?"

In that moment, he didn't think he could deny her anything. "Throw it as many times as you like, Addie. You're a natural."

She smiled shyly as she picked up the pig and threw again. When it went even farther, she laughed. "I know this is likely a silly thing, but I'm so happy. Thank you, Daniel."

"Of course. It was my pleasure."

Daniel realized that he meant that, too. When was the last time he'd been so happy to help another person? When was the last time he'd been so happy just to see another person smile?

The answer was obvious, of course. It had been far too long.

Chapter 11

After debating whether to go before her babysitting job or after, Addie gave in to temptation and visited "their" oak tree at twelve o'clock on the dot. After making sure no one was around to see, she checked their little niche, and found her new letter.

He'd written her back!

Pleased, she put it securely in her purse, then started walking toward town.

It felt like Christmas Day had come again, which was both a good comparison and a rather pitiful commentary on her social life. Her grandmother was right—she should be getting out and meeting available Amish men. Thinking about Daniel, Addie blushed. She had definitely felt a connection with him, which was a surprise. She wasn't sure how two people who had known each other for years could suddenly start enjoying each other's company, but it had happened.

She had no idea where her admirer lived, but she was sure that he must live over in Kidron or Wooster or maybe even near Middleburg. If he lived close, he would surely have approached her like any "normal" suitor would. There had to be a reason he was writing instead of calling at her door.

Of course, the less confident part of her was still worried that their correspondence was just a lark. A simple excuse to play a game at her expense. Then, when the novelty wore off, it would end as suddenly as it began.

A car horn blared.

She jumped. To her surprise, Addie realized she was already near the center of town. Cars were going by on the road, children were playing in the yard of the elementary school, and a pair of men were walking on the street just in front of her.

Unable to wait to read what the note said, she darted into a coffee shop and sat down for a few minutes to read the note.

> *Dear Addie,*
>
> *Have you been enjoying the burst of sunshine we've had lately? What have you been doing?*
>
> *I've been trying to go outside as much as possible. I work at the hospital, so my days are usually spent inside. I don't mind the work all that much in the winter, because if I wasn't working I'd be spending my extra time inside anyway. In the summer, though? Well, I practically have to drag myself out of bed every morning on workdays. On my days off? I'm up like toast with the sun.*
>
> *Now that it's close to April, most everyone seems to be talking about summer vacations. I haven't any plans. Come to think of it, I didn't do anything special last summer either. It kind of makes me wonder when my life will become*

more balanced, though my father says that balanced lives rarely happen. What do you think?

I almost forgot to respond to your words about Snickers. I, for one, like that you have a donkey. Snickers seems like a good companion, and it's a blessing that you could help an animal in need. Wouldn't it be a better world if everyone took in an animal that needed a home?

I'll look for your new note next week.

Your S.A.

"You want another cup of coffee, Addie?" the waitress asked.

Startled, she realized she'd been holding the empty cup between her hands while she studied the letter. "Thank you, but no. I've got to leave in a minute."

"Where are you off to today? Housecleaning?"

"*Nee*. Babysitting Tabby Beaumont."

The waitress smiled. "She's a cutie. Gretchen brings her in every couple of weeks," she commented as she wiped the surface of the table next to Addie's.

"She's as sweet as sugar, which means I'd better get on my way." Quickly she folded her letter. "Thank you for the latte, Melissa."

"Not a problem." Glancing her way again, she straightened. "Hey, Addie, it's none of my business, but are you okay?"

"Of course, why?"

"No reason. It's just the way you were studying that letter. I worried you might have gotten some bad news."

"Not at all. It was just, um, a good letter."

"Those are the best, aren't they?"

"They are, indeed. Have a *gut* day now," Addie said as she hurried out the door.

Four hours later, Tabby was asleep, and Gretchen wasn't due back for an hour. That gave Addie plenty of time to sit in front of the fireplace, reread the note, and think. Boy, she needed to think.

When she'd received the first note, it had been soon after Aaron and June's engagement party, and she'd been feeling rather low. She'd felt as if life was passing her by and that she was practically invisible to most everyone her age. The party hadn't been the first time when she'd felt so awkward, wondering whom to talk to first and what to do when it was obvious that no one had anything to say to her. However, it sure had been one of the most painful experiences in recent memory. She'd vowed then and there to give up. Give up trying, give up wishing things would improve.

The Lord must have been listening and felt differently, because soon after she'd received the very first note. Of course, she'd been skeptical and surprised, but she'd also been excited. It was if she'd had proof that there really was someone in Apple Creek who had noticed her and wanted to get to know her.

Better yet, it even seemed as if this secret admirer was just as socially awkward as she was. That suspicion had given her the courage to write back, just to see what he wrote next. And now, here they were, exchanging notes every week.

Now, instead of being filled with worry and second guesses, she was filled with hope and anticipation.

However, that anticipation didn't hold a candle to her unexpected afternoon with Daniel Miller and his dog Bob. When she'd first seen him at the park, she'd been tempted to simply walk past them. Daniel wasn't mean or rude; they'd never had any occasion to be near each other. He was handsome and popular and had always been.

He was also good friends with girls who had seemed to

find joy in being catty and making her feel foolish. That alone had made her want to keep her distance from him.

But the joy in his face when he'd been playing with Bob had drawn her like a magnet. She hadn't been able to stop watching the pair—and his joy had prompted her to say something to him.

Never in her life had she felt a man's regard so strongly. She remembered every touch, every smile, every word of encouragement that he'd spoken. It had been so, so lovely.

She could barely stop thinking about it.

Which, of course, was silly. Here she was, acting as if she had two suitors, when all she had was a secret pen pal and a few fun minutes with an acquaintance and his dog. Neither signified as an actual relationship.

When the back door opened and Gretchen came in with her arms full of bags, Addie got to her feet. "Did you have a good time with your errands?"

"As good a time as one can have at the Supercenter," she said as she set four plastic bags on the kitchen counter. "Before that, I did go out to lunch with a good friend, though. That was lovely. How's Tabby?"

"She was a good baby, as always. She's sleeping now."

"When did she go down?"

"About thirty minutes ago."

Gretchen smiled. "Great. That means I have a few minutes to work on Howard's birthday present."

"Are you getting crafty again?" Addie teased. Gretchen was always attempting a new project, some with better results than others. Her attempt at knitting had been rather disastrous, though she did have a gift for making stamped note cards.

Gretchen chuckled. "I am, though this time it's just a matter of planning instead of talent. Would you like to see what I'm going to do before you go?"

"Of course."

Gretchen walked over to the kitchen table and got out a piece of cardboard with what looked like a blank jigsaw puzzle on it. "I'm going to write him a note! Then Howard has to put it together in order to see what I have to say."

"That is very cute."

"I'm going to make him a birthday cake, too, and get him a round of golf at a course he's been interested in trying out." Beaming, she said, "Howard is going to have to put together my puzzle to figure out where his gift certificate is! What do you think?"

"I think he's going to like both the puzzle and your gift very much." Of course, Howard's devotion to his wife made Addie believe that anything Gretchen did would be met with effusive compliments and smiles.

"I hope so. It's hard because I don't want to do too much or not enough." She wrinkled her nose. "Do you know what I mean?"

"I do."

She opened her wallet and pulled out Addie's payment. "Do you have any plans for the weekend, Addie?"

"Oh, no. I usually stay home with my grandmother on the weekends."

A little of the excitement that had been shining in Gretchen's eyes dimmed. "I'm sorry."

"It's all right. I didn't expect to have plans, anyway."

Gretchen's expression cleared. "Oh, of course. The Amish don't usually go to a lot of parties or anything, do they?"

She chuckled. "We do." She shrugged. "But I'm not very good in social situations."

Gretchen looked embarrassed. "I'm sorry, I put my foot in my mouth, didn't I?

Addie chuckled. "You didn't. I'd rather be honest than not."

"We've known each other for a while now. Do you have anyone special?"

"I'm not sure. There is someone, but we are taking small steps."

"Good for you. I've always thought that taking things slow is best."

Choosing her words carefully, Addie went on. "I'm not sure what the Lord will choose for my life, but I'm hopeful that the right thing will happen at the right time."

"Me too. You're such a nice girl. I hope you find a man who's worthy of you very soon."

"Me too." After slipping the money into her billfold, she said, "Well, I had better get going."

"Yes, of course. Thank you for watching Tabitha. She never cries when we leave if you're here. You're the only babysitter she's so comfortable with."

"You're welcome, but you know I enjoy being with her." After exchanging a few more words, Addie let herself out, smiling to herself about Gretchen's jigsaw puzzle. She hoped Howard would like it, too. Gretchen seemed so proud of her idea.

Walking home, she passed the park where she'd seen Daniel and his dog, walked by the corner store, and then at last reached her street. To her surprise, there was a car in the driveway.

Worried that something was wrong, she hurried down the street and rushed in the front door. "Mommi?"

"We're right here, dear."

Addie turned to see her grandmother sitting with a man who was wearing jeans, boots, and a thick navy sweater. They were both sipping coffee. Neither looked upset or worried, which was a blessing. When they looked her way, she smiled. "Hello."

"Hello, dear," Mommi said. "Come in here and join us. I have someone you need to meet."

Walking closer, Addie realized that this person wasn't a

stranger to her grandmother. They seemed comfortable with each other.

"Zac, this is my granddaughter, Addie. Addie, this man is Zachary Carr. He came over with news about your father."

Addie could hardly believe her ears. "My *daed*?"

Zac stood up. "It's nice to meet you, Addie. I've heard a lot about you."

That was another surprise. "How?" Looking from Zac to her grandmother, she said, "Have you two been in touch?"

"I was here about six months ago, and we've been corresponding through letters ever since."

"Really? I didn't know that." Feeling hurt, Addie turned to her grandmother. "Why did you never tell me this?"

Looking guilty, Mommi said, "I know you're confused, but I had my reasons for keeping this a secret."

If they'd been alone, Addie would've had a lot to say. Since they weren't, she simply nodded with a jerk of her head. "I see."

"Addie, listen, child. I didn't want to tell you about Zac or your father because I knew you'd be upset. Plus, I didn't want you to get worried if nothing happened."

What would she be upset about? Her father was a complete stranger to her. Now she was even more confused. She was running out of patience fast.

Turning to Zac, she said, "Perhaps you would be so kind as to fill me in. What, exactly, has happened to my father?" *And what could it possibly have to do with me?* she added silently.

Compassion filled his gaze. "I think you'd better sit down, Addie."

Every nerve ending on alert, she sat. Then watched as Zac sat down across from her, opened up a leather briefcase, and pulled out a thick manila folder.

Chapter 12

The air in the living room seemed to crackle with tension while Zac opened the thick folder he'd brought.

"I'm sorry, ladies, but it's going to take me a minute," he apologized as he flipped through several sheets of legal-looking papers. Every so often he held one up and scanned it quickly before flipping through the stack some more.

Sitting by her side, her grandmother held her back as straight as an ironing board. She didn't look as curious as Addie felt, however. Instead, it seemed she was more worried about what the lawyer was going to say—and about how Addie would respond to whatever news she was going to hear.

As one minute turned to two, then three, Addie's anxiety rose. It was now obvious that she'd been kept in the dark for a reason. She couldn't imagine what it could be.

At long last Zac found whatever paper he was looking for. He glanced at it again before placing it back down on the table.

His expression full of sympathy, he spoke. "Addie, I'm

afraid there's no easy way to say this. About eighteen months ago, your father, John Henry Holmes, passed away from lung cancer. From what I understand, after, ah, breaking up with your mother, he became a successful real estate agent in Illinois. He also married again and had two other children. They are twelve and thirteen."

"So I have two half siblings?"

"Yes."

The news wasn't easy to hear, but Addie couldn't exactly say that she was upset. She had no memory of her father, and her grandmother had never spoken of him. She hadn't even known his name. "Okay . . ." It felt as if Zac was waiting for some kind of response, but she didn't have one. At least not at the moment.

Hoping for a hint of what was to come, she glanced at her grandmother. Mommi was still sitting motionless and staring straight ahead.

Disappointed, Addie leaned back against the sofa. "Is there anything else, Zac?"

"Oh, yes." He crossed his legs. "Addie, your grandmother told me that you have had no contact with your father since you were a small child. Is that the case?"

She nodded. "That is true. I have no memory of him."

"It seems that while John Henry never reached out to you, he never forgot about his daughter." He flipped to another sheet. "Addie, it is my responsibility to inform you that Mr. John Henry Holmes left you, as his oldest child, a sizable inheritance."

"He left me money?"

Zac nodded. "That is why I originally reached out to your grandmother. I knew you were legally of age, but I wasn't sure where you were living."

This story was getting more and more confusing. "Why didn't you contact me as soon as my grandmother told you that I was here? Why was I kept in the dark until now?"

Mommi looked pained. "Patience, child."

As far as she was concerned, her grandmother's admonishment seemed like a lot to ask. So she ignored it. Folding her hands on her lap, she turned to Zac. "I'm listening."

For the first time, the lawyer looked uncomfortable. "Your father left a message saying that he didn't want you told until your age and whereabouts could be verified—and that I was able to come in person to tell you the news."

"Because?"

Zac sighed. "Because he was worried about how your mother would react." After a pause, he added, "No one had heard from her for some time. Or so we thought."

He was speaking in riddles again. "My mother is as much a stranger to me as my father. Is she still alive?" As much as that hurt to ask, Addie had no idea about her mother's life.

Her grandmother inhaled sharply. "Addie, you should temper your tongue."

"Is she?" Addie asked again. It might be wrong, but she didn't feel as if she owed her mother much.

"She is," Zac said. "Unfortunately, for several years, she had a difficult time." Still looking uncomfortable, he fussed with the stack of papers in front of him again. "Kate made some poor choices. I guess you could say she also made some pretty negative connections."

Addie was becoming completely confused. "I don't know what that means."

Mommi interjected. "What Zac is circling around, dear, is that after leaving you with me, your mother still didn't get herself together. She made several more bad decisions, each one worse than the last. Eventually, she was incarcerated."

Incarcerated? It took a moment for the meaning of the word to register. "She was in jail?"

"Yes. Kate Stutzman was sentenced to seven years in a minimum security prison." Looking down at the paper he was holding, Zac added, "She served three and a half years. She's been out for some time now."

"My mother was in prison."

"*Jah,*" Mommi said.

Addie felt as if she was living in the middle of a dream. A very strange, very horrible nightmare. Abruptly deciding that she would contemplate how this news made her feel at a later time, she turned back to the lawyer. "Based on all those papers, I'm assuming you know that she dropped me off here when I was a little girl. I haven't seen her since. She's a stranger to me."

"Yes, I imagine she is," Zac murmured.

"Plus, if she was a prisoner while my father was a real estate agent and getting married again, I don't understand why he thought she would be upset that he left me money." Money that Addie wasn't even sure she wanted.

Zac flipped through some pages again. "John Henry knew she had a drug habit and had heard about her imprisonment. When he drew up the will, he wasn't sure what she was like, or how she would react in the event of his death."

This was getting worse and worse. "She had a drug habit."

"Yes. The court documents reveal that she developed an addiction to heroin. It spiraled out of control, and she began, uh, associating with some disreputable people."

"She wouldn't have been imprisoned for that, would she?"

"No. She was found guilty of robbing a convenience store clerk. The clerk was killed during the robbery. Your mother wasn't directly responsible, but she did have to serve time."

"My mother robbed people and played a part in someone's murder?"

Her grandmother's bottom lip trembled. "I'm sorry you had to find out about this, dear."

Addie was, too. Though she was more upset that her grandmother had known much of the information but had never shared any of it. "When did you find out, Mommi?"

"We should talk about that another time."

Addie had been waiting all her life to know more about her mother. Her grandmother had always said she didn't know about Kate's life. Impatient for answers, she turned to Zac. "Did you tell all this to my grandmother when you first met? Is that why she is so . . . so calm?"

Before he could answer, her grandmother spoke again. "I already knew about Kate's troubles."

"How? Did the police call you?"

"Not exactly. Kate wrote me a letter. The warden at the prison reaches out to next of kin, too. Every so often I would receive a message from the prison with an update about Kate-usually there was a parole hearing or some such scheduled." Mommi waved a hand. "Then, of course, Kate would write to me as well."

"Why did you never tell me?"

"Much of it happened when you were a little girl. There was no reason for you to know, especially since your mother had given up all her rights." Looking even more flustered, she said, "I always intended to tell you, but I could never think of the right time."

"Mommi, I'm nineteen. You've had lots of time to tell me this."

"I know. I have no real reason to have kept this from you except that I was afraid."

"Of what?"

"Of seeing you hurt again. Of hearing you ask questions that I couldn't supply the answers for." Softly, she added, "Of having you think worse of your parents than you already did."

Maybe later she would have the luxury of reviewing everything her grandmother had said and really analyzing how she felt. Now, though, Addie was aware that this Zachary was listening to their interplay. And that he was waiting to share even more news.

Though she felt like covering her ears with her hands, she said, "What other news do you have to share with me?"

He looked at her directly, as if she was an adult, as if she was strong enough to handle whatever he had to say. "Your mother was released from prison seven years ago. When she got out, she spent time in a halfway house in Ross County, then took a number of jobs, and eventually obtained both her GED and her associate's degree. She now works in a manufacturing plant and makes a good wage." He paused again. "She's also been sober for ten years."

"Okay. That's good for her. But I still don't understand what this has to do with me." It was a struggle, but she was determined to remain distant. Knowing that her mother had turned her life around but still had never wanted to contact her made hearing the story of her life even more painful.

"Adelaide. Come, now. You should not sound so uncaring."

But how could she sound any other way? "I'm sorry, Mommi, but you obviously know that this is difficult to hear. That's why you kept your silence, right? I'm not going to pretend that any of this is easy when it's far from that."

Zac looked from one to the other, then murmured, "Continuing on, I should tell you that your mother was also listed as a beneficiary in your father's will. He left a small settlement for her, with the stipulation that she had to have changed her life in order to receive it. That is where I originally came in. His estate contacted me to find her, to investigate how she was living, and to determine whether she met the criteria. Only after I talked to her did I seek you out."

"Addie, after all this time, Kate is doing mighty well." She smiled. "It wasn't easy for her to turn her life around, but she did. She hardly seems like the same person. I'm so proud of the progress she's made."

It took a second for her grandmother's words to register. "You've been in contact with her recently."

"Well, yes."

"For how long?"

Her grandmother seemed to steel herself before answering. "Well, um, at first we wrote letters, but then, after *Dawdi* died, we started calling each other." Sounding nervous, she laughed lightly. "Well, you know what I mean. She called and left me a message and then I would call her back. We did this for quite a while. But then, I saw her a few weeks ago."

"How?" Her tone was harsh, but Addie couldn't help herself.

Looking even more uncomfortable, Mommi added, "Your mother came here to see me when you were babysitting at the Beaumonts' one day. It was a shock to see her, but she looks wonderful." She smiled. "So happy and fresh."

"She's happy."

Her grandmother's eyes lit up. "I think she is. We talked about a lot of things. About how she never felt like she fit in here in Apple Creek. About how your grandfather and I never listened to her feelings. She was right about that, too."

"I see." Of course, Addie didn't see anything, but she was so confused, she didn't know what else to say.

"At last, I knew it was time to forgive her and move on. Kate wants to be forgiven. I needed to do that, didn't I?"

"And you still kept her existence a secret from me."

Zac jumped in then. "Addie, your mother asked me to come here and tell you her story, so you can make your own decision about her. That is my other reason for being here. I not only wanted you to know about your father's gift, but also to tell you that your mother is a sweet woman who feels terrible about the pain she's caused you. She wants to meet you."

Her mother, after ignoring her for years, wanted to get to know her. At long last.

Well, actually, her mother wanted to know her now that

Addie was receiving some money. She wanted to have a relationship now that her daughter was all grown up, trying to make her way in the world, and didn't actually need a mother.

"No," she said.

Her grandmother inhaled sharply. "Addie—"

Too angry to even look at her grandmother, Addie continued to stare straight at Zac. "You said this is my choice, correct?"

"*Jah*. I said it is your choice, and I meant it, too."

"Then that is my decision. Now, when will I find out more about this inheritance?"

"I'll be happy to sit down and discuss the amount you'll be receiving. We can set up a time to do that."

"I'd like that. Thank you. Perhaps one day soon?"

"I can meet with you on Monday. Will that work?"

She nodded. "Monday will be fine."

"Would you like me to meet you here?"

"No." She named the first restaurant she could think of. "Could we meet there instead? Maybe at ten in the morning?"

He wrote that down. "I'll be there."

"I will, too. Thank you."

Ten minutes later, Addie walked him to the door. "I'll see you on Monday."

He held out his hand and shook hers. "Miss Holmes, I know this news has been a shock in many ways, but I can't help thinking that your grandmother's heart was in the right place."

"I imagine you are right."

"Perhaps you should let that comfort you instead of making it one more thing to regret."

"I'll do my best."

Addie continued to stand in the open doorway as she

watched Zac stride to his car. While they'd been speaking, the sun had started to set and the wind had picked up. A few snowflakes were swirling in the air. Every few seconds, one would land on her face.

Ignoring it all, she dwelt on her bitterness. Briefly, she even considered Zac's parting words and tried to put them into practice.

But it was no use. She might want to be patient and understanding, but she was also human.

At the end of the day, she didn't care about her grandmother's motives. As far as Addie was concerned, they didn't matter. Mommi's heart might have been in the right place for her daughter, but what about her granddaughter? No matter what explanation or excuse her grandmother might offer, Addie felt Mommi's actions said it all. She'd made her choices and they were telling. From Addie's perspective, they could never be explained away.

"Addie, you're letting in the cold air. Close the door."

"Sorry." She stepped back to shut the door. As tempting as it was to continue to look out at the street and dwell on her own angry feelings, she turned.

Her grandmother was on her feet and clutching her walker. "Come away from the door. How about I turn on the kettle? We can have a nice cup of hot tea. After all, we do have so much to talk about." Looking as if she was delighted by the prospect, she smiled. "We can even sit down in front of the fire. It will warm up these old bones."

Though their years of history pushed her to agree, she simply couldn't do it. "I'm afraid you're going to have to enjoy the fire on your own. I . . . I just can't right now."

Her expression fell. "Child—"

"Oh, *nee*. I am not a child, Mommi. You know that and I know that. I'm a grown woman who's just discovered that one of her parents is dead while the other was once an addict and spent time in prison. But that's okay, because she's all better," she added sarcastically. "My mother just never felt like getting to know me until now."

"That's hardly fair, Addie."

"You're right. It's hardly fair at all." Her voice shook with emotion, but she forced herself to continue. "However, none of that comes close to the way I feel about your keeping all these secrets and then lying to me. For years."

Her grandmother shook her head. "It wasn't like that."

"You might have felt there were a dozen reasons to do what you did, but all I care about at this minute was that you did it."

"You aren't going to let me explain?"

"I didn't say that. I'm saying that I've just received a great many shocks. I'd like time to come to terms with what I've learned. If you won't at least give me that, I'm not sure what it means. Or maybe it means that in your opinion, my feelings don't matter. Maybe they don't matter much at all."

Chapter 13

Dear Secret Admirer,

I almost didn't write you this week. Only our promise to continue to send letters to each other compelled me to put this note in "our" tree. However, I'm afraid today's note isn't a very merry or happy one. Honestly, my heart is so full of pain, I fear that I'm using our correspondence as a way of surviving. I have to tell someone what just happened and try to describe how disenchanted I feel.

No, how devastated I am.

Unhappily for you, S.A., you are the unfortunate recipient of my news.

Choosing to read about my mess is another story, however. Therefore, if you'd rather forgo the experience, feel free to toss this note in the trash. I promise, I won't judge you! I wouldn't blame you for not wanting to immerse yourself in my problems. I am only asking you to give me the grace of allowing me to share what happened with someone else.

If you haven't already thrown away this note, feel free to read on. . . .

The letter was a shock.

Glad no one else was around, Daniel dropped it onto the chair next to where he was sitting and attempted to get control of himself. It was difficult, though. He was stunned by both her story and the obvious pain that flowed through each of her words.

A burst of laughter floated into the room, bringing him out of his reverie. Glad for the nudge, Daniel took a deep breath of air. He'd been so intent on her story, he had practically forgotten to breathe.

"Get a hold of yourself, Daniel," he whispered. "This ain't your story, it's hers."

It was hard to keep any emotional distance, however. Addie's pain was so acute, it was almost tangible. He hated that she was so hurt. He hated that she had no one to share the pain with but him.

No, it wasn't exactly him. She was reaching out to his fictitious counterpart because he'd been too chicken to simply walk up to her in the middle of a party and become her friend.

Daniel wished there was something he could do besides continue to read. No, he wanted nothing more than to hurry over to her house, knock on her door, and pull her into his arms. She needed someone.

She needed more than a made-up secret admirer who'd begun writing to her on a whim and couldn't seem to stop because it would reflect badly on him.

But he had no choice. He was no more able to stop reading her note than he was able to prevent a future illness or his eventual death. Taking a deep breath, he continued.

Here's what happened. I recently learned that not only did my mother live within driving distance of Apple Creek and chose not to see me, but also that she went to prison! And I'm supposed to believe that she actually cared about me.

My father, on the other hand, divorced my mother soon after they had me. He eventually had another family and made a life for himself—all while never contacting me. To make matters even crazier, right before he died, he changed his will and left me some money. And it's a lot, S.A. What do I even do about that?

Daniel put down the letter. He was floored. He couldn't imagine learning all of that at one time—it must have been difficult. But if her father had come to his senses and left her a gift, he wasn't sure why she was so torn up. Was Addie still harboring such bitterness toward her *daed* that she couldn't forgive him or accept his gift?

He supposed it was likely, but it didn't quite seem like the woman he'd come to know through their letters.

Now even more curious and concerned, he picked up the note once again.

Then, to make matters worse, it turns out that my mother has been in contact with my grandmother for months now. Can you believe that? She's even been to the house to see Mommi while I was babysitting. I don't know if I'm more upset by the fact that she only wanted to reacquaint herself with her mother instead of her daughter—or the fact that Mommi didn't see fit to tell me.

No, that ain't exactly true. I think I'm most upset about the fact that Mommi invited her over specifically during a time when she knew I wouldn't be there.

My grandmother now wants me to give my mother a chance and get to know her.

After all this time! After being teased by most everyone because my parents didn't want me, I'm supposed to accept that now the time is "right" for us to meet and form a relationship? It's bad to say, but I'm suspicious.

I mean, why now? Mommi acts like my mother has turned over a new leaf and everything is wonderful and good, but I am far more skeptical.

I'm even wondering if my mother has come out of the woodwork because my father left me money.

Does that make me horrible?

"*Nee,*" he said out loud. "You're not horrible at all, Addie Holmes. I was just thinking the very same thing."

His mind spinning, Daniel focused on the last of the note, determined to finish it so he could see how she was feeling.

It might not come as a surprise to you (Or it might!) but I told my grandmother that I didn't want to talk it all over with her and I didn't want to meet my mother either. Mommi is not happy with me. She looks hurt and sad—and I have a feeling that a stern lecture about not only turning the other cheek but forgiveness is in my future.

I don't know if I've ever felt more upset in my life. My parents have suddenly appeared in my life and the one person I thought I could trust, no matter what, has been keeping secrets from me. I feel completely alone.

Alone, except for you, I suppose. Maybe we don't actually have a "real" relationship, but it certainly feels like a relationship to me. These letters have started to mean a lot to me.

I'm sorry to burden you with my troubles, but please know that I don't expect or need advice. I just wanted someone to give me the chance to be open and honest. So thank you for that.

I'll look forward to your note next week—but if you decide not to write back, I'll understand. You started writing me because you found something in me worthwhile. You might not feel that is the case any longer.

So, if you decide to never write me again, please know that I understand. In fact, I wouldn't blame you one bit.

Addie

Daniel carefully folded the letter, put it back in its envelope, then slipped it in his jacket pocket. Only then did he give in to temptation and close his eyes. She was upset and needed a friend. He wanted to be that friend.

But what was she going to do when she realized that *he* was her secret pen pal? He would be yet another person who had kept secrets from her.

When she found out that he was the author of all these notes, she was going to hate him.

It would be nothing less than he deserved, too. He was kind of starting to hate himself.

"Hey, Daniel, sorry, but your break is gonna have to be done five minutes early," Stefan called out. "There was an MVA on the turnpike. At least four ambulances are heading this way. We're going to need you to stand by in the ER."

Multivehicle accidents were awful. "All right. I'll be right down."

"Thanks."

Daniel didn't bother replying—there was no reason to. Everyone had to come together during emergencies; there were no exceptions. He didn't mind, anyway. He was so troubled by Addie's note—and his mixed feelings about it—he was actually eager to be so busy that he wouldn't be able to think.

He checked his cart and headed toward the main maintenance elevator. When it opened, his coworker Tonya was already inside. She looked resigned.

"Hey, Dan."

He nodded. "Tonya."

"I guess you heard about the accidents."

"I did. What's wrong?"

"My husband is a trucker, so whenever I hear about an MVA, I think about him."

"Ah. I can see that."

"It's silly. I mean, think of all the stuff we see here. It doesn't make sense that these traffic accidents should bother me the most."

Thinking about Addie's letter, he said, "Someone just reminded me how awful it is when your greatest fears have a chance of coming true."

"That's it exactly." The elevator door dinged and opened up. "Of course, I don't know what that means I should do."

"Take things one step at a time?"

"I'll try—Oh, my word," she said with a gasp.

Daniel felt the same way. Although he wouldn't describe the activity as pandemonium, it certainly was the opposite of calm and orderly. Everything seemed to be going at full tilt. The ER's bright lights, loud noises, and rushing people jarred his senses. Following her through the double doors, he asked, "Do you have a preference?"

"You mind being in triage?"

"Nope."

"Thanks, buddy, I owe you."

He didn't have time to reply, since one of the nurses was already waving him over. "Daniel, thank God you're here. Will you help me prepare the first two cubicles on the left?"

"Anything I need to know about?" He had to bring in special containers if there was a lot of blood to clean up.

"It's nothing too bad." She lowered her voice. "Dr. Curtain was in the first cubicle though."

"All right." Dr. Curtain was a good doctor but messy.

They looked at each other and smiled. "We'll get through it, right?"

"We always do," he said as he returned the smile, then pushed his cart into the first cubicle. Sure enough, it held all the signs of Dr. Curtain and his nurse. Blood, bandages, and some kind of nasty-looking fluid in a puddle in the middle of the floor.

"How long is that going to take you, Daniel?" one of the orderlies asked as he peeked inside.

"Longer than a minute."

"Can you make it as fast as possible? We're slammed out in the lobby."

"I'll do my best."

"Thanks."

He'd just poured some disinfectant in a bucket when a toddler started screaming at the top of his lungs.

It was going to be a long afternoon.

Chapter 14

Work had been busy. The emergency room was filled with patients while the waiting rooms were packed with double the usual number of concerned friends and family members. Kristen directed traffic as best she could while every other staff member did their part.

Knowing how integral a smoothly operating triage space was, Stefan had asked Daniel and Tonya to stay in that section. As more and more patients were seen and then either admitted or discharged, Daniel barely had time to gather linens, mop and disinfect a room before he was frantically pulled over to do the same thing for another two cubicles.

Glad for his years of hospital experience, he worked in tandem with Tonya at lightning speed. By the time the majority of the accident victims had been seen, he'd worked two hours overtime. He was also such a sweaty mess, he'd taken a shower in the staff locker room. After seeing some traces of blood on his clothes, he changed into a pair of scrubs to wear home.

He knew he looked a sight, what with his head covered in

his familiar black felt hat and the rest of him in a pair of green scrubs, but he was long past caring. All that mattered to him was that he wasn't wearing contaminated clothes—and that he was on his way home at long last.

Relieved that he'd earlier called his parents' phone shanty and asked someone to help with Bob, Daniel was getting ready to call for a driver when Tonya and her husband offered to take him home. On another night, Daniel might have been hesitant to take them up on the offer. He knew Tonya didn't live very close to him—plus it was likely she was just as exhausted as he was.

When Tonya reassured him that they really didn't mind, he accepted. He couldn't have been more grateful.

While Tonya's husband Cory drove, Daniel sat in the backseat, content to listen as Tonya told her husband all about their busy shift. He found himself fascinated by both the way she'd chosen to describe the scene and the way her husband seemed to realize that she needed to talk it out.

"You're awfully quiet back there," Cory said. "Is Tonya exaggerating a bit too much—or are you half asleep?"

"Neither. Tonya isn't far off the mark," he said. "No, what I was actually thinking about was how nice it must be for her to have you to talk to. Work was really hard today."

"Do you not have yourself a woman, Daniel?" Tonya asked.

He grinned at her phrasing. "I don't, but that wasn't what I was getting at."

Choosing his words with care, he added, "I was just thinking how hard it is to describe days like today to my Amish friends and family. They would understand, of course, but I would be reluctant to share everything for fear that I might shock them." He also had a couple of relatives who would declare that he shouldn't be working in the outside world in the first place.

"I hear what you're saying," Tonya said. "Sometimes I see things at the hospital that I would never tell my mother about. They would either be too upsetting or I would be afraid that I couldn't describe them in the right way."

"Exactly," Daniel said.

"Tonya and I long ago decided that we would always be honest with each other," Cory said.

"It's helped, a lot," Tonya added. "Life is too difficult to go through alone, you know?"

Daniel nodded. "Yeah."

Cory chuckled. "When we started dating, we promised to be each other's sounding board—and sponge."

"I don't get the sponge part," Daniel said.

"You know, the person who absorbs everything so you can clean yourself up," Tonya added.

"I like that description."

"Me too," Tonya said. Turning to face him, she added, "I'm happy to be your sponge, Daniel."

"Careful, I might take you up on that."

She chuckled. "No worries, I promise. If you decide to trust me with your bad, I'll be honored. As far as I'm concerned, no one shares anything too bad—or too good—with people they don't trust."

He liked the way they were talking about such a serious topic in such a fun way. "You make it sound like oversharing is a good thing."

"I think it is. Sharing is caring and all that, you know."

He laughed. "I'll let you know, Tonya. Thank you."

Daniel continued to reflect upon their conversation during the rest of the drive home. By the time Cory pulled up to the front of his house, he felt lighter at heart—and more filled with appreciation for Addie. She might have been reaching out to him so he could be her sounding board, but she'd also awakened something inside him that he hadn't known existed. A need to reach out to others, both as the giver and the receiver.

What he had to do next was figure out how to not only write her a meaningful response but also find a way to see her in person. She needed to know as soon as possible that she wasn't alone and that there were people in her life she could count on.

It turned out that he didn't have to find an excuse to see Addie. She was at the hospital two days later.

An organization within the hospital had contacted her to bring her donkey to the building. Snickers—and Addie—had a reputation of visiting people who were in stressful situations, and the directors wanted to see how the donkey might interact with some of the children and elderly patients. There was a covered patio that would give the donkey a convenient place to stand and the patients a way to see it without being exposed to the elements.

What was interesting was that the entire hospital staff seemed as excited to meet the therapy donkey as the patients were. Everywhere he went, the staff was talking about the sweet Amish girl with glasses and her adorable donkey. Everyone was singing their praises. Daniel had heard more than once that simply being around Addie and Snickers had made someone's day.

By the time he had a break, Addie was finishing up a conversation with a teenage boy in a wheelchair, his little brother, and his parents. Daniel stood to one side and watched as Snickers inclined his head so the patient could run a hand down his mane.

When the little brother impulsively hugged the donkey, Daniel held his breath, afraid that the sudden movement might have startled the animal. But Snickers handled the exuberant hug like a pro. He held still, then did a trick with

Addie. She asked him how old he was, and he stomped a hoof seven times. His ears perked up with happiness when the family clapped for him.

Through it all, Addie was calm, friendly, and informative. She had a way about her that said she genuinely enjoyed being with the patients, didn't mind their questions one bit, but she was also in charge of Snickers and deserved to be listened to.

It was impressive.

When at last the group moved off, Daniel strode forward. "That was wonderful, Addie."

Her eyes widened before she visibly collected herself. "What was?"

"You were so good with that family." He motioned toward Snickers, who was now chomping on a slice of apple she'd just fed him. "And with this donkey, too."

She smiled before glancing away, this time with a faint blush tingeing her cheeks. "I can't take much credit. Snickers is a good donkey. He loves helping others, too."

"I could see that, but you did a great job, too. You handled everyone perfectly."

"*Danke,* but it was nothing."

"It is." He stepped closer. "You know, every time we talk, I learn something more about you. I had no idea that the two of you did things like this."

"Why would you?" When he raised his eyebrows, she added, "I mean, it's not like we know each other all that well. Plus, I know what a lot of your friends have been saying about my having a donkey pet. They think it's really strange, right?"

This time his cheeks were the ones that were heating. He knew what Addie meant. A lot of their friends had made fun of her rescuing the animal, even though they hadn't known the whole story. Actually, they'd made up their own story, seeming to take great enjoyment out of painting Addie in the most disparaging light.

And he, to his shame, had often readily accepted the malicious gossip as the truth.

"I can't speak for anyone else, only myself. But I do want to say that if I have been rude or uncaring, I'm sorry."

She pursed her lips. "I'm sorry. I sound judgmental, don't I? I guess I'm too sensitive when it comes to Snickers."

"For the record, I think he's great and that your work with both him and the patients and staff today is something to be proud of."

"I don't do this to feel good about myself. My needs don't matter much. I simply like the chance to let other people learn more about donkeys. They are underappreciated, I think." Her voice warmed. "Plus, I get to show off Snickers and his tricks." Looking at the donkey fondly, she rubbed his nose. "Snickers likes these visits, too."

"Would he mind if I petted him?"

She leaned closer to Snickers. "What do you think, boy? Do you mind if Daniel here gives you a pat?"

Snickers brayed, making Daniel laugh. "*Danke*, donkey. Now where do you like to be scratched?"

"Scratch him behind his ears, Daniel!" Tonya called out behind them. "I've already been out here once. Snickers and I are buds now."

"It's Tonya, right?" Addie asked.

"It is. I hope it's okay that I came back out. I wanted to see this little guy one more time before you go home."

Snickers wiggled his ears. "I think that means he's delighted you've returned," Addie joked.

Daniel stepped to the side as Tonya sidled in, chatting to both Snickers and Addie with equal enthusiasm.

After a few minutes passed, Tonya gasped. "Oh, my word!

I bet you two don't know each other. Addie, this is my friend Daniel. Daniel, this is Addie."

"We've known each other a long time," Daniel said.

"Is that right? Dan, how come you didn't tell me Addie was going to be here today?"

"I didn't know."

"There is a large Amish population in Wayne County," Addie said. "We all aren't exactly close friends with every other person who drives a buggy."

"I guess you have a point. I hope I don't offend you or anything, but I think you two have a good chance of becoming friends. You seem like the same sort of people."

"Amish?" Daniel teased.

"No, nice. You both are nice, the type of person to go out of their way to help someone in need."

"That's sweet of you to say. Thank you," Addie said. She glanced at him shyly before a man joined them.

"Ready to load up Snickers, Ad?"

"Sure, Joe." Reaching for the donkey's reins, she clicked her tongue. "Come along now, Snickers. It's time to go home."

Looking back, she smiled. "Good-bye, Tonya."

"Bye, Ad!"

More softly, she added, "It was good to see you again, Daniel. Blessings to you."

He inclined his head. "*Jah*. And to you, too."

Realizing that it was time to go back to work, he sighed. Once again, he felt as if he was missing something important where Addie was concerned.

Or maybe it was just that he was being reminded again and again that for so long he'd had everything about her all wrong. Now he just had to figure out how he could finally get things right.

Chapter 15

After much debate, Addie asked Brooke to accompany her to the coffee meeting with Zac. She didn't want to go alone—visiting with a lawyer was just too scary.

Brooke, to her relief, had agreed instantly, though she'd warned Addie that maybe it would've been better for her to go with Mr. or Mrs. Beaumont instead. It seemed even Englischers got a little bit apprehensive when speaking with lawyers.

Addie knew that either Mr. or Mrs. Beaumont would have happily accompanied her and probably would've even thanked her for allowing them to help. More than once Gretchen and Howard had said that they would be happy to help her if she ever needed something.

Maybe their counsel would have been helpful, but Addie knew she needed a friend by her side. She wanted someone who was her equal—not yet another person who seemed to know a whole lot more about finances, wills, and estate taxes than she did. She was tired of feeling at a disadvantage.

At ten in the morning, just as they'd agreed, Zac entered

the coffee shop that she'd suggested. Just as he joined them, his phone buzzed. "One sec, ladies." Turning around, he answered. "Zachary Carr. Yes? Oh, hold on." When he turned back to them, he looked harried. "I'm sorry, but I can't ignore this. Do you mind sitting on your own for a moment?"

Feeling as if she'd just gotten a brief reprieve, Addie smiled. "Of course not. Take your time."

"Someone should be over to take your order. Get whatever you'd like. Both of you. It's on me."

"*Danke.*"

Sure enough, the server came and took their orders. After ordering coffees and a chocolate donut to split, Addie tried to calm down.

Brooke, of course, noticed how nervous she was. She eyed her warily for a couple of seconds before saying, "No offense, but you look kind of a mess. Are you really that scared about today's meeting?"

"I don't know. Maybe." She smiled, though she feared she just looked ill. "I'm really on edge. I am comfortable with English, of course, but sometimes, when I get nervous, I start thinking in Pennsylvania Dutch. Then I have to translate it to have a conversation. It's tiring."

"Well, I don't think you have too much to worry about. Zac seems really nice. I thought he'd be a lot older."

Addie smiled. "If I hadn't met him, I would've thought the same thing."

"Here you go, girls. Two coffees and two donuts."

"We only ordered one donut," Brooke said.

"You two are too cute to have to split one of them. The extra donut is on the house."

"Thank you!" they chirped together, then giggled.

"There's our sign," Brooke said. "Everything this morning is going to go great."

Addie didn't know if two donuts was a "sign" or not, but

she figured that it meant they were off to a good start at the very least. Besides, Brooke was right. Zac did seem nice. Plus, she couldn't help believing that if he was going to tell her bad news, he would've asked her to meet him at an office.

"Sorry about that," Zac murmured as he sat down across from them. "My mother is kind of having a tough time. I don't feel I can ignore her phone calls right now."

And just like that, Addie relaxed. It seemed that was all she'd needed to believe that this Zac was someone she could trust. "I hope she is all right?"

He looked surprised that she'd asked, but he seemed to relax, too. "Yeah." Running a hand through his hair, he said, "She forgot how to reset the Internet at her house. It's all good now."

"Here you are, sir," the server said. "A latte for you and a bagel."

"Thanks." Zac paused while the server approached with the coffee and the treat, then got back to business. He opened a folder, scanned it briefly, then said, "As I told you earlier, there is nothing for you to be worried about. This is all pretty cut and dried. Your father went to great lengths to make his gift something easy to receive instead of another form of stress."

"That was kind of him. I mean, I suppose it was." She still had no idea how, exactly, she felt about John Henry Holmes. Should she feel anything for a man who'd never paid her any attention until he was near death?

Brooke reached out and gripped her hand. "Hang in there," she whispered. "You're not alone."

The lawyer's expression softened. "Your girlfriend is right, Addie. It might feel like you don't have any support, but that's the furthest thing from the truth. I don't mind answering any questions or explaining things more than once.

Not just today, either. You can call me up two months from now and I'll be happy to go over everything again."

"Thank you."

"Let's continue, then." He opened up a folder, pulled out two stacks of neatly paper-clipped sheets, and handed one to her. The top of the paper said The Last Will and Testament of John Henry Holmes.

Feeling a wave of emotion surge deep inside her, Addie forced herself to push it back. How could she be sad about the passing of a man she'd essentially never known? She needed to concentrate on the papers and the meeting at hand, not the past.

"You can read along with me, Addie. I'm not going to read this whole thing right now, but I did want to look at one section with you. Turn to page five."

She did as he asked.

"If you look at the fifth paragraph, it says, 'In addition, I am bequeathing the sum of ten thousand dollars to my daughter Addie. Though this sum—nor any sum—will never make up for the pain and suffering I have put her through because of my neglect, I do hope that this amount will assure her that she was never forgotten. This amount is to be paid in two-thousand-dollar installments for the next five years.' "

"Two thousand dollars every year for five years?"

"He was worried if he gave this all to you in one lump sum, the taxes would take most of it. This way the taxes will be lower. Perhaps it might make it easier to accept, too? Two thousand dollars is a lot of money, but not an overwhelming amount."

She nodded. His words made sense, but it was a very big amount to her. She did many, many odd jobs just to earn half that amount. Her throat felt dry. She swallowed hard.

"What do you think?" Brooke asked.

"I don't know. There's a part of me that doesn't want to accept any of it. Perhaps I should just give it to my grandmother instead."

Zac folded his hands on the table. "Addie, there are no strings attached. Every time you receive the check, you can do whatever you want with it, but I would caution you to at least take some time to think things through before you start giving it away. Maybe think of some things you might want to do. Or get. Or perhaps you'd simply like to save the money for a rainy day."

"That's good advice, Ad," Brooke said. Her voice was encouraging but firm.

Buoyed by her friend's opinion, Addie felt some of her panic fade away. But then she remembered her mother. Mommi might think otherwise, but Addie still didn't trust Kate's sudden reappearance in her life. "Zac, what about my mother?"

He studied her intently. "What about her?"

"I'm pretty sure you said he left some money to her as well. Is that correct?"

"He did leave a small amount. A much smaller bequest than he left you. The majority of the money went to his widow and the children that he, uh, raised."

"Addie, what are you thinking?" Brooke asked.

"That maybe that's why my mother has surfaced. Maybe she wants some of it." Why else would she only now want to know Addie? No other reason made sense.

Her girlfriend shrugged. "You don't know that."

"For some reason I feel guilty. Like she deserves it more than I do."

"It doesn't matter if you 'deserve' it or not," Brooke said. "Your father bequeathed it to you as a gift. He's not giving you money that he owes you."

"Brooke has a good point," Zac interjected. "It's not my

place to say whether John Henry should have given you a lot more or nothing at all. That was his prerogative. Just as it's your decision as to how you want to spend it. There are no rules here."

"But there is probably a right way to handle this as well as a wrong one."

Zac shook his head. "Not necessarily. You don't have to give your mother any of the money you inherit—or your grandmother. It's yours. I don't know if this advice helps, but perhaps you should also remember that this will was also your father's decision. He wanted you to have this money. If you ignore his wishes, you might regret that one day."

She understood what the lawyer meant. Her emotions were so raw, Addie feared that she wasn't thinking about anything with a clear head. Instead, everything was tainted by a lifetime of confusion, bitterness, and even fear. For so long, she'd been afraid that there was something wrong with her, that maybe she was unlovable.

"You've given me a lot to think about."

"I'm sure I have," he said with a smile. "It's a lot for anyone to think about."

Standing up, he handed her an envelope. "Here is your first check. As I said, you should take a few days to think about the pros and cons before you make a decision about what to do with it. Call me any time."

The envelope felt like hot metal in her hands. All she wanted to do was get rid of it. "I will."

"Good." He held out his hand and shook hers. "You have my card. Please don't hesitate to call me at any time. Even if you just want another person to listen to you weigh those pros and cons."

"That is very kind of you."

"I'd like to see you happy, Addie. I don't come across too

many people with as giving a heart as you have—or who have been through so much."

After shaking hands with Brooke, he pulled on his overcoat and exited the coffee shop.

When he was out of sight, Brooke fell back into her chair with a dramatic sigh. "Wow, Addie. That was intense."

Sitting back down as well, Addie placed the envelope on the table. Staring down at it, she said, "It's incredible. Every bit of it."

"You look so sad. This has really torn you up inside, hasn't it?"

"Yes. I feel like I've gone my whole life wishing that I had parents. Or, at the very least, wanting to know more about them. Now, I'm hearing from both of them, and I don't know how I feel about it."

"So far, I don't think there is anything you need to do. Just put that check into your bank account and go on with your life."

"It's not that easy."

"Are you sure it isn't?" When Addie didn't say anything, Brooke's expression turned even more serious. "Listen, if you'd like me to just take you home and never mention this again, I will. You asked me to go with you and I did."

"But . . . ?" she prodded. It was obvious Brooke had a whole lot more to say.

Brooke's voice gentled. "But . . . I'd like to share my opinion, if you want to hear it."

"I would."

"All right, then." After taking a fortifying breath, she said, "Addie, I think you might be making all of this more complicated than it has to be. Yes, your father abandoned you, and you've got strong feelings about that."

She rolled her eyes. "I've got a little more than strong feelings, Brooke."

"Okay. But he also happened to give you some money."

"Which I don't want."

"I get that, but you might one day." She waved a hand, cutting off Addie's next protest. "Also, it is a lot, but it isn't a fortune. I mean, not really."

"It doesn't matter if it's two dollars or two million. It's guilt money."

"It might be, but who cares? It's obvious that he regretted his actions. He regretted them so much, he was afraid to even reach out to you in recent years because he knew he'd feel even worse."

"See? He was selfish his whole life."

Brooke lifted one shoulder as if that was beside the point. "Maybe he was, maybe he wasn't. You didn't have a relationship with him, though. You didn't know him." She lowered her voice. "The saying really is true. One never knows what other people are going through."

"I hear you, but I didn't know him at all." Addie swallowed hard, trying to control her emotions, but it was hard. Really hard. "That's why—"

"It doesn't matter what you want or what you wish had happened five or ten or even twenty years ago. You can't change the past. Plus, he's dead now, Addie."

She gasped. "I can't believe you said that."

"It might be rude to mention it, but it's the truth. He can't make any more amends, Addie. The only thing he felt he could do for you was remember you in his will."

Brooke's frank words were jarring, but Addie also had to admit that there was truth in them. Besides, forgiveness and retribution were the Lord's territory, not hers. "You're right," she whispered.

"I'm sorry that I am. I wish I could make a lot of things different for you, but I can't."

Since they'd already started down the advice road, Addie murmured, "What about my mother? Do I need to see her?"

Brooke waved her hand. "Sorry, but I can't answer that one. All I can say is that she waited to reach out to you, so I think you can take your time deciding if you want to see her or not."

"Take my time? Like take a week?"

Brooke shook her head. "No. Take a month. Take a year. Take two years."

She laughed. "That's not taking my time. That's . . . well, I don't know what that is."

"No, that's taking your time, not anyone else's. You need to have some control in your life right now, don't you think?"

"*Jah,* but I'm not sure what I want. Everything in my head just keeps spinning. I feel like it's a washing machine on the spin cycle."

"Then let your mind spin for a bit. I mean, what's wrong with that? You're a grown woman and you have choices." She smiled. "Besides, don't forget that everything in that washing machine might get tumbled around a lot, but it all gets clean in the end."

The analogy was convoluted, but it also kind of made sense. "That's true."

"You need to pray about this, Addie. Ask God what He thinks." She softened her voice. "There has to be a reason He brought this all together at this time in your life. Ask Him to help you understand and to guide you."

Suddenly, everything felt as if it was clicking into place. "I do need to pray about this."

"Praying is always a good idea." Looking pleased, Brooke said, "Do you feel better?"

"Almost. I still don't know what to do about my grandmother."

"Addie, sorry, but I don't think there's much to figure out. I like Lovina a lot. I think she's a nice lady. Plus, don't you think the woman who took you in and raised you as her own deserves the chance to explain herself to you, at the very least?"

"Yes, but it's so hard."

"Yep. But you've told me this before—not everything that is right is easy."

"I cannot believe you just threw that back in my face."

"Sorry, it was the truth."

When they stood up again, Addie gave Brooke a hug. "*Danke*. I don't know what I'd do without you."

"Hopefully you won't have to worry about that any time soon. Now, are you ready to go home?"

"I'm not ready, but that's where I need to go."

"Good girl. You'll feel better after that tough conversation is over."

"I hope so."

"Hey, did you tell your mystery man all about this?"

"I did. I wrote him a whole, long note."

"What did he say?"

"I don't know yet. I should receive his next letter later this week."

Brooke grimaced. "I don't know how you're surviving this letter writing thing you two have going."

She chuckled. "Survive? Brooke, it's nice. You've said so yourself."

"It is, but it also seems that you have to wait forever every time you want to hear some news. I'd hardly be able to stand it!"

Addie couldn't deny that the waiting was difficult, but the anticipation was also exciting. Waiting for each letter felt like waiting for Christmas Day to arrive. "On some days, it does feel that way. But I always remind myself that the waiting isn't actually forever. It just seems that way." She winked. "Plus, I've heard that waiting builds patience."

"You and your Amish wisdom," Brooke teased.

"Sorry, but I can't help having some of that. I am Amish, you know."

"At least you know that for sure."

"You said it, Brooke. At least I have that." Their laughter filled the air as they walked outside. It filled her heart, too.

Chapter 16

Addie's grandmother wasn't home when Brooke dropped her off. It was such a surprise, Addie hurried to Mommi's room, looking for signs that she'd hurt herself. It was clean as always.

Confused, she wandered through the living room and little sitting area off the kitchen—then finally spied a neatly written note on the kitchen table.

> *Addie, my friend Bonnie invited me to go with her to Shipshy on a bus trip. Bonnie's sister got sick and she asked if I'd like to take her place. A trip outside this house might do me good, and Bonnie don't even care that I can't get around too good. I'll be back in three days.*

Feeling guilty, Addie stared hard at the paper. It was obvious that Mommi was avoiding her because Addie had been so hateful. Her leaving on a spur of the moment bus trip was not just unexpected, it was something of a shock. Addie couldn't remember her grandmother ever leaving on a trip without carefully planning every moment of it for weeks in advance.

She felt so guilty . . . until she reminded herself that it wasn't a bad thing for her grandmother to go on a bus trip with a friend. Until her hips had gotten so bad and she'd started losing her balance, her grandmother had been active.

Plus, Mommi was probably right. A short break from each other might be just what they needed.

Thinking that she would take Brooke's advice, she got an apple out for Snickers, carefully sliced it into quarters, then headed out to the barn.

The donkey sauntered right over when she entered and stuck his nose over the top of the metal gate to his stall.

"Hi, Snickers, how are you today?"

He nudged her shoulder in response.

"I missed you, too. But I wasn't gone very long, right?" She handed him a quarter of an apple. "I had an important meeting with a lawyer, of all people. Brooke took me and was even kind enough to stay at the coffee shop so I wouldn't have to face the man alone."

Snickers chomped his apple slice, then nudged her again. After she gave him the second piece, she knew it was time. "Snickers, Brooke gave me some good advice. She said I need to do more praying and less fretting. I think she's probably right, too. I mean, all of a sudden I have some really big problems—too big to try to figure them all out on my own."

Snickers chomped again, then wiggled his ears, which Addie believed was his way of telling her to get on with it. "All right, fine." Lifting her chin, she said, "Dear God, I know I'm standing in a barn with my pet donkey, but I have a feeling that you won't mind me praying this way one bit. After all, donkeys are part of your world, too, right?"

She pulled over a plastic bucket, turned it upside down,

and sat. "Honestly—and you probably know this too—sometimes I think that Snickers might have a stronger faith than I do. He had to have a lot of faith in order to believe that he'd get rescued."

When Snickers blew out a breath of air with a noisy snort, just as if he agreed wholeheartedly, she gave him another piece of apple.

"Anyway, Lord, I'm really struggling with the reappearance of my parents in my life. Though my father is gone, and I haven't actually seen my mother, it sure feels like they're as present in my life as if they'd come knocking on the door. I'd almost stopped thinking about them. To be honest, I'm struggling with that, too. Is it bad that I haven't thought of either of my parents in a long time?"

Feeling more and more at ease, Addie continued to talk, pouring out her heart and her fears and asking Him to help her find strength, clarity, and peace.

When at last she finished, Snickers had eaten the last of his apple and appeared to have drifted off to sleep. Addie figured she couldn't blame the donkey. Her prayers and storytelling had lasted almost twenty minutes.

Deciding to go back into the house to clean, she left the comfort of the barn, braced herself against the wind, and hurried across the yard.

After she finished cleaning, she thought she would bake some bread for her neighbor Maude, and write her secret admirer a note. She decided to leave it in the tree for him later in the afternoon. Sure, she might be breaking the rules a bit, but there wasn't much she could do about that. This was one of those times when she had to listen to her feelings rather than the rules. She needed to trust someone, even if it was a secret letter writer.

Boy, did she hope that her impulsive action didn't end up being a mistake.

* * *

After writing her letter, Addie walked to their oak tree, deposited the letter inside, then headed about a mile in the other direction. The elderly lady named Maude lived there. Addie always worried that she spent too much time by herself.

"Addie, it's so nice to see you," Maude said when she answered the door. As gracious as ever, she added, "Won't you come inside for a spell?"

"I'd love to. *Danke.*" Holding the loaf of dried-cherry walnut bread she'd neatly wrapped in waxed paper, Addie smiled at the older woman.

Maude seemed to be in pretty good shape today. Her dress and apron were free of stains and the pins were neat and straight. Addie was relieved about that. "I brought you a loaf of bread. I made it this afternoon."

"*Danke.*" Maude held it up to her nose. "Cranberry?"

"Dried cherries and walnut."

"I am sure I will enjoy it."

"I hope so, Maude." Following the older woman into the kitchen, Addie looked around. The sink was full of dirty dishes and the countertops were dirty. Even the cabinet doors had a few smudges on them. Whoever had come over to help Maude shower and dress hadn't taken the time to clean the kitchen as well.

That was a pity.

Taking off her coat, she said, "How are you feeling today?"

"Good enough. I can't complain."

"Me neither. That's a blessing, *jah*?"

"Uh huh." Maude clasped her hands in front of her and looked confused again.

"Why don't you sit down for a spell? I'll make us some hot tea and we'll eat some of the bread I brought."

"Okay." A moment later, Maude's gaze settled on the loaf of bread again. "Oh! You brought me bread? That is so kind of you. What kind is it?"

"Dried cherry and walnut," she repeated patiently.

"I think I like that."

"I hope you will." After making sure Maude sat down, Addie put the kettle on, then rinsed off two plates and sliced thick pieces of the bread onto them. "Here you go. Start if you'd like."

"Not without you, Addie."

Though Addie was tempted to clean instead of sit, her heart told her that Maude needed conversation as much as a helping hand.

She carefully set two cups down as well and joined her. They bowed their heads and gave silent thanks before digging in. Maude smiled at her sweetly. "It's so nice to see you, Addie. And you brought bread, too. What kind is it again?"

Unable to help herself, Addie reached out and squeezed Maude's hand gently. "It's dried cherry and walnut, dear. I hope you like it."

Two hours later, she departed from Maude's house knowing that she'd left it in better shape than she'd found it. After they ate the bread and chatted, Maude dozed in front of the fireplace while Addie put the kitchen back to rights.

While she was doing that, she was relieved to see that someone had left Maude a few meals. It seemed that Maude was able to heat up her food, just not do the dishes.

Just before she left, she unfolded a worn quilt and wrapped it around Maude's lap.

"You are a *gut* girl, Addie," Maude whispered.

Addie smiled at her as she put her coat back on. She wasn't sure what was going to happen to Maude in the future, but at this moment, she was clean and resting peacefully. That was all Addie could do for now.

By the time she got back home, Addie was feeling very grateful for her own blessings and much more sympathetic toward her grandmother. Mommi might not have done the right thing, keeping so many secrets, but Addie's visit to Maude had reminded her that each person had their own struggles to get through.

Most people didn't broadcast their pain to anyone who walked by. Sometimes they didn't even share it with people who genuinely cared. It was easier to simply hold it inside.

Hadn't that been what she'd done for most of her life?

"That's what you've done for all of your life—until very recently," she reminded herself. "Only now, when your back is against the wall and you feel overwhelmed, are you confiding in Brooke."

And her secret admirer.

Her stomach pinched as she wondered again who her mysterious pen pal actually was. Boy, she hoped he wasn't going to make her regret sharing so much with him.

"You've already made that decision, Addie," she said out loud. "You made your choice, and you can't go back in time—just like your father couldn't."

Or her grandmother.

And that, in a nutshell, was what remained true. The Lord gave each person twenty-four hours in one day. How a person decided to use those hours was up to him or her. It didn't matter if those hours were filled with good decisions or bad. Filled with good works or evil.

The simple truth was that they couldn't be made over. They were done. All anyone could do next was deal with the consequences.

And, perhaps, hope and pray that the best they were able to do was good enough.

Chapter 17

Dear S.A.

A funny thing happened to me today. I met with a lawyer at a coffee shop. Don't worry, I wasn't alone. I brought my English friend Brooke with me. Brooke is friendly. She's patient with me, too. She never gets upset if I ask her what something is, or if I take too long at a store or during an errand. Every time I thank her for being so patient, she waves it off though. She says that she and I are friends and that's what friends do for each other.

Anyway, I asked her to accompany me to this meeting because sometimes when I get flustered I start thinking and speaking in Deutsch. Do you ever do that?

For some reason, I bet you don't.

Just to let you know, the meeting went well. The lawyer had some information about my father, who recently passed away. I didn't make a fool of myself—though now I wonder why I was so concerned about that. If the Lord doesn't expect us all to be perfect, why do I feel like I need to be?

Hope you don't mind seeing an extra letter from me.

Addie

Dear Addie,

I was glad to see this letter in our tree today. Write me whenever you feel like it, and I'll do the same. I don't think we need to have too many rules about our correspondence. Whatever we're doing is working for us, right?

I was interested to read about your visit with a lawyer. I've never met with one. I'm not sure why I would. Unless something bad happened at work, of course.

I nodded when you mentioned that you sometimes think in Deutsch. That has happened to me, too. Unfortunately, since I work in a hospital and I speak English all the time, I sometimes have to remind myself to speak Deutsch when I'm visiting my family.

Don't worry, everyone's brain gets scrambled sometimes. I hope you have a nice weekend, Addie.

Your S.A.

Daniel might have written to Addie that his brain got scrambled sometimes, too, but he was pretty sure that he was doing a good job as a secret admirer.

Feeling that he'd neglected his other friends lately, he made plans to hang out with Bradley and Roman after church on Sunday.

Last year, Roman had bought an older house near

Daniel's. Its proximity was the good thing about it. The bad part was that it was in great need of just about everything.

However, it was all Roman's, it had a nice fire pit and sitting area in the back, and the property was a full acre. Until recently, Daniel had enjoyed nothing better than hanging out with his two best friends at Roman's. Unfortunately, all he could think today was that he'd rather be at home with Bob.

Church had been the same as always. It had been a long service made even longer because his least favorite preacher had spoken for the majority of the two-hour service. Joshua was only a few years older than Daniel and had drawn the lot last year. Both the fact that the congregation had selected Joshua to be in the lot—and the fact that he'd been the one to pick the marked Bible—had been the focus of a lot of talk and speculation among most everyone they knew.

Daniel, Bradley, and Roman all agreed that they would want nothing less than they wanted to be named preacher. After all, that honor was filled with much responsibility. Not only did the preachers take turns giving the sermon every other Sunday, but they were expected to counsel members of the church district, sometimes join the deacon to reprimand members who didn't adhere to the *Ordnung,* and generally be at every one's beck and call. They were not paid to carry out those responsibilities.

Finally, the job was also for life.

Though he believed that the Lord never gave a person more than he or she could bear, Daniel often worried that performing such a job to the best of one's ability year after year could drain even the strongest of men.

And, while many men handled the position with grace, rumors abounded about how the cloak of responsibility weighed heavily on some of the preachers' hearts over time. Some men couldn't seem to handle it and took to drink in private—or eventually left the order.

Daniel knew that he would feel as if he had been stepping off a dark ledge if he'd been chosen. Joshua, on the other hand, had seemed to relish every bit of it.

"Joshua preaches the worst sermons," Roman said as the three of them sat in his living room. Roman was in the process of refinishing the floors and woodwork in his spare time, so there were tarps and pieces of wood all over the place. He'd arranged three folding chairs in front of the fireplace and flipped over a cardboard box to use as a makeshift coffee table.

It had started raining just before they'd gotten to Roman's house, canceling their plans to sit in front of the fire pit. At least the indoor fire was warm, and it cast an inviting glow about the space.

Daniel nodded. "Not only are they the most boring sermons on earth, but he's far too full of himself. Did you catch that part when he insinuated that some people needed to pray more—or to seek his counsel if they ever felt their faith wobble?"

"That's the problem with him," Roman agreed. "While Preacher Elias could tell me to pray and I'd nod and promise to do so, when Joshua tells us the same thing, he does it in such a way that it feels like he doesn't think any of us pray enough." He coughed. "Not that I would seek his advice for my troubles. Ever."

"Joshua's ridiculous," Bradley said. Even though Bradley was Mennonite, he knew Joshua from when they all used to play kickball together. "I canna believe that Ruthie is allowing him to court her."

"Ruthie is desperate to be wed," Roman said. "And desperate to be settled."

Daniel didn't disagree, but he was surprised to hear his friends speak so harshly about her. "I'm surprised to hear you two talk about Ruthie like that."

"I canna help it if it's true," Bradley said. "Ruthie isn't a very happy person inside. I think she's hoping that getting married will change that."

Roman stared into the fire. "I have no wife, but I don't know if marrying a woman for all the wrong reasons brings happiness."

For some reason Daniel continued to feel honor bound to stand up for the courting couple. "Come now. They could be in love."

"They could also not be," Bradley quipped.

As interesting as the thought of Ruthie and Joshua getting married might be, Daniel thought his friends were missing the point, which was that Joshua was no one's favorite preacher. "What are the chances of Preacher Elias counseling Preacher Joshua to sound a bit less smug? Do you think he'd have much success?"

"My guess is that the odds aren't good at all. Joshua don't seem to be too good at taking advice." Bradley stretched his arms behind his head. "He sure didn't back when we were in school."

"Today was especially bad. Did you guys see how annoyed all the older men looked at the end of the service?" Roman asked. "Joshua needs to start watching his mouth a bit more. Even my *dawdi* looked irritated, and he is the most patient man I've ever met."

"We really ought to start praying for Joshua," Daniel said. "He needs our prayers and support, at the very least."

Roman smiled at him. "There you go again, Daniel. Putting us firmly back in our places."

"Stop. You know I'm not like that."

Picking up his cup of coffee, Roman sipped. "Switching subjects, what is going on with you and Addie Holmes?"

Daniel, who'd been sipping his coffee, too, nearly choked. "What are you talking about?"

"Come on, don't play dumb. More than one person has seen you speaking with her around Apple Creek."

"I fail to see why that is noteworthy. Don't you speak to her when you pass on the street?"

"Of course I do, but that ain't what I'm talking about. You've been seen not just saying hello but having a conversation." He raised his eyebrows. "A real conversation, Daniel."

He was horrified that those brief chats had been noted and discussed. "Do you hear what you're saying? Not only are you being disrespectful, but you're gossiping about the most inane things."

"I'm not being disrespectful about anyone. I'm just asking about the two of you. You're the one who's deflecting."

Bradley winked at Roman. "Why do you think Daniel is getting so riled up? Could it be that there are strong feelings involved?"

"Stop. I'm not riled up."

"Sorry, but you are."

"Fine. Whatever. But, even if I am, I have reason to be. You two are being ridiculous."

Roman stood up to refill his coffee cup. "All I'm saying is people have noticed that after years of ignoring Addie Holmes, you have been seen speaking with her several times." Joining them again, he added, "I even heard that you were chatting with Snickers the donkey."

He yearned to close his eyes and pretend he was someplace else. "Honestly, Roman."

Bradley's eyes were lit with mirth. "Come on, man. Could that actually be true?"

"It is. And there's nothing wrong with Addie."

"Not if you like girls who only have donkeys for friends," Bradley said.

Daniel was getting mad. "I don't believe that is true, but if it is, that says more about us than her, don'tcha think?"

And just like that, the air felt different. His two best friends weren't pleased with his insinuations.

"Are you turning sanctimonious now, too?" Bradley asked.

"It's not sanctimonious to say that I've changed my mind about Addie, and I feel guilty that I haven't been a better person around her."

Roman coughed. "Come on, Daniel. It's Addie."

Daniel put his coffee cup down, and against his better judgment, said what was on his mind. "*Jah*. It is Addie. We've all grown up with her but hardly gave her the time of day. She's a sweet girl who's had a difficult life. She also has a giving heart—giving enough to continue to try to be friends with everyone in spite of our not being friends to her."

"And the donkey?" Bradley asked.

"She rescued that donkey when it was about to be put down, trained it, and now takes it to hospitals to visit patients and medical staff. While you two are finding fault with everything she does, Addie is going to a great deal of effort to help make other people's days brighter."

Roman's expression went slack. "I didn't know about her hospital visits."

"She and Snickers came to the hospital I work at recently. If you could have seen the way the people responded to that little donkey—and how grateful they were to Addie, you would feel as ashamed as I was." Unable to stop himself, he added, "Here you two are making fun of me for talking to her when everyone should be scorning us because we always left her out. We never gave her a chance."

Roman looked taken aback. "But her parents—"

"Are her parents," Daniel finished. "Do you take responsibility for all of your parents' faults? Or do you simply take credit for their strengths?"

"That is hardly fair."

"Neither is your narrow-minded perspective. Her parents might not have been there, but her grandmother was. At the end of the day, we've all forgotten that she was just a little girl when that happened. No one deserves that. Especially because it's not her fault."

Daniel got to his feet. "Look, we've all been friends for a long time. I know you don't want or need a lecture from me about how to treat Addie. If you don't want to change your attitude, that's your choice. But I've decided that I'm not going to keep my mouth shut anymore just because I don't want to cause waves."

All traces of humor left Bradley's face. "All right, then."

Daniel didn't understand. "All right, what?"

"You're right. I've been wrong about her, and I need to be better. I'll do my best to start making amends as soon as possible."

"Are you serious? Because I'm not going to be okay with you joking about her anymore."

"Of course." Lowering his voice, Bradley added, "Daniel, I might be a jerk, but I think I can be redeemed from time to time. At least, I hope I can be. Everything you've said is right. I'll do better. I promise."

Roman nodded. "I've been thinking some of the same things. Especially since Ruthie was so cruel at the engagement party. Every time I spoke with her, I felt dirty, like I needed to be cleansed—after I confessed all my sins." He stopped, then smiled slightly. "To someone besides Joshua, of course."

Daniel laughed. "Understood."

"Seriously, if you are her friend, then I'll try to be her friend, too," Bradley said.

"It's as easy as that?"

"Of course. She might not ever want to speak to me, but I'll make an effort."

"*Danke.*"

Roman studied Daniel. "Hey, Dan, you like Addie, don't you?"

"Of course I do. I just said we were friends."

"*Nee,* Daniel. Even though I sound like I'm fifteen again, I have to say it. You obviously do like her in a way that's something more than mere friendship."

"I never said that."

"You didn't need to. Your actions—and your reprimands—speak for themselves. You like her."

"*Jah*. I might," he allowed at last.

Bradley shared a look with Roman. "You know, now that I'm seeing Addie for who she really is—I don't think this is a bad thing. I can see them together."

"I can, too. She obviously has a good heart. And, no offense, but I've never said she ain't pretty. Addie Holmes has always been a pretty thing. Green eyes are a rarity, and hers are striking."

Roman had noticed her eyes. He had noticed that she was pretty and sweet. But that didn't mean that Daniel wanted Roman or Bradley—of all people—to start playing cupid. "Don't you start matchmaking."

"Daniel, no matchmaking is needed. The match is done. She might not realize it, and you might not want to admit it . . . but it's done."

Roman nodded. "I'm looking forward to getting to know her better, Daniel. And . . . throwing your engagement party one day."

"Stop. Just stop."

When his buddies only laughed, he knew that whether or not he wanted it, everything had just changed.

It was only when he was walking home that he realized everything in this blossoming romance between him and Addie was not rainbows and sunshine.

He was still her secret admirer, and when she discovered the truth, she was going to be very angry.

Very angry indeed.

Chapter 18

It was raining when she finished babysitting Tabitha, so Addie took Gretchen up on her offer of a ride. "I'm so glad you agreed to let me drive you," Gretchen teased. "I thought I might have to arm wrestle you or something."

Addie giggled at the image. "I'm not that stubborn. I just really like to walk, but not in the rain."

"I know, sweetie, but Howard and I do worry about you walking from our house by yourself. It's a long way."

"Not too long. Just thirty minutes or so. Besides, I usually stop off at the store on the way home."

"Do you need something? Tabby is sound asleep. I can wait in the car with her while you shop. Then you won't have to carry any groceries home."

"*Danke,* but I am fine. Just taking me home will be enough today."

"I understand." Gretchen drew up at a stop sign, then turned right. "Addie, do you need anything at all? I have to be honest, sometimes I worry about you. You sure carry a lot of responsibility on your slim shoulders. It's a lot, especially for someone your age."

"I am all right. It's nothing that the Lord and I can't handle."

"I do hope you find yourself a young man soon. Having a good partner in life is such a blessing," she added as she pulled into the driveway.

Addie was struck by the way Gretchen referred to her husband. "Is that how you think of Howard? As your partner in life?"

Gretchen smiled. "I think of him as all sorts of things, as my husband, of course, but also my friend. And . . . sometimes as my sounding board. But yes. Howard is my partner in life. Everyone needs someone they can depend on, no matter what, right?"

"Did you know Howard was the one for you right away?"

"No. I knew I liked him, but I didn't know he was the man for me until I realized that I could depend on him for just about anything. I knew Howard would make me smile when I was sad, give me a hug when I needed it . . . even tell me the truth when I really needed to hear the truth. He knew he could count on me for those things, too. When I figured all that out, I knew he was the one for me."

"I hope I find someone like that."

"Me too, dear. Take it from me. Don't settle for less. Wanting to love someone isn't the same as love, right?"

Thinking that bit of advice said everything, Addie nodded. "You're right. Thank you for the ride—and the advice."

"You're welcome to both. See you soon."

When she walked inside, the house was quiet. When Mommi had returned from her trip, the two of them had reached a truce of sorts. Mommi wasn't going to apologize for keeping secrets, and Addie wasn't going to pretend that the episode hadn't hurt her feelings.

However, Addie was old enough to understand that neither of them was perfect, and it was wrong to expect that they'd never have disagreements.

Addie knew that one day they'd have to discuss everything again. Until then, she was okay with simply continuing on.

Concerned that her grandmother hadn't called out a greeting, Addie peeked into her bedroom. Mommi was dozing in her favorite chair, her knitting needles and a ball of yarn resting on her gray dress.

Glad for a few moments to herself, Addie went upstairs, washed her face and hands, and then decided to write to her S.A. again. It wasn't going to be an easy note to write, but she had a feeling it was the right thing to do. Gretchen's words about her husband had struck a chord with her. She had a feeling that her last comment had been very true, too. Wanting to be in love wasn't the same as love.

The truth was that she and this mystery man actually didn't have a relationship. As sweet as the letters were, they weren't a substitute for something real.

It was time she remembered that.

Dear Secret Admirer,

I'm beginning to wonder if we should continue our correspondence. As much as I've enjoyed exchanging letters with you, I am beginning to be uncomfortable with the secrecy, especially since it is so one-sided.

Do you ever intend to reveal your true identity? Or do you plan to continue this correspondence indefinitely?

I hope and pray that you will give me the courtesy of a truthful reply.

Addie

* * *

Addie put her pen down and reread the letter again. It was short and to the point and conveyed some of the irritation that she'd begun to feel.

But it also made her feel a little sick, both at the thought of the letters ending and at the thought of hearing his response. What if he simply told her that he would stop writing but relayed nothing else?

Or what if he said that he did intend to reveal himself—and then did just that?

Or what if he promised to reveal his true identity but then didn't after all. If he continued to string her along with false promises, he would be no better than a real boyfriend who did such a thing.

And she would be just as dishonest if she would let him do that.

"What should I do, Lord?" she asked out loud. "Is there an obvious course of action that I am ignoring?"

When no real solution came to her, she shook her head in frustration. Not with the Lord, of course, but with herself. Faith didn't work that way. She knew it. One couldn't shoot off questions to a higher power and then wait impatiently for a response as if waiting for change at the grocery store or something.

Yes. This was the right thing to do. It wasn't easy, but she would be glad when she left the note for her pen pal in their tree.

Getting off the bed, she folded the letter, slipped it in the envelope, and sealed it. She would put it in their tree sometime that afternoon. Before then, though, she was going to rouse Mommi, make a pot of split pea and ham soup, and then maybe even clean Mommi's bedroom.

Heading down the stairs to the kitchen, she was brought up short by the sight of her grandmother lying on the ground. Her grandmother wasn't unconscious, but she did seem to be on the verge of it.

"Mommi!" Running to her side, she crouched on the ground and reached for her hand. "Mommi, what happened?"

"I got dizzy and fell. I think."

Addie felt for her grandmother's pulse. It seemed steady, but she wasn't exactly sure what it was supposed to be like. Wishing she had more medical knowledge, she knew she needed help. "You need to go to the hospital."

"I think . . . I think that would be *gut*," Mommi said before her eyes closed.

"Mommi?"

Her grandmother didn't open her eyes.

Scrambling to her feet, Addie tried to decide what to do. Go to the neighbors first and ask one of them to sit with her grandmother while she ran to the phone? Or just go to the phone first?

Throwing on her coat and boots, she ran outside, electing to go to the phone shanty first. The ambulance needed to get there as quickly as possible.

The phone shanty that they shared with four other houses was a half mile down the road. Feeling as if her heart was in her throat, she ran on the gravel path as fast as she could, praying with every step for the Lord to watch over Mommi while she couldn't.

Running into the small shack, she picked up the phone and dialed 911. The moment the operator answered, she relayed her name, her grandmother's name, and their address.

"Stay on the line until someone gets there."

"I can't. I'm Amish. I need to get home. I'm at a phone shanty down the road."

"Who is with her?"

"No one." It was hard even saying the words. What if she'd made the wrong decision and her grandmother was suffering all alone? "Is someone on the way?"

"Yes, Addie. They are en route. But stay on the line, okay?"

"I can't. I just can't. I've got to go." She hung up, then ran back toward the house.

Tears were in her eyes by the time she got back to her grandmother's side. Hating that Mommi seemed so still and pale, she knelt down again and felt for a pulse. "Mommi, can ya hear me?"

"Cold."

Praise God. She was alive. "I know," Addie said. "It's cold outside and I didn't have my gloves on. My fingers are likely freezing." She rubbed them against her wool coat, hoping to warm them at least a little bit.

"I called for the ambulance. The dispatcher said it should be here real soon. In just a few minutes. So, you have to stay strong. Stay real strong. We have to pray and keep hoping, right?"

When silence fell between them, Addie felt a sense of peace. She didn't know what had happened, or what the doctors would find. But she did know that God was with her and that was enough.

Maybe that's what He had been trying to let her know all along? That all her worries and disappointments had been hard, but she hadn't been tackling them by herself. In the midst of all those hard moments, she hadn't been walking alone. He'd been there, too.

Hearing sirens in the distance, Addie got to her feet and ran to the door. When the ambulance pulled in and two paramedics jumped out, she opened the door and waved them in.

"She's here!"

A man with steel-gray eyes scanned the entryway. "Do you know what happened, miss?"

"*Nee*. I mean, no, not really. I came out of my room and found my grandmother collapsed over here," she said as she led them to her. "I found her on the floor."

Immediately, they got to work. "Has she said anything to you? Given you any indication of what is the matter?"

"She's spoken, but hasn't said much. I'm really worried," she added as she watched the two men kneel by her grandmother and check her vital signs.

The older man started calling off instructions in a clipped, rapid-fire voice as he started attaching monitors to Mommi.

"Is . . . is she going to be okay?" she asked at last.

"Hope so, ma'am," the younger said as the older man spoke on his radio.

When their expressions became even more concerned, it took everything she had to keep her distance.

Less than five minutes later, her grandmother was on a stretcher, with an IV in her hand. "We're taking her over to the hospital in Wooster, miss."

"Can I ride with you? I have no other way to get to the hospital."

"Of course, but we need to go now."

"I understand." While the men first secured her grandmother to the stretcher, then carried her grandmother out to the ambulance, Addie grabbed her purse, double-checked that no candle was still burning and that the stove was off. Seconds later, she locked the door and hurried to the ambulance. "Do you want me to get in the back with her?"

"No. Over here, miss." The younger man helped her into a side door. "Buckle up."

She did as she was told and merely held on as the other

doors locked and they tore down the road, lights flashing and sirens blaring.

The driver was on his radio, calling out codes.

All she seemed to be aware of was the fact that they'd attached an oxygen mask to her grandmother's mouth.

Addie began to pray harder.

Chapter 19

"Hey, Daniel? Daniel, are you available?"

Surprised to hear Stefan reaching out for him so soon after starting a shift, Daniel strode over to the radio attached to his cleaning cart. "I'm here."

"Where are you at?"

"I'm in admissions." He'd just finished cleaning the lobby bathrooms and was about to wipe down the glass doors.

"Are you in general admissions or in the emergency room?"

"Regular. Why?"

"Kristen just called. They need you over in emergency."

Already thinking of the mess he was going to have to clean up, he frowned. "What happened?"

"It's not to clean. An elderly Amish lady was just brought in. Her granddaughter is with her, but she seems rattled. No one is sure if she understands much English or not. Head over there, will ya?"

"I'll be there in a few." Being asked to interpret or calm an

Amish person didn't happen daily or even weekly, but it was a regular occurrence.

Because Pennsylvania Dutch was the first language most Amish learned, it was still their preferred speech, especially in times of stress. He'd seen some of the most fluent English-speaking members of his church district become confused when the doctors or nurses tried to direct them or give them instructions.

"Try to get there as soon as you can, Daniel. I'll get someone else to take care of your cart."

"I understand." After explaining his exact location and being assured that no one would question why he'd left his cart in the hallway, Daniel rushed through the halls, exiting the main hospital into the emergency area.

When Carol, the emergency room charge nurse, saw him approaching, she motioned him over. "Thanks for coming over so quickly. We've got an elderly woman who collapsed at home and her granddaughter. The girl is beside herself. I think she understands English but I'm not sure."

"I'm happy to help."

"Thank you so much. Go to Triage Seven, 'kay? You'll see Doctor Klein or Rob nearby."

Daniel headed where Carol directed. The curtain divider around the seventh cubicle was partly open. Seeing the familiar dress, apron, stocking-covered legs and black loafers, he knew he was at the right place.

"Hello?" he said in Pennsylvania Dutch. "My name is Daniel and I work here at the hospital. I'm here to help in case you have any questions about your relative's care."

The woman turned. "Oh, *danke*! I'm so glad you're . . . Daniel?"

"Addie!"

"I can't believe you're here." She got to her feet and stepped toward him. "You're an answer to prayer."

Unable to stop himself, he reached for her hand and gently squeezed. "What's going on?"

"It's my grandmother."

Stepping into the cubicle, he spotted Lovina. Several monitors were attached to her as well as an IV and an oxygen tube. Her eyes were closed and she looked pale. "I'm so sorry, Addie. What happened?"

Moving to his side, Addie released a ragged sigh. "She collapsed while I was in my room. When I came out, I found her on the floor. I was so scared!"

"I'm sure you were," he murmured. "But if you got her here, you must have done something right, ain't so?"

"I hope so. I didn't know what to do at first. I was afraid to leave her."

"How did you manage?" he asked, still hoping to calm her down a little.

"I ran as fast as I could to the phone shanty and dialed nine-one-one, then ran back, praying the whole time."

"You did the right thing. Now, what did the doctors and nurses say?"

"They're running tests." Her bottom lip trembled. "I don't know what I'm going to do if she's really bad off, Daniel."

"I know, but you have to think positive. It could be anything."

"That's what Rob said."

Rob was one of the more experienced registered nurses who worked in the emergency room. Daniel liked the fact that he never seemed to lose his cool—or took out his frustrations on other people. "If Rob is her nurse, then your grandmother is in *gut* hands. He's the best."

"He seems nice."

"He is. Now, who is your doctor?"

"A man with glasses . . ."

"Dr. Klein. He is a *gut* doctor. You'll be able to trust him, Addie."

"I hope so." Looking more worried, she peeked out through the opening. "I wish someone would come back in here soon. Do you think they forgot about us?"

"*Nee*. Getting results takes time, *jah*? Why don't you have a seat?"

"Are you going to leave now?"

"Nope. I'm going to stay with ya in case you need me to translate something either Dr. Klein or Rob says."

"How did you know we were here?"

"If an Amish person comes in while I'm on shift, they try to send me over. I make sure the patient understands everything."

"It's nice that the doctors ask you to come over . . . and so kind of you to help out."

"Believe it or not, the staff tries to make all the patients and their families as comfortable here as possible."

"I believe it." She smiled before her attention returned to her grandmother again.

They sat side by side next to Lovina. A pair of monitors beeped on the other side of the bed. After a few moments passed, he asked, "What have you been doing today?"

"I babysat this morning. Mommi was napping when I returned home. So I went to my room to freshen up, then I was going to make some soup and clean her bedroom when I found her."

He felt so sorry for her. Though he often saw at least a dozen worried family members every time he was at work, it was completely different when he knew the people involved. And Addie had become special to him. He hated to see her so upset. "See? That's the Lord's timing right there," he murmured. "You were home when she collapsed. I'm thinking that things could've been much worse."

Her green eyes widened. "Daniel, you are right. I should be counting my blessings instead of worrying."

"I wasna criticizing, Addie. I promise."

She nodded, then hurried to her feet as Dr. Klein and Rob entered.

Catching sight of Daniel, Dr. Klein's smile widened. "Good to see you, Daniel. I'm glad you were on shift today."

"Me too, especially since me and Addie here know each other."

"I'm sure that's a blessing," Rob said.

"*Jah,*" Addie said. Visibly gathering herself together, she said, "Do you know what happened to my grandmother yet?"

"We have a pretty good idea." Looking at a computer attached to the cart, Dr. Klein cleared his throat. "Addie, your grandmother has a kidney infection. There are a couple of other numbers and results that are a bit concerning, but I'm pretty sure that this infection is what made her collapse."

"I don't understand."

Dr. Klein glanced at Daniel, obviously ready for him to interpret.

"Do you understand about the kidney infection, Addie?" he murmured in Deutsch.

"I understand, but I don't understand why she is still unconscious."

After he translated, Dr. Klein said, "I'm guessing she's had the infection for a while. It could be that she stood up too quickly and got dizzy or disoriented, then lost her balance, fell, and hit her head."

"That could happen?" Addie asked.

"All the time," Rob said as he checked more numbers and read them off to the doctor.

Daniel was studying Addie. She looked concerned but not quite as frantic as before. "Do you understand, Addie?"

"I think so." Looking bleak, she adjusted her glasses on the bridge of her nose. "What happens now?"

Dr. Klein answered. "We're going to admit her, make sure she doesn't have any kidney stones, and work on fighting this infection. Watch this concussion. If all goes well, you'll get to take her home in two or three days."

"She's not going to like sleeping in the hospital."

"I know," Rob said, "but I think she'll change her mind as soon as she realizes that this is the best place for her. She's not out of the woods yet, Addie."

"Can I stay with her?" she asked Daniel in Deutsch.

"She wants to know if she can stay here overnight with her grandmother," Daniel translated.

"I'm sorry, no. Your grandmother needs to rest and you do, too, miss," Dr. Klein said.

When Addie looked about to protest, Rob spoke again. "When your grandmother gets home, she's going to need quite a bit of help. You'll need your strength if you'll be taking care of her all the time."

"He's right," Daniel said in Pennsylvania Dutch.

"We'll see you tomorrow when you visit, Addie," Dr. Klein said. "Please try not to worry too much. Rob, please make sure she has all the paperwork and emergency numbers."

"Yes, Doctor."

"Get some rest," Dr. Klein said. "I promise, we're going to do our best for your grandmother. Before you know it, she'll be back home and being here will be just a memory."

"Danke."

He smiled at Daniel, then walked out between the gap in the curtains.

After checking Lovina again, Rob filled out some papers, then handed a clipboard to Addie. Briefly, he explained what the papers said and instructed her about how to call and get updates.

"Do you have any questions?"

"*Nee.*" She looked at Daniel, conveying that she was going to ask him questions and not Rob.

"I'll make sure she's good before I go back to my shift."

"Great. Thanks, Dan. Will you go ahead and walk her out? We need to transfer Lovina."

Addie went to her grandmother's side, whispered to her and clasped her hand, then turned back to Daniel. "I'm ready now."

When they were out in the hall, Addie, in her gray dress, neat white *kapp,* and clean face, looked like a breath of fresh, clean air in the chaotic area. Only the worried look in her eyes conveyed just how upset she really was.

"Thank you for your help," she said formally.

"No need." Reaching for her hand again, he pressed it between both of his. "I'm glad I was here. Hey, are you going to be all right?"

"Of course. I am not sick."

"You know that's not what I meant." Thinking quickly, he added, "I get off in about three hours. If you'd like, I could stop by your house. You know, just to see if you need anything."

"I won't. I'm used to taking care of things on my own."

Somehow, that made him feel even worse for her. "Are you sure? Do you have someone who could come over?"

"I'll be fine." Her voice was as firm as her expression.

He still didn't like the idea of her going back to an empty house by herself, but didn't want to argue. "All right. Hey, I can ask whoever takes me here tomorrow if we could go to your house and get you, too. I need to be here at nine, so it would be early. How about that?"

"I'm sure I'll hire a driver or ask my friend Brooke. There is no need for you to go out of your way for me."

He felt that she was neatly putting him back in his place. Though he would've thought that would be a relief, all he felt was frustration. "Addie, you don't have to go it alone, you know."

When she met his gaze, her eyes were carefully blank. "Daniel, we have known each other for most of our lives. Just because we've talked a few times recently, it doesn't mean that everything has changed between us, right?"

"But it has."

"To what end?" Looking frustrated with him, she added, "Do you really want me stopping by your house to chat? Visiting with you after church services? Standing with you during the next engagement party we are both invited to?"

"Yes. Yes to all of that."

"If you really believe that, I'm impressed."

"It's not just words. I've changed."

"I think we both have, Daniel."

"Look. I know I haven't given you a lot of reasons to trust me, but I'd still like you to try. It would mean a lot to me if you would."

She met his gaze. "You mean that, don't you?"

"Very much so. Addie, will you at least think about it? I know you have a dozen reasons to say no, but I really hope you will say yes anyway."

She stared at him, seemed to be trying to read all sorts of things in his expression.

Then, to his relief, she nodded at last. "All right," she whispered.

"Danke."

Later, when he was cleaning patient rooms on the fourth floor, Daniel's conscience reared its head. How was Addie going to react when he admitted that he'd been her secret admirer all this time?

More important, how was he ever going to break the news to her without ruining the fragile bond they'd just forged?

Chapter 20

The house felt dark and dirty when Addie returned home from the hospital. Though she was tempted to just feed Snickers and check on the chickens before collapsing in bed, there was so much more to do.

She lit two kerosene lanterns, put on a kettle for some hot tea, then hurried back outside. The flashlight cast a wide beam across her path. The bright light was helpful for walking but irritated the hens something awful. They squawked in annoyance about the beam but calmed considerably after she tossed out their feed.

Snickers was asleep when she entered. He opened one eye long enough to watch her refill his water and fill his bin with oats and some fresh hay. "*Gut naught,* donkey. Sleep well and I'll see you in the morning, *jah*?"

He wiggled his ears in response.

Satisfied that all was well outside the house, she entered it again, this time taking a minute to put away her coat and boots. The kettle was whistling. She poured herself some tea, pulled out a couple of oatmeal cookies that she'd made a few days ago, and sat down. At long last.

To her surprise, she realized that her whole body seemed to be filled with some sort of adrenaline rush. A low-grade buzzing had settled into her limbs. It was a strange sensation. She felt she needed to either collapse into bed for the next ten hours or use that time to run in circles around the house. She didn't know which was the better option. Maybe it was neither?

Ack! Everything about the day had been so confusing. Addie still didn't understand how her grandmother could've been so sick for so long without her knowing. Had she really been that bad a caregiver?

It seemed so.

She shivered as she recalled the sight of Mommi on the floor. She'd been so pale, and her head had been bleeding. She'd looked so weak when Addie had tried to talk to her. Addie had been so scared and hadn't known what to do—stay by her grandmother's side or seek help. Of course, going to get help had been the right answer, but she'd never felt more alone during her run back and forth to the phone shanty.

Just as the panic she'd put to bed began to awaken, she pushed it away again—this time with the truth she'd almost forgotten. "You weren't alone, Addie. The Lord was with you and Mommi, right?"

She nodded to herself. If her faith had ever faltered, the day's events would've surely reaffirmed it right then and there. The Lord was big enough to look after her and her grandmother at the same time. He'd kept watch over Mommi while giving Addie two good legs to run to the shanty. He'd helped the 911 operator on duty radio for help. He'd been with the ambulance driver and the EMTs and the doctors and nurses and everyone else who had helped so much. She might have felt alone, but she hadn't been alone. Not for one minute.

And just like that, a new sense of peace filled her body, stilling the trembling in her limbs and easing her mind.

What she needed to do was sit for a spell and count her blessings. There were a lot of them, to be sure. Her grandmother was going to be fine. The doctors and nurses had been kind and patient with both Mommi and herself; they'd even called over Daniel to assist in case Addie had been too upset to completely understand all the English terms she was hearing.

Which brought her to yet another blessing: Daniel. She still wasn't sure how a man she'd known for most of her life—and had barely ever spoken to for most of that time—had suddenly become so important to her. She didn't know if she'd changed, or he had. All Addie did know was that instead of him ignoring her and her avoiding him, they were not only talking, but having enjoyable conversations. It was a blessing and a mystery all at the same time. Today, when he'd stayed with her in the cubicle, she had gotten the sense that he wasn't there out of a work obligation. He'd wanted to help her. No, he'd wanted to be with her. Like they were friends.

Or maybe even something more?

She lifted her cup, ready to take another fortifying sip of tea before realizing that it was empty. She sighed. It was time to make her choice. Either sleep or clean.

Standing up, she knew there wasn't much of a choice to be made. The kitchen was in disarray. On the floor was another stain that she hadn't noticed before she'd left with the EMTs in the ambulance. Whether it was from blood or just mud, she wasn't sure. Pushing her exhaustion away, she turned on the faucet and got to work.

Thirty minutes later, the kitchen was spic and span again and she was on her hands and knees near the stairs, scrubbing the floor. Once that was clean again, she strode into her grandmother's room.

It smelled musty, giving clues that her grandmother had been fighting off a sickness but keeping it all to herself. Refusing to once again wallow in guilt, Addie stripped the sheets off the bed and tossed them into the hall. She then gathered clothes and towels and took them down to the basement. After starting a load in the gas-powered washing machine, she debated about her next choice. She could either start dusting or simply wait until the sheets were done and hang them up on the line in the basement.

Not eager to dust in the dark, she carried a kerosene lantern to the bathroom and took a hot shower, letting some of the stress of the day gradually make its way down the drain. After slipping on a fresh nightgown and brushing out her hair, she walked back to the basement and pinned sheets to the line that ran the length of the space. Tomorrow, if the day was clear, she'd carry everything upstairs to the line outside.

At last, her day was done.

After making sure that the doors were locked and both kerosene lamps were extinguished, Addie turned on the flashlight and went upstairs to bed. Only after she climbed under the thick white quilt that covered her mattress did she notice the paper and pen that she'd used to write to her secret admirer.

To her surprise, she hadn't given that letter or her troubled, chaotic worries a second of thought. *Nee,* that was putting it in too general terms. The truth was that she'd forgotten all about *him*, even after leaving the hospital. Instead, she'd thought about Daniel.

That was puzzling. Or maybe not? Did a mystery correspondent writing caring phrases matter as much as a real person in her life who was willing to give her a helping hand?

It seemed the answer was no.

For some reason, her pen pal—and Daniel—made her think of her life with her grandmother and how both grateful and resentful she'd been over the years.

And, for some reason, she thought of Snickers, too.

That little donkey served as a good reminder that nothing was wanted and appreciated all the time. Sometimes the value of a creature or person fell to the wayside . . . or the opposite happened. Something forgotten only needed fresh eyes to see its worth. That had certainly been true for that little donkey.

When she'd first seen him, he'd been deemed worthless by his owners. Even she hadn't been sure of his value. Only a fierce need to protect a being in need of protection had propelled her to offer for him. She'd even had to haggle with his owner, who had made no bones about declaring that the donkey was worth more dead than alive.

But now, all these years later, he was a therapy animal, bringing joy to so many. For herself, he was a treasured pet.

He'd come into her life without warning and changed it dramatically. He'd been a gift from the angels. Just as her grandmother was.

Just like Mommi had said Addie was to her—an unexpected gift that she hadn't even realized she wanted.

Each situation was like a mirror. One side was nothing—only something dark and flat. A smooth surface.

But on the other side? The reflection brought in light and allowed one to see oneself clearly.

"Both the good and the bad," she whispered.

"You, Addie, have finally flipped that mirror, and you're

seeing the world around you—and yourself—in all its flawed, imperfect, and beautiful glory."

That was the truth. At least, it was to her. She wasn't anyone special, but she had worth. A lot of worth. As did most everyone around her.

Even little donkeys—if they were given the chance to shine.

Chapter 21

Preacher Joshua had been preaching for ninety minutes, and by the look and sound of him, he didn't seem to be in any hurry to stop soon.

Coughing loudly, Roman's seventy-one-year-old grandfather got up and strode outside.

Daniel and two other guys beside him watched the old man leave with what he was sure were matching looks of envy. Wisdom really did come with age.

"*Mei dawdi* is the smartest man in this barn," Roman muttered under his breath.

Daniel nodded as he shifted uncomfortably. He'd made the mistake of sitting in the middle of the fourth row of bleachers in the Hershbergers' barn. He had no way to take a break without making everyone else move and creating a ruckus. If he left, he'd likely be the focus of Joshua's next sermon.

As if the preacher could read his mind, Joshua raised his voice. "All of you sinners, thinking you can have everything you desire? It is time you stopped looking at the outside world and instead give praise for everything you have. Or, better yet, each of you should reach into your soul and ask for His forgiveness."

The youngest Hershberger son, who was sitting on his left, sighed.

Preacher Joshua paused, seemed to look Daniel directly in the eye, then declared, "You know I am right."

Daniel squirmed in his seat. Not because he thought Joshua was right, but because he was beginning to realize that he was guilty of trying to do too much, and it was all backfiring. He was exhausted from work. From trying to be the friend that Roman and Bradley were used to, trying to be the friend to Addie that she needed. . . .

All while wondering what to do about Addie's latest letter.

She was giving him up. Didn't trust him.

He should be thanking his lucky stars. She was giving him a way out, and he had begun to wonder if such a thing was even possible. Now, all he had to do was write her one last letter, agree that it was time their correspondence came to an end, put it in that tree trunk . . . and be done with it. His career as a secret pen pal would be over and he could concentrate on deepening his friendship with Addie. In time, he might even be able to forget that he'd ever done such a crazy thing.

But, ironically, that whole scenario felt wrong. Now that he'd gotten to know her, he was sure that if he did break things off so abruptly, it would somehow hurt her.

Whether it was right or wrong, Daniel felt that he must somehow find a way to tell Addie the truth. He felt that she needed to know that his intentions had been sincere.

He had no idea how to do that, however. It wasn't as if he could tell her the truth in a letter, then show up at her house the next day and assume that she would be happy to see him.

"The word of the Lord is righteous and true!"

"Oh, boy," Roman muttered next to him. "Preacher Joshua is in a chatty mood today."

"*Jah*." That was the problem, too. It wasn't about the message so much as the man delivering it.

"Shh," muttered a man below them on the risers.

"Sorry," Roman said.

Daniel knew if he'd been with his coworkers at the hospital, one of them would've added that they were "sorry, not sorry."

Inwardly amused by his train of thought, he looked across the aisle to where all the women sat and caught sight of Addie. She was sitting in the middle of some ladies who were all about five or six years older than her. Her grandmother wasn't there. He'd assumed Lovina would stay home, but her absence was still strange. The district counted on Lovina Stutzman to keep everyone in line. She always presided over every community activity with a stern eye. No matter the age, no one dared antagonize Lovina.

Without the formidable woman sitting beside her, Addie was undoubtedly feeling a little lost.

"Daniel, aren't you going to get up?" Roman asked.

He blinked. The service was over, and he was blocking the four men to his right who were waiting for him to get up so they could move.

He surged to his feet. "Sorry," he muttered as he followed the rest of the men on his row to the aisle and down the steps to the barn's cement floor.

"You sure don't seem like your normal self today," Roman chided as they started walking outside to where the luncheon was being set up. "What's going on?"

Oh, nothing beyond adopting another personality and

hoodwinking a woman he was starting to have feelings for. "Nothing."

"Nothing?"

"All right, fine. I think I'm tired. That's all."

Some of the concern shining in Roman's eyes lifted. "You been working a lot, haven't you?"

"*Jah*. Seven hours overtime this week. Plus, I've been visiting my parents, like usual."

"That is a lot," Roman murmured, though he didn't exactly look like he believed Daniel. Scanning the crowd, Roman brightened. "Come over here. I know what will wake you up."

"What will?" he asked as Roman darted around two toddlers chasing each other.

"This." Roman grinned. "Hiya, Addie."

Addie, who had been speaking with a new couple who'd recently moved into the area, turned with a smile. It slowly faded as she realized that it was Roman who had called her name and not him. "Ah, hello, Roman. Daniel."

"I saw you across the way and thought it had been far too long since we've talked," Roman added. Just as if he hadn't ignored her for years.

Her eyes darted toward Daniel before she spoke again to Roman. "*Jah*. It has been a very long time."

Daniel was fairly sure if they'd been standing in the middle of an ice storm, her tone couldn't have been chillier. Hoping to save the moment, he smiled at the couple she'd been talking with. They were either visitors or new to the area.

He'd been rude. "I'm sorry if we interrupted your conversation. I know we met a couple months ago. I'm Daniel Miller and this is Roman Schablach."

"I'm Matt and this is *mei frau* Tricia."

"It's *gut* to meet ya. *Wilcom* to Apple Creek. I hope you are settling in all right."

"*Danke,*" Matt replied. "We are, though I must admit we're anxious for warm weather to arrive."

"We moved from southern Indiana," Tricia added.

"It does feel like spring takes its own sweet time to visit," Roman joked. "Here it is April and we're still getting more cold, wet days than not."

"I told Tricia and Matt not to give up. After all, we've already seen our first hints of spring. Now all we have to do is look for signs that planting season is just around the corner."

"Lambs are my sign," Roman said.

Daniel nodded. "Lambs, to be sure. And the ducks."

Tricia brightened. "Ducks, did you say?"

"There's a pond near my *haus*. It's thawed of course, but still bitter cold. However, whenever the ducks that come every year return, I know I've made it through another winter—and that *mei daed* will soon be needin' *mei* help to plant alfalfa."

"I'll be on the lookout for those ducks, then." Tricia smiled at her husband. "It will give us a reason to walk by the creek more often."

He chuckled. "Indeed." After exchanging a few more words, Tricia and Matt went on their way. Afraid Addie was about to leave, too, Daniel stepped closer. "How is your grandmother?"

"Cranky," she said with a laugh. "Mommi doesn't like me fussing over her so much. Or watching her like a hawk to make sure she eats right and takes her medicine." Looking flustered, she added, "Daniel, if I never said a proper thank-you, please forgive me. We are both mighty grateful for your help in the emergency room."

"I was glad to have been of help."

"I'm sorry she was in the hospital," Roman said.

"Me too. *Danke*." She blinked away a tear and swiped it

with her hand. "Sorry, I don't know what's wrong with me. I think I'm tired."

"That's going around," Roman said.

Daniel grunted. Noticing that Addie was wiping her eyes again, he fumbled for a handkerchief that he'd stuck in his coat pocket. When he pulled it out, a piece of paper fell out as well.

Except, it wasn't exactly a piece of paper. It was an envelope.

No, it was Addie's envelope, addressed to her secret admirer.

And of course, it landed with the letters *S.A.* on the front. He gaped at it, wondering how in the world he was going to pick it up without Addie noticing.

Time seemed to move in slow motion. Addie glanced at the envelope, then inhaled sharply. Roman knelt down to pick it up. And Daniel? He just stared, doing the best he could to think of something.

No, *anything* to rectify the situation. But there really wasn't anything he could do. It was un-rectifiable. For sure and for certain.

"Here," Roman held it up. "What's *S.A.*?"

This was every one of his worst nightmares come to life. "Uh . . ."

Addie was staring at it like it was a rabid bat. "Where did you get that letter?"

"Um . . ." What could he say? His mind still seemed to be mired in tar or pudding or something. Even the smallest words seemed to be stuck in transit. All he wanted to do was ask the Lord to turn back time. To get him back to a place where he had some control over the situation.

Roman, who was still holding the note, looked at Addie. "Addie, are you saying that you know what *S.A.* means?"

Looking crestfallen, Addie nodded. "I do."

"Really? So, it's yours?"

"*Jah.*" She held out her hand. "If you could give that to me, please? I'll go dispose of it."

Hearing that Addie was about to throw out that letter, throw out *his* letter, hit him hard. "*Nee.*"

Roman looked from one to the other. "Wait a minute. Daniel, are you saying you know what this *S.A.* letter is?"

For some reason, having to confess the truth to Roman in front of Addie made everything even worse. "I do. But it ain't none of your business. Hand it over, if you please."

"*Nee,* please give it to me," Addie said. Her voice sounded brittle, as if it was about to break into a thousand pieces. "You see, it's a letter I wrote to someone who I thought was special. Obviously, he was not."

"Addie, wait."

She ignored him. Standing in front of him, she lifted her chin. She was transformed from the shy, timid girl he'd known all his life to someone quite different.

In place of that girl was a woman who would make Lovina Stutzman proud. She was fearless.

She was also incredibly mad.

Her voice lowered. Each word shot out of her mouth like tiny darts. "Did this amuse you, Daniel? Is this why you brought Roman over? Because you found a silly note I wrote and decided to embarrass me?"

"*Nee!* Not at all." Finally realizing what she thought—that he'd somehow found the note in the secret hiding place, read it, and then made a joke of it . . . and had planned to reveal all after church, he started to sweat. "Addie, you have it all wrong."

She turned to Roman. "May I have the note back, please?"

He didn't hesitate. "Here."

She was going to turn around. He couldn't let her do that. He couldn't allow her to think for another moment that their letters weren't genuine.

Or that he was the type of man who would knowingly embarrass her like that. "I didn't steal that note."

Her glasses seemed to accentuate the pain shining in her eyes. "Daniel, don't lie to me. Stealing is the only way you could have had that."

"It was not the only way." He looked at her intently. "Addie, do you hear what I'm saying to you? I. Did. Not. Steal. That. Letter. From. The. Oak. Tree."

Addie froze. "What are you saying?"

This was it. Never had he imagined that he'd reveal the truth to her like this, without forethought or finesse. Or with a witness. "Roman, give us some space, will ya? Me and Addie have something to discuss."

Looking worried, Roman turned back to Addie. "Is this what you want? Do you want to be alone with him? If not, I will stay."

Daniel couldn't believe it. Now, Roman was actually acting as if Daniel was capable of hurting Addie! And on purpose, no less!

How had this awful situation flipped and somehow managed to get even worse?

"I would never hurt Addie," he bit out. "She is safe with me, Roman." Glaring at his buddy, he added, "Please. Go."

Roman folded his arms over his chest. "Addie has every right to decide what she wants to do—without your interference." His voice turned gentle. "Addie, if you don't feel comfortable being alone with Daniel, I can stay."

"You're being ridiculous, Roman. You are also being offensive. Addie and I are friends. Of course, she's fine being alone with me. You need to walk away."

"Don't tell me what to do—"

"Stop speaking for me!" Addie blurted. When they both gaped at her, she took a deep breath. "Roman, *danke,* but I am fine. Though it seems we are attracting a lot of attention, Daniel."

"We can go wherever you want." Thinking quickly—thank the good Lord, his brain was working again—he added, "I'll be happy to drive you home in my buggy." When she hesitated, he added, "Please say yes to that, at least. We've got a lot to talk about."

She stayed him with a hand. "Daniel Miller, are you really my secret admirer? Are you really the man who has been writing me those notes?"

"I really am. Now, will you please allow me to see you home and explain?" He could tell she wasn't sure whether she should or not. "Please, Addie. You need to hear what I was thinking."

"All right. I, ah, I need to say good-bye to the Hershbergers first, though."

"I'll wait in the driveway." Wanting her to know that he was serious, not just about the ride home but about his explanation, he said, "I'm not going anywhere without you, Addie Holmes."

Her eyes widened before she turned and walked away.

"Did I really hear her ask if you were her secret admirer?" Roman asked.

"*Jah.*"

"Daniel, what in the world have you done?"

"I'm already going to have to try to explain myself to Addie, Roman. There's no way I'm going to relay it all to you, too. You're just going to have to wait your turn."

He walked to the driveway to wait for Addie. And to think about how he was going to find the words to describe his intention. To find a way for her not to hate him for the rest of his life.

Given the way his brain was working, he figured each one of those goals was going to be next to impossible to achieve.

Almost—he realized—as impossible as it was going to be to find hope that Roman wouldn't tell pretty much everyone in Apple Creek about what he had just witnessed.

Chapter 22

Addie felt as if everyone's attention was on her as she moved through the crowd to thank Marianne Hershberger for the morning's hospitality. If she hadn't been so hurt by Daniel's actions, the whispers and the looks of pity might have felt worse than they did. She might have even hung her head in shame.

Not any longer. As far as Addie was concerned, she'd done nothing wrong except trust Daniel. He was the one who'd reached out to be her friend. He was also the one who'd come up with the underhanded scheme to be her secret admirer.

She hadn't instigated either.

Even though she knew she'd likely spend the next weeks or even months castigating herself for being foolish enough to respond to an anonymous author, she had written him back in good faith. So, she was guilty of being hopeful and naive as far as the letters were concerned.

She wasn't going to accept any blame for believing in Daniel's kindness.

Addie wasn't sure why he'd decided he had nothing better to do than to play this foolish game with her heart. Maybe she never would. However, the shame lay with Daniel, not her.

Marianne headed toward her when she saw Addie approach. "Are you all right?" She wrapped an arm around her shoulders. Marianne was an older woman who'd always been kind to Addie. "It looked like you and Daniel and Roman were in the middle of a big argument."

"I don't know if I'm all right or not. I'll be okay, though. Daniel and I are about to discuss some things."

Marianne looked even more concerned. "The timing of this is hardly fair. You just got your grandmother out of the hospital!"

Marianne didn't know the half of it. "I'm okay. I just came over to thank you for hosting church today."

"Do you want me to go with you? I don't mind."

"That's kind of you, but I'm fine."

"All right, but I hate for you to think that you have to deal with everything on your own. I'd be happy to help if I'm able."

"*Danke,* but there's nothing you can do. Like I said, I just wanted to thank you for hosting. Everything was really pretty, and your cookies were delicious."

"*Danke,* Addie. If you need anything at all, just let me know."

"I will." Pleased that she had done the right thing, Addie walked back toward Daniel. A few people were still staring at her, but most everyone was sitting down to eat the simple meal of sandwiches, macaroni salad, berries, and cookies.

"Are you ready?" Daniel asked when she returned to his side.

"*Jah.*"

He looked stung by her tone but simply led the way to his

buggy. It was freshly painted and parked off to the side. "I hitched up Hero while you were saying good-bye to Marianne," he explained. "Now you won't have to wait while I do that."

"All right."

Daniel frowned again, but he didn't say anything else. Only opened the buggy door, helped her in by gripping her elbow, and then untied the reins from the hitching post.

Minutes later they were on their way. He kept silent as he turned right. There were several buggies already on the street, as well as vehicles attempting to pass. Daniel kept a safe distance from the buggy in front of them and a firm hand on his horse.

Little by little, as Hero *clip-clopped* along, some of Addie's cold bitterness dissipated. Maybe it was because of the comfort of the buggy. It was far warmer inside the conveyance than it had been when they were standing in the yard. There was only a scant six inches separating the two of them. In addition, he had a thick wool blanket on the seat. It made the enclosure feel even more cozy.

Then, too, she might be finally thawing because she saw how upset he was. Daniel was not acting upset that he'd been caught. Instead, he was acting upset because she was mad at him.

Or maybe he was simply mad at himself.

"Do you want me to take you straight home or could we talk?"

"I thought that had been decided. You may take me directly home."

"May I come in when we get there?" His voice sounded even more strained.

"My grandmother will be inside."

"Do you have someplace where we could speak privately in the house?"

"I suppose so. Or you could try to explain yourself now."

"There's a lot to explain."

"Oh, I bet there is."

"Addie, please. I know you are mad and hurt, and I don't blame ya for either. But I do need you to give me the time to try to explain myself. I can't properly do that while driving a buggy."

They were almost at her house. She wanted an explanation—no, she needed one. That meant she was going to have to be reasonable. "Fine. You may come in, but do not involve my grandmother."

"I won't."

They drifted into silence again. Maybe Daniel was lost in his own thoughts—she didn't know. Addie's own head was in such a mess, she had started hoping that she wasn't about to dissolve into tears. The situation was bittersweet, though. She'd imagined more than once being on a man's arm after church and being given a buggy ride home.

After they'd talked so much of late, she had even wondered what it would feel like to ride in Daniel's buggy. She'd imagined how it would feel, being alone with just him in the small enclosure. She'd imagined the skirt of her dress rustling against his coat, imagined feeling like they were snug together while the rest of the world continued on the outside.

And here she was. It was happening. However, it was such a twisted version of her girlish dreams, it was painful.

"Okay if I hitch Hero to the post next to the barn?"

"Of course." After he set the brake, she climbed out of the buggy and stood to the side while Daniel got out on his side and attached the reins to the hitching post. Then she led the way to the house, wondering all the while how she was going to be able to explain Daniel's presence to her grandmother while not leading her to believe she had a beau or making her upset because something was obviously wrong between them.

She decided to simply be as straightforward as she could be. There would be plenty of time for tears and explanations later.

Hesitating at the door, she said, "I'm going to do my best to make sure my grandmother knows this is a private conversation."

"I understand."

Thinking what conclusions Mommi would draw, Addie winced. "Ah, just to warn you, she might assume that your visit is of a different nature."

Regret filled his eyes. "I know what you mean."

She led him inside. "Mommi, I'm home!"

"I'm in the kitchen, Addie. Come in. How was church? You can keep me company while I wash dishes."

"I have company. I'll wash the dishes after he leaves."

"He? Who is here?"

Addie groaned to herself. She might as well have just rung a bell and clapped her hands. Having a male visitor was practically the only thing that she could have done to create such a burst of excitement in her grandmother's voice.

"Daniel, I think I'd better go talk to her. Please sit down." She gestured to the living room before hurrying to face her grandmother.

As she feared, the kettle was on the stove and her grandmother already had a tray on the counter. "Addie, you see, dear? I knew your dreams would come true one day. You finally have a caller."

Addie's cheeks were on fire. Of course, her grandmother was practically yelling. "Mommi, this isn't what you think. Daniel Miller is here, but he hasn't come over to uh, court." She mentally groaned. How much more embarrassing could this moment get?

"How did this happen? Did you see him at church?"

"*Jah*. We ah . . . had something to discuss, so I suggested that we speak here."

Her grandmother's eyes were shining. "I'm so happy he brought you home, dear. Well, you go visit. When the tray is ready, I'll call out and you can help me carry it in."

"We won't need a tray."

"Of course you will."

"Mommi, I'd rather not serve Daniel anything. He won't be staying long."

She shook her head. "Child, that is not the way to treat a new beau. I know you don't have any experience in courting, but I promise, this is how it is done."

Her grandmother had not only ignored everything Addie was saying, she was still yelling like they were in the middle of a field. Daniel would have to be outside in the barn not to have heard. She had thought her day couldn't get worse, but somehow it had.

Realizing that there was no way she was going to be able to settle her grandmother down without telling her the whole story, Addie sighed. "*Danke,*" she said at last. "Call me when you are ready. You may not try to carry a tray."

"I'll call you. Go on, now," she said with a smile.

Daniel was standing in the living room with his hands in his pockets when she returned. He was still wearing his coat—just as she was still wearing her black cloak.

"I have been rude. Would you like me to take your coat?"

He shrugged it off. "Tell me where to hang it." When she pointed to the hooks near the door, he held out his hand for her cloak. There was no reason not to hand it over, but yet again, she felt as awkward and out of control as she had for the last hour.

When at last they were both sitting down, Addie was eager to get the conversation over and get him out of her house. Taking care to keep her voice down, she began. "Daniel, I can't begin to tell you how I'm feeling."

He grimaced. "I'm sure you are confused and mad at me."

"I am, but mainly, I don't understand." She took a deep breath. "You told me that these notes of yours weren't a game?"

"Not at all. I wasn't playing you for a fool, Addie. I promise, I wouldn't do that to you." He leaned forward, resting his elbows on his knees. "You see, it all started during Aaron and June's engagement party."

"What about it?"

"I was bored, so I was looking around at all the people, wondering who else I could talk to. I ah . . . do that from time to time. I scan crowds." He grimaced. "Anyway, I ended up looking at you. You were surrounded by several people as well, but I could see that you were standing alone. Like I was."

"And?" Daniel was acting as if his words had some kind of great meaning, but all she could vaguely remember was feeling as awkward as she always did during large social gatherings. She'd been wishing she was at home reading a book or talking to Snickers.

He averted his eyes. "A couple of my friends started talking about everyone else we knew. . . ."

"And my name came up?"

"*Jah.*"

The acknowledgment shouldn't have been painful, but it was. "And?"

"And I realized that I didn't appreciate how everyone was practically acting as if you were an old maid." His cheeks flushed. "And so I decided that what you needed was a bit of confidence."

She was incredulous. "Daniel, you decided this all by looking across a backyard at me?"

"*Jah.*" He swallowed. "That's when I decided to be your secret admirer."

She sucked in a breath. "Daniel—"

"Addie! Come get the coffee and snacks."

She jumped to her feet. "I need to get that."

He was on his feet as well. "May I help you?"

"*Nee.*" She needed a moment to get herself together. Besides, things were only going to get worse if Daniel started talking to her grandmother.

Feeling as if her insides were shredded, she walked to the kitchen. Her grandmother was standing by the door, peeking out.

"How is it going?"

"It is fine." Catching sight of Mommi's best tray loaded down with the coffee carafe and snacks, Addie's stomach clenched. "I wish you hadn't gone to so much trouble."

"It's never trouble to show someone you care. Ain't so?"

Addie nodded. "I need to take this out. Thank you again, Mommi."

Walking down the hall carrying the heavy tray, she felt as if she might as well be walking into a lion's den. So far, everything that she'd heard from Daniel had made her heart hurt.

"Here, let me help you," he said, meeting her halfway. He easily took the tray from her hands and carried it to the coffee table.

"Would you like a cup of coffee?" As irritated as she was with him, Addie couldn't refuse to offer him something—especially since it would spur another lecture from her grandmother.

"That's not necessary."

"If we don't drink any, we'll be disrespecting my grandma." She poured herself a cup, adding a healthy splash of milk. "Please, help yourself."

"*Danke.*" After filling his own cup, he sat down with it between his hands. "Addie, as I was saying, I decided to write you a letter on an impulse, but my motives weren't wicked. I really didn't intend you any harm."

"Where did you expect it to end?" She shook her head, frustrated that she wasn't conveying her thoughts quite right. "I mean, how did you expect it to end? Did you ever intend to tell me the truth?" Hating how vulnerable she sounded, she added, "Was that why you suddenly started talking to me?"

"I didn't *suddenly start talking to you*. Come on, Addie. I wasn't that bad."

He was wrong. From her perspective, his behavior had been like a switch being flipped. One day she'd been standing on the other side of a party, watching Daniel with his crew of friends—and the next, he was starting a conversation with her at the post office. "Daniel, that first time we talked at the post office, had you already decided to start writing me letters?"

His throat worked.

As Addie watched him, her mind spun. Was Daniel thinking about lying again? Or was he only doing what she was doing—attempting to navigate one of the hardest conversations of her life?

"*Jah,*" he said at last.

"I see." So it had been all a game to him.

"*Nee*, don't look at me like that. I wasna—" He shook his head. "Addie, I wasn't pretending to want to talk to you. That ain't it at all."

He lowered his voice. "That day you're talking about? The day you and me started talking in front of the post office? Well, I had your letter in my hand and I couldn't figure out how to hide it with you standing right there. If you thought I looked uncomfortable, it was because of that."

"You couldn't have just given it to me? Or, better yet, simply come over and told me what you were thinking?"

"You and I both know that wouldn't have gone well."

"Are you sure about that?"

"Are you sure it would have?" His tone turned pleading.

"Come on. Addie, think what you want about me, but while you're doing that, be honest with yourself, too. If I had shown up on this doorstep, asking to sit with you for a spell, how would you have reacted? Would you really have smiled, invited me in, and served me coffee?"

"Is that what you think has happened today?"

"Of course not. But what I do think is that you've come out of your shell these last couple of weeks. You smile more, and not just at me. At everyone. You seem more open to conversation, and not just with all the people you've helped, but the people you went to school with. All of us."

Addie wanted to shake her head. To protest that she was still the same woman she'd always been. The same woman he'd ignored and whispered about behind her back.

She couldn't.

"You're right." Her throat felt thick, as if all her emotions were stuck in it. Maybe it was really just her tears that were stuck until she could release them in the privacy of her bedroom. Suddenly, she realized that there wasn't anything else to say. There was no reason to push for the truth. Now she had it. It was just a real shame that the bare truth didn't make her feel any better.

Actually, the truth was something ugly, like an unsightly scar on her arm or face. Something for her to be reminded of on a daily basis, something for everyone to notice the minute they looked her over.

This secret admirer silliness was now a part of who she was. *Nee,* of who *they* were.

She stood up. "I . . . I appreciate your honesty, but I think it's time for you to go."

"*Nee.*" He stepped closer. Wrapped his hands on her elbows, bringing them closer than they'd ever been before. Except maybe in her dreams. "Addie, I might have admitted the truth about those letters, but we are not done. We haven't really talked about them."

Flashes of the sentences she'd written appeared in her head. How honest she'd been. "I don't think we should ever talk about them. Honestly, I think it would be best if you gave the letters back to me."

"Why?"

"You know why, Daniel."

He shook his head. "*Nee,* I do not."

She resented that he was making her say the words. But why should she be surprised? After all, he'd been playing her for a fool for weeks now. "Since we have no relationship, I'd rather not have the things I've written available to you."

His blue eyes flashed. "*Available?* What do you think I am going to do with them?"

His hands were still clasping her elbows. Not hard, not enough to bruise—but firmly all the same. He was holding her in place. Making her face him. Making her reveal what was in her heart all over again.

Oh, she could step backward, and the connection would be broken. Of that, she had no doubt. But maybe she felt the need to have this one last moment when it was just the two of them. When they were being honest and forthright. When there was no one else around to judge or listen or comment or even approve.

"I couldn't begin to guess," Addie finally said.

Something appeared in his eyes, then. Something close to disappointment, or maybe even bitterness. He dropped his hands and stepped back. "I suppose I deserve that."

She felt his loss. Felt suddenly chilled, even though the fire was crackling in the fireplace and the room was warm. She was tempted to apologize. To tell him that she was sorry for being so harsh. For not being more sympathetic to his point of view.

But how could she do that? Didn't she need to hold on to at least a portion of her pride?

"Daniel, I appreciate your coming over, but I think it is time you left."

He stilled. Froze for a moment, then stepped backward. "All right, I'll leave. But this is not the last you're going to see of me, Addie. We've come too far to throw away something that has been so good and true. I'm not going to let you do it."

While she attempted to think of a good retort, of anything to say, he walked to the front door, took his coat off the hook, pulled it on, and then walked out.

Never looking back at her once.

He'd done what she'd asked. He'd left the room and the house.

So why had she never felt more alone?

Chapter 23

Standing at the door, watching Hero pull Daniel's buggy down her drive, Addie pressed a fist to her mouth so her grandmother wouldn't hear her cry out.

Her heart was broken. She felt so fractured, she wouldn't have been surprised if the doctor at the hospital pronounced it severed in two. Daniel had left. Of course, she'd forced him to leave.

But that didn't mean there wasn't a tiny part of her that had been wishing he would refuse to depart until things were better between them.

Closing her eyes to try to stall a flood of tears, Addie attempted to pull herself together. Daniel's departure was probably for the best anyway. How could things between her and Daniel ever get better? Was there even a slight chance?

"Addie Holmes, what did you just do?"

Startled, she opened her eyes. Her grandmother was standing in the living room, her hands clenched around her metal walker, glaring at her.

Facing yet another confrontation was almost more than she could bear. "What are you talking about?"

Mommi shuffled forward. "You know exactly what I mean, girl. Why did you just kick Daniel Miller out of here? And what is all this nonsense about secret admirers?"

"You were eavesdropping on our conversation? Our private conversation? How could you?"

Her grandmother almost looked embarrassed as she joined her. "I didn't mean to. I only happened to overhear a few things."

"It sounds like you heard a great deal more than that." Pushing away from the door, Addie strode toward her grandmother. "And I'm sorry, but it's obvious that you didn't only happen to do anything. I'm surprised you didn't come in and join us."

Mommi didn't back down even an inch. Lifting her chin, she pushed her walker to the couch and then sat down in the spot where Daniel had been sitting. "If I had, things might have gone better."

Angry tears were now running down Addie's cheeks. "You are unbelievable."

"Adelaide, calm down and stop with this nonsense. I am not the source of your problem." She waved a hand. "Now, come sit down and talk to me. Tell me what has been happening."

"*Nee.*" She turned to walk upstairs.

"I'm sorry, Addie, but you don't get that choice."

"Mommi, I canna do this—"

"Oh, yes you can." When Addie turned back to her, Mommi gentled her tone. "Do you remember when I tried to help you in the kitchen and you told me to go sit down?"

"Of course. You didn't want to rest like the doctors suggested."

Her grandmother nodded. "I wanted to pretend that I was

just fine, when in truth I felt weak and out of sorts. When you made me sit back down, I realized that I wasn't fooling myself or you."

In spite of the seriousness of both the current conversation and the last, Addie felt like smiling. Her grandmother was still as sharp as a tack. "I guess you're trying to tell me that I'm not fine?"

"Not even a little bit." Looking a bit placated, her grandmother crossed her legs. "As far as I'm concerned, your kidneys might not be hurting, but your heart sure is. And, as hard as it might be to hear, you need to listen to some advice for your own good." She lowered her voice. "In order for your heart to be better."

How had Mommi turned the tables so easily? And how in the world had she known that Addie's heart was broken?

Swiping her eyes again, Addie sat down beside her at last. "Go ahead and tell me what you think. I'm all ears."

"*Nee,* child. You talk to me, *jah*? Now, tell me about these notes that you and Daniel exchanged. What were these letters and how did you receive them?"

"I don't want to tell you. You're going to think the worst of me."

"Never."

"Mommi, I promise, you're going to think I was the biggest fool. And I was!"

"Because you believed in the words that someone wrote to you? Addie, child. What type of person would you be if you didn't believe them? Not someone I would want to know."

Her grandmother's words were so sweet—and were the perfect example of why it was such a blessing that the Lord had put Addie in her hands. She said the things that Addie needed to hear. Everyone said that Lovina Stutzman was a formidable woman. Addie reckoned that might be true. But she never considered the description to be a negative one. Yes, *formidable* could mean difficult or intimidating, but it could also mean inspiring and impressive. Her grandmother would always be those things to her.

"Addie, dear. Just tell me."

"All right. It all started when I received a letter soon after Aaron and June's engagement party. It came in the mail, was short but full of praise . . . and was signed *Your Secret Admirer.*"

Mommi blinked slowly. "You have a secret admirer?"

"I did. I mean, I thought I did." She shook her head slightly. "What I'm trying to say is that the letter seemed sincere enough that I wrote him back and we began exchanging letters about once a week."

"For how long?"

"It's been over a month now."

"I see. And during all this time you never had any idea who was writing you? This person never gave you any hints?"

"*Nee*. Though . . . now I realize that was likely my fault as much as his. I don't think I wanted to know who this person really was. If I found out, I'd have to face what might happen next."

"I don't understand. You didn't think the relationship would have a good outcome?"

As hard as it was to be truthful, Addie shook her head. "While I hoped it might, I couldn't see how it would. After all, if the writer was someone who knew me well, wouldn't they have already tried to form a relationship?"

Her grandmother nodded slowly. "I don't understand how Daniel came into the story."

"Mommi, my secret admirer *was* Daniel. He wrote me those notes, but I don't think he ever intended to reveal his identity."

Her grandmother looked as confused as Addie felt. "But you've gotten to know him better of late. Why was he writing letters, too?"

"I didn't think to ask him that." Not wanting to reveal too much more, she said, "The reason he came over today was because he had one of my notes with him at worship and it fell on the ground. In the middle of the Hershbergers' backyard, no less. That's when I saw the front of the envelope of the last letter I'd given him. I'd written *S.A.* on it. I saw the envelope—and his friend Roman saw it, too."

Mommi gasped. "Oh, my word."

"*Jah*. That was how I felt, too. I was so confused . . . and so crushed. *Nee,* I am crushed. Not only did I think he was my friend, but I had imagined that this secret admirer might even be someone I would eventually have a relationship with."

Thoroughly ashamed, she looked down at her hands, not wanting to reveal just how smitten she'd become. "And now everyone in Apple Creek is going to know how pathetic I am."

Mommi's expression hardened. "Don't say such things. You are not pathetic."

"I canna help it. Besides, it's the truth."

Reaching for one of Addie's hands, her grandmother carefully enfolded it in hers. "Child, I said this to you at the beginning of our conversation and I'm going to say it again. You have nothing to be ashamed of. Daniel Miller is the one who should be ashamed, and I'm going to make sure he is, too."

"*Nee,* Mommi. You mustn't get involved." When her grandmother looked ready to argue, she added, "I am a grown woman. The only thing worse than what has already happened would be having my grandmother zoom in and try to save the day."

"I think I'm a bit old to do any zooming, child."

"Exactly. You've been ill. Mighty ill. Remember?"

"I haven't forgotten." She leaned over and picked up one of her famous Russian tea cake cookies. "It's a shame Daniel didn't try a cookie. They really are tasty."

Picking up one as well, Addie took a bite and smiled. "I'm sure he is already regretting his decision," she teased. "You really do make the best cookies, Mommi."

She shrugged. "I've been blessed. I've had someone to make cookies for."

The smile they shared spoke volumes. A good reminder that even in the darkest moments, there were still stars in the sky and still wonderful things at home.

Chapter 24

Daniel had ruined everything. No, *ruin* wasn't a suitable descriptor for what had happened. He'd never forget the look of pain on Addie's face when she'd asked him to leave. He'd put it there, too. She'd looked so devastated, he'd felt his heart rip in two.

If his heart remained in two pieces, he would certainly deserve it! He had hurt Addie terribly. So much so, it was possible that his actions would prevent her from ever being able to trust another man.

He was so ashamed—and couldn't even imagine what his parents would say if they ever found out what he'd done.

Feeling as if he had a fifty-pound weight on his shoulders, he mechanically unhitched Hero, rubbed him down, and led him to his stall. Hero was technically his parents' horse. They had four horses, a pony, a pony cart, and both a buggy and a courting buggy as well as a wagon. With ten children, there was always a need to take someone somewhere.

When Daniel had bought his house two years ago, his brother Jack and Daed had helped him build a small enclosure. Now, if he borrowed one of the buggies or a horse, there was someplace to keep the animal until he could take him back home.

It was obvious that Hero wasn't exactly pleased with his temporary lodging, but he settled into the stall well enough, especially after Daniel gave him an extra scoop of oats and fresh water.

Now that the horse had been seen to, he was more than ready to go sit inside and try to figure out what to do next.

As he headed out of the barn, he discovered Roman and Bradley waiting for him on the front porch. Their expressions were solemn and troubled. No doubt he looked the same way.

"Hey," Roman said.

"Hey." Daniel wanted nothing more than to shut the door in their faces. "Sorry, but you guys need to leave. It's, um . . . a bad time right now. I'm not up for company."

"Too bad," Bradley said. "I just heard about what you've been doing."

Daniel wasn't sure if he'd ever been more irritated at Roman. "Boy, you've been busy. It hasn't even been two hours since that letter fell on the ground. What happened? You couldn't wait to spread the news?"

Roman scowled. "That isn't why I went and got Bradley and you know it."

"You should be glad he came and got me," Bradley said. "I think you're going to need all the help you can get right now."

Daniel turned away and started toward the house. "I don't want to hear it, Park. You have no idea what you're talking about."

"Then you'd better explain it to me."

He opened the door. Bob, who'd obviously been waiting for him, wagged his tail and raised his nose for attention. Unable to ignore the hound, Daniel bent down and stroked his head. "Hiya, Bob. Go on out now."

As the hound trotted out, barely stopping by his friends' sides for greetings, Daniel turned back to Bradley. "Listen, as much as I appreciate what you're saying, I don't need—"

"Face it, Daniel," Roman interjected softly. "You need us right now."

As tempting as it was to put them off, it was a fact that his friends weren't going to go away—and neither was his problem with Addie. "Fine. Come on in."

They walked right by him as he waited for Bob to do his business. For the first time in his life, he hoped that Bob would take his time and sniff every plant and shrub before wanting to come back in.

Bob, that traitor, returned to his side in no time at all.

Bradley walked right over to his fireplace, knelt down, and started putting in kindling. "I don't care that it's April. It's cold in here."

Daniel stuffed his hands in his pockets as he watched Bradley light a fire and Roman turn on a kerosene lantern. When they were finished, he pulled off his coat and tossed it on the back of a chair. "Continue making yourselves at home," he said sarcastically as he sat down.

"That's what we're doing," Bradley replied as he pulled off his coat as well and sat down across from him.

Roman took a seat on the couch. "I told Bradley as much as I knew," he said. "How did your talk with Addie go?"

"Not well. She's hurt."

Roman nodded. "Of course she is. Did she let you explain?"

"More or less. It doesn't matter though. My excuses are terrible. She doesn't trust me. I don't think she's ever going to trust me again." Feeling even worse, he muttered, "I don't even know if she'll ever trust another man."

"I doubt you've put her off all mankind. Likely just you," Bradley said. "I mean, you were the one who lied to her, not the rest of us."

Lines formed around Roman's eyes, but he didn't say a word. It was obvious that he was trying not to smile.

Honestly, sometimes his friends were simply too much to take.

"Listen, you two. It wasn't just a lie. I did a whole lot more than that." He waved a hand, frustrated with both his motives and his explanations. "Guys, it wasna that I told Addie a bunch of lies—it's that she thinks I took one of her biggest weaknesses and made a game out of it."

Bradley frowned. "You didn't do that though, did you?"

"*Nee!* I might be a jerk, but I'm not evil. I . . . I really was trying to make her life better. It just somehow all blew up in my face."

"And hers," Bradley muttered.

Daniel flinched.

Roman was still studying him. "Daniel, did you apologize to her?"

"Of course I did! But surprisingly, my apology didn't seem to mean much to her." He knew his voice was thick with sarcasm, but he couldn't help himself.

Bradley leaned back and folded his arms over his chest in annoyance. Roman, on the other hand, continued to remain calm. "Would it have been enough for you?" he asked quietly.

"Probably not." Realizing he wasn't telling the truth, he shook his head. "I mean no. It wouldn't have been enough for me at all." Figuring that he might as well get everything out in the open, Daniel added, "Addie wants all of her letters back."

Bradley raised his eyebrows. "How come?"

"She's worried about me using them against her." His voice was thick with shame. He could maybe accept that his efforts to be her friend had backfired, but he was mortified that she now thought he was capable of such a thing.

"What does she think you're going to do?" Bradley asked. "Pull them out and make fun of her or something?"

"I guess. Or show them to other people. I wouldn't, of course."

Bradley looked horrified. "I hope not. No offense, but I don't ever want to read your private correspondence."

"Me neither," Roman said.

Daniel rolled his eyes. "*Danke* for that. The worst of all this is that I thought she and I had become friends. You know, outside of the letters we were exchanging. Now that's gone, too. She wonders if our friendship was yet another way I was intentionally toying with her. It wasn't that at all, though!"

"I told you the other day that I thought you were smitten with Addie," Bradley said. "Do you remember that?"

"Of course I do."

"Have your feelings changed?"

"*Nee*. I mean, I feel guilty and ashamed and horrible . . . but I still like her. I can't simply turn my feelings off and on like a light switch."

Bradley's lips curved. "There you go. Finally, the truth is out. You like her a lot."

Wasn't that what he'd just been telling them both? "Uh, yeah."

"You're going to have to go courting," Roman said. "But this time, on the up and up. You know, out in the open," he added, as if Daniel wasn't capable of understanding what he meant.

"Guys, she hates me now. I've hurt her."

"I know. But that doesn't mean you should give up," Bradley said. "If you're smitten, you're smitten. You need to go courting and get her to take you back."

Bradley might as well have told him to race to the moon and back. "How am I supposed to do that?"

"Honestly, man, do we have to figure everything out for ya? Next time you're at church, walk to her side and visit people with her. As a couple."

"You don't think everyone is going to wonder what is going on between the two of us?"

"*Nee,*" Roman answered. "All anyone is going to think is that you have finally become open and honest."

"It's not that easy. People are going to wonder about what happened, because Addie and I never did much together in the past."

"People aren't going to be dwelling on your messed-up romance as much as you think they will," Bradley said. "As entertaining as it might be, they've got troubles of their own to worry about."

"It's not me I'm worried about. What if people are rude to her? I mean, think of all the unkind things that Ruthie and Mary Jo said."

"Walk over to Roman if you're at church. Or, if you're out among a big group of people, come over to me. I'll be glad to be Addie's friend and support your relationship," Bradley said. "I don't think we're alone in that either. Addie is a good person. I'm realizing I should have recognized that from the beginning instead of letting a bunch of gossip and childish rumors sway me."

"I feel the same way," Roman said.

"You are both serious, aren't you?"

Roman folded his arms over his chest. "You aren't the only person who has made mistakes . . . or who can grow and change."

"I hear ya." And Daniel finally was hearing them, too. Mending things with Addie wasn't going to be easy, but it wasn't going to be impossible—because he wouldn't give up on them.

"Hey, Dan?" Bradley murmured after a couple of minutes passed.

"*Jah?*"

"How did you know what to write, anyway? I mean, when you first started writing Addie notes."

"I didn't know what to say. In the end, I simply told her that I thought she was worth getting to know and that I thought writing letters might be a good way for us to get to know each other."

"And she wrote you back."

"*Jah,* she did . . . and those letters were great. Perfect." He smiled. Those letters were a gift. He also knew that he wasn't going to give them up. They meant too much to him to simply give back.

Chapter 25

Addie reckoned that she was the only Amish woman around who had a social calendar for her donkey. It couldn't be helped, though. Snickers had become an extremely popular animal. Not only did the hospital want him to visit once a month, but two nursing homes did, too. Then, after seeing her and Snickers in action, a trained counselor had asked if they would visit a conference she was hosting and describe not only the job Snickers did as a service animal, but also share some stories about their experiences.

At first, she'd been reluctant. She was still emotionally drained from the secret admirer drama. She also hated to leave her grandmother for too long. Mommi was getting around better than before, but Addie now knew that she was very good at hiding discomfort and sickness.

She eventually gave in, though. Her little donkey loved his field trips and the attention. If there was ever an animal who had been meant to be a service animal, it was Snickers.

As always, the organization she was affiliated with took care of both arranging their transportation and the cost. They made it easy for her to take Snickers out and about.

As she unloaded him from his donkey trailer, she smoothed his bridle and the jaunty red ribbon she'd threaded in his mane for today's nursing home visit. They were going to be seeing some long-term care patients who needed a bit of an emotional boost. Some were so sick that they wouldn't be able to get too close to Snickers. With that in mind, Addie had decided to dress up her donkey a little bit. Ribbons always seemed to do the trick.

"Hey, Addie."

Surprised to hear someone calling out to her, she turned toward the voice.

And then froze.

Daniel was walking toward her with a determined expression. He was dressed in dark gray trousers, boots, a black wool coat, and a dark navy-blue shirt that seemed to make his eyes appear even bluer.

Yes, she had noticed all of that in about ten seconds. It took about the same amount of time as it did for her heart to feel a little zing just because he was standing in front of her.

Hating that her body seemed to forget just how much he'd hurt her feelings, she forced herself to wait a moment before responding. "What are you doing here?"

"Someone happened to mention to one of my siblings that a cute Amish girl and her donkey were coming over to visit their mother today. Jack told me. I decided to come over to see if I could help."

"I don't need any help with Snickers." Her donkey moved his head, as if he was agreeing completely.

"How about this, then? I wanted to be near you and thought coming here might be a way to do that." Snickers nudged Daniel's shoulder with his nose. "Hey, buddy. Don't you look fancy with your ribbons on? You're looking mighty handsome."

Watching Daniel gently pet the donkey, Addie knew she couldn't send him away. Snickers loved being helpful and tending to people in need. What he did not like was being around men he didn't trust. It stemmed from his years of being abused, of course.

For the donkey to playfully nudge Daniel for attention spoke volumes. It was like he was giving Daniel his seal of approval. There was no way she could send him away now.

"Come along then."

His lips twitched, but he didn't relax into a full smile. "What may I help you carry?"

Though her pride might have wanted to refuse all of his help, her arms told a different story. "You may take my tote bag, if you wouldn't mind."

He took it from her. "Lead the way and I'll follow."

Fighting off another warm sensation, Addie led Snickers toward the entrance to the Healing Hearts Nursing Home. Snickers *clip-clopped* by her side, his brown eyes actively scanning the area. "You're about to go make a lot of people happy today, Snick," she murmured. "I'm so proud of you."

Snickers appeared to be nodding in response.

"I'd swear he understands everything you are saying," Daniel said.

"I'd be surprised if he doesn't. Donkeys are smart animals. I even met a horse trainer who told me that he thought Snickers was exceptionally intuitive."

They'd reached the front entrance. "What do you do now?" Daniel asked.

"Open the door for us. We'll go on in."

"They'll let him inside the building?"

"Oh, *jah*. Don't worry. He won't make a mess."

He opened the door, and they walked through. There were several staff members in the lobby, and they each had big smiles on their faces.

"Snickers! You're here!" Molly, the administrator, called out.

When she headed Snickers' way a little too exuberantly,

Daniel headed her off. "He's a wonderful-*gut* donkey, but he can get a bit skittish, you know?"

Molly stopped in her tracks. "Oh! Of course. I'm sorry." Approaching more slowly, she reached out a hand to Snickers' nose. "He's so good with our residents, I forget that he's still a horse. May I pet him?"

He is a donkey, not a horse, Addie mentally corrected. "Of course."

Scratching Snickers between his ears, Molly turned to Daniel. "Are you Addie's helper?"

"Today I am. I'm also her friend."

"Ah. Well, isn't that so nice?" The administrator smiled at her. "I'm happy for you, Addie."

Oh, no. Molly thought the two of them were a couple. After debating the pros and cons of correcting the woman's mistake, Addie simply smiled. She was here to do a job, not explain her messed-up relationship with Daniel Miller. "Where would you like us to go?"

"Cameron here is going to take you over to the community room. Like last time, we'll be bringing in a patient or two at a time for a few moments each. Cameron, you remember Addie?"

"I sure do. She's hard to forget."

"I can't imagine you have too many Amish girls leading donkeys around here," Addie teased.

He grinned back. "You might be surprised."

Chuckling, she smiled back at him. Cameron was English, appeared to be about her age, and seemed to be all muscle. Over time, they'd become a good team at the nursing home. "Morning, Cam."

"Morning to you, Addie. And to you, Snickers." He ignored Daniel. "Addie, I was glad to see you were on the schedule today."

"Thank you. I'm glad to be here. Will we still be able to visit some of the other residents in their rooms?"

"I think so. You're only here for two hours though, correct?"

"Correct."

"I guess we'll have to do the best we can, then." His voice was deep, and with a bit of shock, she realized that he was flirting with her! Right in front of Daniel! "Well, um, I am grateful for your help."

"It's not a problem." He gently ran a hand down the donkey's short mane. "I volunteered to help you today."

Daniel stepped forward. "That ain't necessary if you have other work to attend to."

When Cameron looked at Daniel as if he was just noticing him for the first time, Addie said, "Cameron, this is my friend Daniel."

"Hi," Daniel said. He was not smiling.

"Good to meet you." After seeming to exchange a measured look with Daniel, Cameron cleared his throat. "We'd better get on our way. We're on a pretty tight schedule."

"Of course. Lead the way."

For the next ninety minutes, she, Daniel, Snickers, and Cameron fell into a routine. Every ten or fifteen minutes, Cameron would escort a new resident to the multipurpose room. The resident would then get to spend time with Snickers, petting him and chatting with Addie. Daniel would stay near the donkey, helping to hold his lead and reassure him, especially when a resident was in a wheelchair.

Addie hadn't thought she would ever need an extra pair of hands, but Daniel's steady presence was so helpful. Not only did Snickers seem reassured, but she found herself able to relax. She not only shared information and stories about Snickers, but about being Amish, too. When one or two of the residents' questions turned a little too personal, Daniel easily took over the conversation.

Later, when Cameron escorted the three of them to some of the residents' rooms, Daniel showed just how patient he could be, especially with the last woman they visited. Sally was sitting in a chair but was obviously in a lot of pain and had trouble speaking. He knelt in front of her and helped her pet one of the donkey's front legs, just as if it was one of the most natural things in the world. Even Cameron looked impressed.

Addie had wanted to stay mad at Daniel, but she realized she couldn't—not after all that. She might not trust him with her heart, but she was no longer eager to think the worst of him.

After she'd loaded Snickers into the horse trailer, Max, the driver, asked if she could wait a few minutes for him to take a phone call.

When Max moved away, she knew it was time to say something from her heart. "Daniel, thank you for joining me today."

"It was amazing. I'm glad I did."

"You were so kind and patient with all the residents. I guess I should've assumed you would be since you work at the hospital, but it still was a nice surprise."

"I do work at the hospital, but I usually spend my days mopping floors and cleaning bathrooms. Not helping patients."

"Well, I still appreciate it."

"Hey, since we have a minute . . . I know I have a lot to make up for . . . but are you still really mad at me?"

"Kind of." She lifted her chin. "I mean, I should be."

"What are you doing on Saturday night?"

"Why?"

"I want to come calling and take you out to supper."

"Daniel, that isn't necessary."

"It is. Addie, I know I made mistakes. I know I kept secrets from you, and I know it is going to take time to mend our relationship. But . . . the things we said to each other in those letters meant something to me. Didn't you feel the same?"

She wasn't able to lie. "I did."

"Then, don't you think we owe it to ourselves to at least see where things could go in the future?"

"I don't know."

"I promise, I'm going to take care of your heart this time. I'm not going to hurt you."

"Addie, I'm all done. You ready?" Max called out.

"Almost, Max. I'll be right there." She looked back at Daniel. "I've got to go."

"So, Saturday night?"

"I'll give you my answer in a note by tomorrow afternoon," she said with a smile.

He smiled back as he tipped his hat to her in a salute.

She was chuckling about it as she climbed into the passenger side of the truck.

"You're looking pleased as punch," Max said. "I'm guessing today's visit went well."

"It did. One of the best visits ever."

"That donkey of yours is getting to be quite the celebrity, Addie."

"I agree. Snickers deserves it though. He really is a mighty special donkey."

"You might deserve some credit for that, Miss Addie. I'm pretty sure Snickers feels that he can do anything by your side."

Addie only smiled in response—but she did smile the whole way home.

Chapter 26

Dear Daniel,

It feels strange not calling you S.A. Maybe it always will?

Thank you for coming to Happy Hearts with me yesterday. You did a good job, and I appreciated your help. I feel certain that Snickers was grateful, too. He likes to be of service but can sometimes be skittish around unfamiliar things, like medical machines and wheelchairs. And men. He likes you.

I suppose I like you, too. As much as I want to stay mad and hurt, I cannot.

So yes. I will go out to supper with you on Saturday night.

Addie

If Snickers hadn't looked so tired, Addie would've gone to his stall and discussed this whole new development with him. Snickers might not have been able to dispense advice, but at least he would've listened and looked sympathetic. She could surely use some sympathy at the moment.

Because she couldn't believe she'd been so foolish as to have told Daniel she would write him another note. Hadn't that just gotten her in such a mess of trouble?

"You have no one to blame for this foolishness but yourself," she grumbled as she walked to their tree. The mail tree. "Why couldn't you have simply told him yes to his face?"

Because you're still too afraid of rejection, she whispered to herself.

And, perhaps, because she'd also enjoyed exchanging letters with him. No, she'd loved it. She'd loved the process of writing her feelings on paper. Debating about the perfect word choice. Imagining what her correspondent would look like when he read her words. Imagining what his response would be.

Imagining who her admirer was . . .

It had all been so romantic.

Well, romantic in an awkward, convoluted way.

Realizing that there was no way to take back her words unless she knocked on his door, she walked up to their tree and deposited the note.

Then, needing a break from her thoughts, she walked to the market to get a few things to make spaghetti pie for supper.

Tiny Treetop Market was fairly bustling when she entered. The two cash register lines were three deep and there were lines at both the bakery and the deli counter.

Addie figured it was a good excuse to wander around a bit. She'd rather see what interesting things were on the shelves than stand in line at the register.

She'd just added some Italian sausage and fresh lettuce to her basket when she turned the corner and came upon

Bradley and Mary Jo. Both were close friends with Daniel. Though Mary Jo had been with Ruthie when Ruthie had asked Addie all about being abandoned by her parents, she'd never gone out of her way to be cruel to her. She hadn't given Addie the time of day.

Addie only knew Bradley by sight. Since he was Mennonite, they'd never had much of an occasion to speak to each other.

When it was obvious that they'd all seen each other, there was nothing to do but continue on. She nodded in their direction as she walked by.

"Hey, wait a moment, Addie," Mary Jo called out.

She stopped and turned around. "Yes?"

Mary Jo walked closer. "How are you?"

"I am well. *Danke.*" She was also feeling pretty confused, but she wasn't going to mention that.

A faint blush appeared on Mary Jo's perfect complexion. "*Nee,* I mean, I heard your grandmother was in the hospital. Is she feeling better?"

Though it was tempting to ask why Mary Jo cared, Addie pushed that response away. The other girl's concern was for her grandmother, anyway. Everyone respected Lovina Stutzman. "She is doing much better, *danke*. I'll tell her that you asked about her."

"Thank you. Yes, tell her I hope she will be feeling better very soon."

"I will." When Mary Jo continued to stand there, Addie cleared her throat. "So, I am getting ingredients to make her supper."

"She is blessed to have you looking out for her," Bradley said.

Feeling almost as if she was talking to two strangers, she murmured, "I am blessed to have her. I'll, um, tell her that you both asked about her health. She will appreciate that."

Addie fidgeted. "Well, it was good seeing you." She smiled tightly. It was time to get out of the store as soon as possible.

"Hey, Addie, wait," Bradley called out.

Wondering what he could want, she paused. "Yes?"

"I owe you an apology."

He looked so sincere, she was caught off guard. "For what?"

He shared a look with Mary Jo. "For essentially ignoring you for years. I'm sorry."

"I feel the same way," Mary Jo said, her voice contrite. "Addie, I really hope that we can be friends again."

Again? The polite thing would be to say okay and go on her way. Her grandmother had told her time and again that one never knew what was going on in other people's lives. Who was she to judge their decisions?

But her experience with Daniel had made her both suspicious and vulnerable.

"Why?"

Mary Jo blinked. "Why?"

She nodded. "Why, after all this time, have both of you decided to reach out to me? I don't mean to seem ungrateful for your concern, but it doesn't exactly make sense."

They exchanged glances. "Well, no reason in particular," Bradley said at last.

"I mean, there's nothing wrong with wanting to make some changes in one's life, right?" Mary Jo added. She met Addie's eyes but then quickly looked away.

"So this doesn't have anything to do with Daniel?"

"It might." Bradley stuffed his hands in his pockets. "But is that a bad thing?"

It was obvious they both knew what had happened between Daniel and her. She didn't know why she was surprised—it was likely half of Apple Creek was aware of her humiliation.

Up until a few weeks ago, Addie would've started crying or maybe just run away. But that wasn't who she was anymore. For some reason she had become stronger and more self-confident.

In addition, after all her words to Daniel about honesty and open communication, shouldn't she be glad that two of his best friends were trying to make amends?

"*Nee,*" she said at last. "You both are right. There's nothing wrong with reaching out to someone or trying to make a new friend. I'm sorry to be acting so waspish."

"You have every reason to be that way," Mary Jo said. "I wish I hadn't given you so many reasons to distrust me. But maybe we can get to know each other, little by little."

"I'd like that."

"You would?"

Mary Jo's incredulous expression was almost comical. It made Addie smile in spite of how awkward the conversation was. "I would. I . . . well, I recently decided that one can't have too many friends."

"*Danke,* Addie. I'll be in touch soon."

"And I'll look forward to speaking with you more often," Bradley said.

"Me too."

After they parted ways, she picked up a few more items, then got into line. The teenager in front of her groaned. "Oh, no," she said.

"What's wrong?" Addie asked.

She pointed out the window. "I just looked outside. It's started raining."

"It's raining?" Addie looked out the window and frowned.

Sure enough, rain was falling softly. It wasn't close to being a downpour, but her sweater and dress would likely be very wet by the time she got home. "Yuck."

"Did you bring your buggy or ride your bike?"

"Neither. I walked," Addie replied.

"I hope you don't have to go far."

"About a mile. You?"

"About the same, but I rode my bike." She smiled in sympathy. "We're both going to get soaked," she said as the checker started ringing up her groceries.

"Be careful. The streets can get slick, right?"

"I will." The teen smiled at her again. "At least it's April so it's not snowing."

"You're right. At least there's that."

Liking how they were both looking on the bright side, Addie felt her spirits lift. It seemed she had many things to be pleased about. Many things to be grateful for. She needed to remember that.

When she was about halfway home, Brooke's familiar blue sedan pulled up beside her. "Addie, I'm so glad I found you! Hop in."

Stunned by her good fortune—it actually wasn't all that fun walking in the rain while holding two grocery bags—Addie hurried around to the passenger side and got in. "What in the world are you doing here?"

"I finished a test early and had some extra time, so I went by your house. Your grandmother told me that you were at the store, so I thought I'd try to find you. I can't believe I did!"

"I can't believe it, either, but I'm so glad." Realizing how wet her clothes were, she added, "I really hope I haven't messed up these seats."

"They'll be fine. I hope you won't get sick." Brooke turned around in a driveway, then headed back to Addie's house.

Noticing that her girlfriend did look troubled, Addie said, "Want to tell me what's really going on?"

"I guess it's that noticeable?" Pulling to a stop, she wrinkled her nose.

"I'm afraid so. What happened?"

"Cameron and I broke up."

"Already?" When Brooke shot her a look, Addie flushed. "That didn't come out right. I meant, I'm sorry that things didn't work out."

"Me too." Brooke sighed. "I know he wasn't very nice to you, but sometimes he was really great."

Addie was far from an expert on relationships, but she thought that Brooke adding the word *sometimes* was awfully telling. "What happened?"

Brooke pulled into Addie's driveway. "We were going to go to one of my friends' house and he didn't want to go. He acted like she wasn't worth knowing. I realized then that Cameron was full of himself and kind of spoiled, too. He really liked things his way."

"In that case, I suppose you're better off without him."

She shrugged. "It doesn't feel like that, though." Putting the car in park, she added, "Why are relationships so hard?"

"I don't know. I've been struggling with that question myself." She smiled. "Would you like to come inside for a spell?"

"No, I better not. I've got another class in two hours."

"Oh. Well, okay. Thank you for picking me up. I'm glad I didn't have to walk all the way home in the rain."

"Me too. See you on Tuesday."

Addie got out of Brooke's car feeling like something had happened between them, but she wasn't sure what that was. Were things better or worse?

It seemed this was yet another one of her relationships that was on the rocks. As she walked into the house, Addie hoped that everything would settle real soon.

Chapter 27

"I appreciate your coming in on such short notice, Daniel," Stefan said as he walked over to shake his hand. "Jose is on vacation and Logan's daughter is sick. Then, when Catalina didn't show up, I was in a real bind."

"It's not a problem. What happened with Catalina? Is she all right?"

"I think so. She didn't call me directly, just sent word through the front desk."

"Uh oh." The staff was so large, everyone knew better than to call the front office reception staff. One of the first things everyone learned when they were hired was whom to contact if there was a problem. He'd learned from the very first not to bother the main reception desk if he could help it. Emergencies were one thing—but taking a day off from work was a different story.

"Yeah. They weren't happy." Looking troubled, Stefan sighed. "I don't know what I'm going to do about Catalina, Daniel. She's a good worker when she's here, but she's not dependable."

"I hear what you're saying."

"I know. I feel sorry for her troubles and want to be there for her, but I also have a hospital to keep clean."

"I guess you've tried calling her?"

"After I got chewed out because someone on my team didn't follow proper protocol, I sure did. I've called her twice but she's not answering." After a pause, he shook his head. "Sorry. You came in here to help me out, not counsel me."

"No, I'm glad you shared. I'm concerned about her, too. I hope she answers her phone soon. So, where would you like me to start?"

Stefan walked back to his desk and looked over the schedule. "Do you mind mopping the second-floor hallway? No one's cleaned there since early this morning."

"It's time someone did then," Daniel joked. "I'll head right up."

"Thanks. Take the radio. I'll buzz if you're needed somewhere else."

"Will do." Going to the storage room, he pulled out his cart, filled it with supplies, and then headed over to the service elevator. The doors opened immediately.

As he rode up to the second floor, Daniel wondered again about Catalina. Ever since she'd first been hired, drama seemed to surround her every move. All the janitorial staff had had run-ins with her at one time or another.

In addition, rumors about the reason for her frequent absences were always flying around. Some of the workers thought she had an abusive husband. Others were sure she had a second job and was simply having a difficult time keeping up with them both. He really had no idea, but he reckoned everything was going to come to a head soon. Either Catalina was going to have to make a change or Stefan would.

He was still thinking about Catalina three hours later when he was helping out in the emergency triage area. Stefan had asked him to help gather laundry, dispose of trash, and assist the orderlies who were wiping down some of the monitors, cabinets, and other frequently shared pieces of equipment.

He'd just walked into one of the curtained areas to gather trash when he came up short. A woman with shoulder-length blond hair lay on the table with a gash in her arm. Several bloody-looking rags were lying next to her. She looked up at him in surprise.

"I'm sorry to disturb ya," he said as he backed out.

"Hey, wait a second, would you please?" She looked upset. "Do you need something? I'm sure someone will be here shortly."

"No, it's—are you Amish?"

He was never thrilled to answer questions about his religion in the middle of a shift. When someone asked him about being Amish when he was obviously trying to help them? Well, it was irritating. "*Jah,*" he muttered before turning to leave.

"*Nee*. Halt."

There was something in her voice that made him stop as she'd asked. Was it because she sounded desperate? Or was it that she'd just asked him to wait—in Pennsylvania Dutch. "You know Deutsch."

"*Jah*. I grew up Amish," she said.

"Whereabouts?"

"Near here. In Apple Creek. It's a really small community," she added, still speaking in Pennsylvania Dutch.

"*Jah*. I know it well."

Looking anxious, she added, "Do you really? Have you been there many times?"

"I'd say so. I live there. Why?"

She blinked, not even attempting to hide her surprise. "I guess that's my cue to say it's a small world."

"I reckon so." He had other cubicles to attend to, but she seemed inclined to talk. Because she was also injured and obviously waiting for a nurse, he figured he had a reason to linger a little longer, especially since she'd grown up Amish. "What brings you out this way? Did ya come to see where you grew up?"

"Kind of, but mainly I came here to make amends," she replied in English. "I made a choice a long time ago that I'm still trying to come to terms with." Switching to Pennsylvania Dutch, she added, "I let my parents raise my child and now she hates me."

Could this woman be Addie's mother? Warning bells were ringing in his head, but he pushed them away. Everyone had secrets of some sort or another. "Who hates ya?" he asked slowly. "Your mother or the child?"

"My daughter." She laughed softly. "The truth is that my mother isn't too fond of me, but I don't think she could ever hate me. A mother's love is eternal, don't you think?"

"Since I have a mother, I'll say I hope it is." When she smiled at his comment, he murmured, "Is it that way for you? Do you still love your daughter?"

Pursing her lips, she nodded. "I really do." Looking down at her lap, she added, "I left my daughter because I loved her so much, and I knew I couldn't care for her. It was a bad time in my life and she was suffering for it. So, even though it broke my heart, I asked my parents to raise her for me." She released a ragged sigh. "As much as it still hurts, I know it was the right thing to do. From what I hear, she's become a special woman."

"From what you hear? You don't know for certain?"

"Nope. She won't talk to me."

This had to be Addie's mother. Had to be.

Staring at her, Daniel felt his mouth go dry.

"Hey, did I shock you?"

"*Nee.*" He wanted to say more, but what could he say? Should he share that he knew both Lovina and Addie or say nothing? If he said nothing, would it make things better—or worse? If he said nothing and Addie later found out, would she feel betrayed?

For that matter, if he said nothing, would he be able to live with it? A secret like that would be hard to forget. *Nee,* to pretend to forget. He was never going to be able to forget this moment.

Still wavering, he met her eyes. Was startled to realize that they were the same exact shade of green as Addie's. *Nee,* they were her daughter's eyes, slanted slightly up, just so. "Do you wear glasses?"

"Contacts. Why?"

He couldn't *not* say anything. Not when it felt as if the Lord had placed them together for this very moment. "Because your daughter wears glasses."

She inhaled sharply. "You know Addie?"

The curtain was pulled back, and Dr. Klein stepped in with a nurse. "Kate Stutzman?"

"Yes." Turning to face them, she attempted to regain her composure. "I mean, yes, that's me. Sorry. We were just chatting."

"Do you need something, Daniel?" the doctor asked.

"*Nee*. I'll be on my way. We just struck up a conversation."

"Wait, Daniel?" Kate called out.

"Yes?"

"Would you please wait for me? Please?"

There was so much pain in her eyes, he couldn't have refused even if he had wanted to. "*Jah*. Ask the receptionist to call for me on the radio. She'll know what you mean."

Turning to the doctor, he explained, "She's former Amish."

"That makes sense." Dr. Klein smiled at Daniel. "I'm glad you can help her today."

"Me too." But as he walked out of the room, he wondered whether helping this woman was going to benefit Addie or make things a whole lot worse for her.

Mentally debating how their next conversation was going to play out, Daniel cleaned the other cubicles as if he was on autopilot. He gathered linens and placed them in the proper container. Did the same with the trash. Sprayed the counters and doors with disinfectant. Did the same with the examining tables. Finally, he gave each floor a quick mop.

And then he did it all again.

Working quickly and efficiently didn't help to ease his worries, but it did help to clear his mind. It gave him clarity. There were simply some occurrences that couldn't be explained away as coincidence; they had more significance than that. He knew all the way to the depths of his soul that meeting Addie's missing mother was one of these moments.

He had cleaned three more rooms by the time Kristen radioed for him to come to the reception desk.

"Yes?" he asked.

"There's a Kate Stutzman here. She says she needs to speak with you."

He noticed Kate was sitting in one of the visitor's chairs. "Yes. We ran into each other in one of the triage cubicles. She's former Amish, you see."

"Ah. Now I understand. When do you get off work today?"

He glanced at the clock. "Two more hours."

Kristen brightened. "Me too. Want a ride home?"

"I do. Thank you."

"Great! I'll meet you at the door in two hours. I can't wait to catch up."

"*Jah*. Me too." Motioning to Kate, who'd just stood up, he said to Kristen, "Is there someplace private that we could talk? We won't be long."

The receptionist pointed to one of the small rooms that was put aside for visitors needing private moments. "Use one of those rooms."

"We can talk over here," Daniel said to Kate. "I only have a few minutes."

"That's perfectly fine."

Noticing the sizable bandage on her arm, he motioned to it. "How is your arm?"

She held up her forearm. "It's sore but okay. Twelve stitches, but hopefully I won't have too much of a scar."

"We men call those battle wounds."

She chuckled. "I like that description, though I doubt tripping and falling is ever going to be classified that way."

They sat down. "What may I help you with?"

"Daniel, I know it's a lot to ask, but I'm wondering if you could help me contact Addie."

"Don't you think that should be her decision rather than mine?"

"I'm not going to bother her if she really doesn't want to know me. All I want is just a chance to meet her face to face. Could . . . could you encourage her to see me?"

"I could, but I don't know if it will help." He wasn't inclined to push too hard. Besides, it wasn't as if Addie was feeling all that good about him either these days.

Kate looked devastated. "Addie really does resent me that much?"

"I couldn't say for sure if she does or she doesn't," he hedged.

"It sounds like you know her. Do you?"

"I do." Feeling that he was in between a rock and a hard place, he said, "Look, I don't know exactly how she feels, but I do know that Addie hasn't had an easy time of it.

Whether your decision was the best thing for her or not, she grew up thinking that she was unwanted by her parents. That's a heavy burden to bear, you know."

"That wasn't how it was."

"I'm just sharing what she's told me."

"As much as I wish things had been different, I can't change the past."

"You're right. But you might have to accept the consequences," he said gently. "Ain't so?"

She nodded. "I'm not going to give up. Will you at least take my phone number and pass it to her?"

Liking the idea that Addie would be in control of any meeting between her mother and herself, he nodded. "*Jah*. I can do that."

Kate opened her purse, pulled out a card and pen, and circled her phone number. "Please tell Addie that this is my cell phone. If, for some reason, I miss her call, I'll call her back."

He studied the name on the business card. "You're Kate Stutzman. What is it you do?"

"I work at a manufacturing plant in Wooster. I'm a shift manager now."

He was impressed. "It's a *gut* job."

"It's a good one for me. I've always been grateful that they gave me a chance. Everyone needs that, don't you think?"

"Yes, I do." Carefully placing the card in his pocket, he said, "I need to go."

"I have my car. I'd be happy to pick you up in two hours."

"Thanks, but I've got a ride already."

"I know. I just thought . . . Well, never mind. I guess I need to stop pushing, right?"

"There's nothing wrong with offering. At least, I've never thought there was. Good day to ya."

"No matter what happens, *danke*, Daniel."

"I haven't done anything."

Looking at him intently, Kate shook her head. "No, you did a lot. You listened to me and gave me your time. Even if Addie never wants to talk to me, it's appreciated."

Walking back to his cart, he wondered how he was going to talk to Addie about meeting her mother without getting her upset with him. He hoped there was a way because he really, really didn't want to lose Addie. That wasn't an option.

Chapter 28

"Why aren't you waiting by the door for Brooke?" Mommi asked. "It's Tuesday, you know."

Looking away from the bookshelves she'd been dusting, Addie shrugged. "She's picking me up late today. She's got a big test or something to study for."

"It's a shame she couldn't have done her studying last night. This is your time with her."

"Mommi, you know studying ain't like that. Besides, she's a college student. I have a feeling those tests are difficult."

"Meh. Maybe so." She sat down on the couch with a sigh. "What are you going to do until then?"

"Now that I've dusted in here, I'm going to visit Snickers. Do you need anything before I head out to the barn?"

"Maybe some hot peppermint tea?"

"Of course, Mommi. I'll be right back."

Walking to the kitchen, Addie thought about Brooke's phone call. As was their habit, Addie had walked out to the phone shanty at eight that morning to check for messages. Months ago, they'd come up with that plan, in case Brooke was sick or something unavoidable came up. Sure enough, there had been a message waiting for her.

Addie had called her back and they'd discussed the later pick-up time. Brooke had sounded regretful and had even asked if the change would be a problem. Of course, Addie had told her that it wasn't.

Things were a little different between them these days. Brooke had broken up with Cameron a couple weeks ago, and she still seemed a little lost. She was quieter and more reflective, seemed a little bit more distant. She didn't seem as eager to talk and chat while they were together. Now their interchanges felt more like a driver/client relationship than two girls about the same age spending time together.

Addie was disappointed by the change in their relationship but didn't know how to make things better. She still wasn't sure whether Brooke was mad because Addie had made it known that she didn't like Cameron from the start or because they were now in different situations romantically. She had a strong feeling that Brooke was having a difficult time dealing with the fact that Addie was the one with someone special instead of her.

Carefully pouring the hot water into a large mug, Addie shook her head in wonder. It was still amazing to her that she was currently in a relationship.

Though, were they actually in a *real relationship*? She wasn't exactly sure.

After adding the tea bag to the mug and three sugar cookies to a plate, she carried it all to her grandmother. "Here you are, Mommi. I'm going to the barn now." She needed to figure things out about her and Daniel. Snickers was the best sounding board—probably because he simply let her talk.

Mommi smiled at her. "Take your time. I'm all settled here."

Glad that the weather was relatively mild, she wrapped a

bright pink shawl around her shoulders and walked out to see Snickers. The bright color made her functional gray dress seem less drab.

Snickers' ears perked up when she entered the barn and walked right over to the front of his stall.

"*Gut matin*, Snick. I thought I'd visit with you for a spell." She gently rubbed the little donkey's nose. "What do you think? Are you ready for another nursing home visit soon?"

Snickers pawed the ground with a hoof.

Addie chuckled. "You're right. I should stop thinking about the future and concentrate on today." Which was exactly how she should be thinking about Daniel Miller, she decided as she focused on him once again.

"What do you think, Snickers? Is Daniel my beau?" Unfortunately, the donkey just stared at her.

She supposed she didn't blame him. It was hard to tell if Daniel was her beau or not. Though Daniel had been very friendly and attentive, they were a long way from being in a romantic relationship. But maybe that was her inexperience talking?

Irritated with herself, she hung her pink wool shawl on a hook and decided to clean the donkey's straw. After wheeling over the barrow, she opened the stall gate and tossed some of the soiled straw into the barrow with a pitchfork. It was a dirty job but not a big one. She was almost done when the donkey turned his head and brayed.

Looking to see what had caught his attention, Addie gave a little gasp. Daniel was standing right outside the barn door, wearing a straw hat, a long-sleeved light green shirt, and dark gray pants.

It was as if all of her fanciful thoughts had summoned him to her side. "Hi."

He smiled at her. "Hiya, back. How are you?"

"I'm *gut*. I didn't expect to see you today."

"I was hoping to catch you before you went out with Brooke."

"She's delayed. Why are you here? Did you happen to be nearby?" It was a foolish question, she knew. It wasn't as if they passed each other's houses while walking or anything.

"I stopped by because I wanted to talk to you about something. If you have time, that is."

"I have time. Brooke isn't coming to pick me up for two more hours."

"Ah. That's good." He glanced at Snickers, who was still watching them. "Are you done in here?"

"Just about. Let me finish taking this straw to the back; then I'll be ready."

"I'll do it." Before she could try to stop him, he had picked up the pitchfork and tossed the last of the straw into the wheelbarrow. "Where does this go?"

"This way." She put the pitchfork back on its hook, patted Snickers one last time, then led the way to the compost pile a few yards away from the barn.

"This a big job, Addie."

"What? Cleaning up a horse stall?" When he nodded, she shrugged off his concern. "It's nothing. It's part of taking care of Snickers. Honestly, I'm a little surprised you handled that pitchfork so easily, Daniel. You don't have a horse."

"I borrow Hero from time to time though. And I've done my fair share of barn cleaning over the years."

"I guess stall cleaning is like riding a bike, hmm?"

Daniel smiled at her joke. "My parents have four horses, as well as some lazy *kinner* who are still at home." He upturned the barrow, neatly depositing the straw onto the refuse pile. "That it?"

"*Jah*. I'll put the wheelbarrow back in the barn now."

"What do you do with the refuse?"

"Once a month two strapping boys come over and take it to one of their fields. It works well for both of us."

They continued to walk side by side as they returned the barrow and then headed into the house. "When I see you do things like this, I realize I've never thought about how much you had to do on your own."

"Why would you have thought about it?"

"I don't know. Because I visit my parents once a week and help out. But here you are, the only one helping your grandmother."

"It's not a burden," she said as they stopped outside the back door of the house. "I take off my boots here."

"I'll do the same."

They sat side by side, removing footwear. It was nothing she hadn't done a thousand times. Next to him, seeing his easy movements, watching the way he carefully untied his laces before removing his boots, the everyday habit felt intimate.

Such thoughts embarrassed her. She turned on the faucet at the mudroom sink. "I usually wash my hands here."

"Of course."

Yet again, they stood side by side. As the water gradually turned warm, they passed the soap to each other.

"This smells *gut*."

"It's lavender oil soap. Mommi and I make several bars of it every summer."

"Addie, who are ya talking to?"

"Daniel is here."

"He is in the *haus*?"

Addie met Daniel's eyes and saw amusement in them. "*Jah*, Mommi. He came over to talk for a spell. I'll bring him into the living room to say hello."

"Don't forget to offer him some *kaffi*."

"I won't."

"Addie, don't forget—"

"I don't need anything more, Lovina," Daniel called out.

"Oh. Of course not."

"Would you like to sit in the kitchen? My grandmother is in the living room."

"That is fine."

Addie served Daniel coffee and they sat down at the kitchen table. It occurred to her then that he'd come over to speak with her, but she'd kept him waiting another thirty minutes while she finished her chore and cleaned up. It was on the tip of her tongue to apologize, but she decided against it. After all, his visit had been a surprise.

"The *kaffi* is *gut*."

"*Danke.*" She sipped her own cup, grateful for the hot brew. It took the edge off her apprehension.

After taking another sip, he placed his cup back on the table. "I guess I canna put this off any longer. Addie, I met your mother yesterday at the hospital."

If she'd been holding the coffee cup between her hands, it would've fallen to the floor. "What are you talking about?"

"I was working in the emergency room, cleaning cubicles, and when I went into one of the rooms to get trash, a woman named Kate Stutzman was in there."

"And you knew she was my mother just like that?"

"No, it wasn't that easy. But when we started talking, things began to come together. It's hard to believe, right? But that is what happened."

"And you just knew she was my *mamm*?"

"It wasn't like that. I mean, of course it wasn't." He sipped the last of his drink. "As I said, I was cleaning and we started to talk. She asked if I was Amish. She asked it in Deutsch."

That surprised her. "She's not Amish. Is she?"

"No, she ain't. But you know that."

She'd told him that her grandmother had talked to her mother. Had seen her more than once. But had Addie ever asked about her appearance? She hadn't. Instead, she'd brushed off every one of her grandmother's attempts to give Addie information. "I don't know much about her. I haven't wanted to know anything about her."

"Well, she sure wants to know you."

"I still don't understand . . . wait. Did she go to the hospital to see you and ask questions about me?"

Daniel shook his head. "Not at all. She had a bad cut and was waiting for stitches. Because it wasn't life threatening, she had to wait a few."

"What was the cut from?"

"I think she tripped or something." He shrugged. "Anyway, as I said, we started talking, and one thing led to another. She said she'd grown up in Apple Creek. We were both surprised that we had that connection. And then she said that she had a grandmother and a daughter there. It wasn't hard to put the pieces together then."

"I guess not." Addie was so flustered, she stood up. "Would you like more coffee?"

"*Jah*. Sure."

Picking up both of their cups, she busied herself with them. Unfortunately, the small task only took a few minutes. All too soon she was sitting across from him again. Daniel was studying her, watching her every move. "I'm sure hearing this is a shock."

"It is, but I guess it was to be expected. I mean, she sees my grandmother from time to time. Who knows—maybe they had plans to talk together while I run errands with Brooke." She was a little embarrassed about her tone, but it couldn't be helped. She was human, not perfect.

"She didn't seem like a bad person, Addie. She seemed full of regret."

"I should hope so. I mean, if she has things to regret."

His eyes filled with compassion. "Addie, I know you're upset, but I really think she was sincere."

What did that even mean? "I appreciate your coming over to tell me. I'm glad you did." Struggling for words, she added, "I . . . I would be upset if I found out one day that you'd spoken to her and never told me."

"She asked that I give you her phone number and encourage you to call her." He shifted, pulled out a slip of paper from one of his pockets, and slid it across the table. "I think you should."

"This isn't any of your business." Hadn't he already done enough?

"Of course it is. I care about you."

"You know my feelings. I've told you. If you cared about me, then you would've told her that you didn't want to get involved."

"I couldn't do that."

"Because she means so much to you?"

He leaned closer. "*Nee,* Addie. I'm involved because you mean so much to me."

His words were sweet . . . but on the heels of this revelation? She wasn't sure what to do or think. She bit her bottom lip as her mind spun.

Daniel continued. "She's your mother and she was visibly anxious. Whether you want to know her or not, I couldn't ignore her request."

She ached to lash out, but knew it wasn't fair. He'd been in an impossible situation. If their positions had been reversed, she wasn't sure what she would've done.

"Please don't be mad."

"I'm not . . . but please don't expect me to feel the way you want me to feel right this minute. Your words are a bit of a shock, you know."

"I know." Still looking worried, he stood up. "Addie, I knew telling you wasn't going to be easy, but I had no choice."

"I understand." Well, she kind of did. She got to her feet as well.

He stepped closer. "Don't use this as a reason to push me away. I came over here knowing that you were going to be mad, but I came anyway."

"That is not praiseworthy."

His gaze heated. "I think you're wrong. I think coming over here to do the right thing, even though you might blame me for something that wasn't my doing, does deserve praise."

He'd stepped even closer. She could feel the heat coming from his body. Or maybe it was just the tension that she'd felt radiating from him. She could also smell the soap on his skin. His eyes were dark, and his voice was deeper than usual. Almost husky.

Another note of unease shot through her as she wondered how to react. Wondered if she was supposed to. It was all so confusing. "If you are aching for praise, then you're going to be disappointed. I've got nothing for you, Daniel."

"That is where you're wrong."

Before she could say a word, before she could sputter a response, Daniel Miller had wrapped his hands around her back, his fingers half digging into her shoulder blades. Pulling her closer. And then he lowered his head and kissed her.

Her lips had been parted in shock. Every sense seemed to be ignited, affected. Heated. She felt his lips. They were slightly chapped, dry. She tasted him, his own flavor mixing with the coffee . . . and maybe her frustration, too.

Or maybe it was just her imagination. Next thing she knew, her hands were gripping his shoulders and she'd raised herself on tiptoe. Seeking more.

Maybe they stood together for two minutes. Maybe it was twenty. It didn't matter. Neither did their letters or her family or the lies or even the promises. All that mattered was that moment.

Addie knew it was perfect. No, it was perfection.

Suddenly, he pulled away.

They were both breathing heavily. Her lips were still slightly parted as they stared at each other.

"That . . . I didn't come over here for that. But I'm not going to say I'm sorry."

"I'm not either."

"Addie, call your mother or don't. But don't let this come between us. Not now. Not after everything we've been through together."

"I won't. I'm not sure what I'm going to do, but I'm not going to push you away, Daniel."

"*Gut.*" He stared at her, as if he was trying to identify every emotion in her eyes. Every thought in her head. "I'm going to leave. Otherwise I'm going to pull you into my arms again."

She nodded. "I understand."

"Tell your grandmother . . ." He chuckled. "Never mind. I have no idea what to tell her. I still want to take you to supper Saturday night, okay?"

"*Jah.*"

"I'll be here at five."

"Sure. Okay."

He chuckled then, brightening the atmosphere. Then he walked out of the kitchen, and into the mudroom.

Addie guessed he was sitting back down on the bench they'd shared and was putting on his boots. Maybe slipping on his jacket by now. Then she heard the door open and shut.

She was alone again.

"Addie, what are you two doing?" her grandmother called out. "When are you bringing Daniel in here to chat?"

Praying for strength, Addie got to her feet. She'd been mistaken. She wasn't alone at all. But for that one moment, it had felt that way.

Chapter 29

Addie debated about whether to tell her grandmother Daniel's news but ultimately decided against sharing it just yet. She wanted time to really think things through. She hoped time would enable her to see her mother's request clearly, instead of through the haze of disappointments and regrets that both she and her grandmother always felt when discussing any topic relating to Kate Stutzman.

Much as she adored her grandmother, she wanted to make her decision based on what she wanted, not what her grandmother did.

She did tell Brooke, though. Even though she and Brooke were adjusting to some changes in their dynamic, they were still friends. Plus, Brooke was the only person she could talk to who wasn't emotionally invested.

While she drove, Brooke listened attentively as Addie told her all about Daniel's visit and his news about her mother. She'd been as shocked as Addie was and even commented that the Lord must have put her mother and Daniel together for a reason.

"So that's how things stand now," Addie finished as Brooke pulled into the Walmart parking lot. "I'm keeping another secret from my grandmother, Daniel seems a little put out with me, and I'm scared about calling my mother . . . and what will happen if I never do."

"You sure never do things halfway, do you? This is a big deal."

"I know. What do you think I should do?"

Brooke shook her head slowly. "Oh, no, Addie Holmes. I'm sorry, but this one is on your shoulders, not mine."

"Come on. You don't have any suggestions?"

She pursed her lips. "How about this? What do you *want* to do?"

"Uh, that isn't helpful."

"Hey, hear me out. I like that you're trying to think about yourself for a change, but you're not going far enough. What you need to do is isolate the variable."

"You want me to do what?"

She grinned. "Sorry, I guess I was putting everything in terms of my chemistry class. How about this? If you took everyone else out of the equation, and you didn't have to worry about your grandma, Daniel, or even what your mother wanted . . . what would you do?"

To Addie's surprise, she knew the answer immediately. "I'd still want to call my mother."

"Why?"

"Why?" She pushed herself a little bit more. "Because . . . because I think I deserve the chance to talk to her. I want to hear what she has to say." She gulped. "And maybe I want her to hear what I have to say, too."

Brooke smiled. "There you go. See, you've already made your decision. This is your choice, right?"

She was right. Addie might be nervous, but no one was going to make her do something she didn't want to do. Calling her mother was her choice. "Do you really think it's that easy?"

"I don't think what's going on is easy at all. But, Addie, isn't it time you put yourself first?"

Brooke had a point. Scared to put the phone call off any longer, Addie said, "Could you take me someplace where I can use a phone?"

"I'll do you one better. You can use mine." She handed it over. "Do you want me to get out of the car so you can have privacy?"

"*Nee*. Could you stay nearby in case I need you?"

"Of course. I don't mind."

Staring at the numbers on the slip of paper that Daniel had handed her, Addie took a deep breath. "This is the right decision, isn't it?"

"Yep. If you don't call this lady, you're always going to regret it. It's like your secret admirer notes, right? I mean, just think about what would've happened if you had tossed that first letter in the trash."

Addie knew what would've happened: nothing. "Daniel and I might not have ever become friends."

"He sure wouldn't have kissed you in your kitchen this morning!"

She was sure her face was bright red. "I can't believe I told you about that—and that you're bringing it up."

Brooke grinned. "How could I not? That was the best part of today's story. It sounded amazing." She tapped the slip of paper balanced on Addie's knee. "All right, it's time. Make that call."

"Here we go." Carefully, Addie pressed the numbers on Brooke's phone, hit Send, and held the device up to her ear. She had to remind herself to breathe. The phone rang twice.

"Hello?"

Eyes wide, she stared at Brooke.

"Say something!" Brooke whispered.

"*Jah*. I mean . . . this is Addie Holmes. Is this . . . is this Kate Stutzman?"

"Yes! I mean, oh, my goodness. I mean . . . I'm so glad that you called!" The words were tumbling out like snowballs down a hill. Each was practically falling on the next. "I've been so afraid that you wouldn't. You sound so good, too."

"*Danke?*"

Kate laughed. "I'm sorry. I'll try to calm down. I don't want to scare you away before we even get the chance to talk."

The woman's voice was lovely. Full of emotion. Honest. Addie wasn't sure what she'd expected, but it wasn't this. "You won't scare me. I . . . I wasn't sure if I was going to call or not."

"What made you decide to do it?"

"A couple of things. The way Daniel talked about you. He said you were nice." Looking at Brooke, she added, "I also got advice from another friend. She suggested that I should call ya so I wouldn't have any regrets."

Brooke gave her a thumbs-up. Addie smiled at her but wondered if maybe she'd been too honest with Kate.

"I think your friend is right," Kate replied in a far softer tone. "Regrets are so overrated." Her voice cracked. It was obvious she was trying not to cry. "Sorry! Sorry, I . . . well, there have been a lot of days when I wasn't sure if I'd ever talk to you. I'm just so glad you called."

Addie felt like crying, too. The sudden rush of emotion she was experiencing overwhelmed her. Holding Brooke's phone tightly in her hand, she didn't know what else to say. "Yes. Well."

"What are you doing today? Where are you calling from?"

"On Tuesdays my English friend Brooke helps me run errands. This is Brooke's phone. We're in a store parking lot."

"Hey, could you hold on a moment? I'm at work."

Addie heard the rustle of paper, a muted conversation, then Kate was back on the line. "Sorry, I had to tell my supervisor that this is important."

"You work in a manufacturing plant."

"Yes. I'm on the line. I've been here ever since I got better. I mean, since I got out of prison." She lowered her voice. "Mamm told me that she told you about my past."

"Jah."

"Listen. Addie. I want to tell you this real quick. Before we run out of time or something. I just want to tell you that I wish I had been a better mother to you. I'm sorry that you had to deal with a lot of things a little girl never should have to. I had a lot of problems, and you had to deal with the consequences. All I can say is that back then I did a lot of things I wish I hadn't, but I'll never regret asking my mother—your grandmother—to raise you. All I could think about was that you didn't deserve me or John Henry. You needed something better than me."

"It hurt you to give me up."

"Of course it did." Her voice sounded thick with emotion. "I loved you. I still love you even though we don't even know each other."

"Is love like that even possible?" Addie was speaking to herself as much as to her mother.

"Of course it is. The Lord loves us, right? Even when we don't believe in him, he loves us."

"You're right. Would you like to come over soon? To, um, get to know each other?"

"Oh, Addie, yes." She laughed softly. "Can you tell that I'm sitting here bawling?" She sniffed. "Sorry. Name the day and time and I'll be there."

"Sunday in the morning?"

"What time?"

"Whenever you want. I'll be up early."

"Then I'll be there around nine. *Danke*, Addie," Kate whispered before she hung up.

Feeling dazed, Addie handed the phone back to Brooke. "I guess it's happening, Brooke. I'm going to meet my mother on Sunday."

"You sure are." Brooke looked just as dazed as Addie felt. "What do you think? Are you going to be okay?"

"You know what? I think I am. It kind of feels like I've finally made a decision. I've stopped spiraling out of control."

"You've made a lot of decisions, right? About Daniel and your grandmother and now your mother." She brightened. "I think big decisions are supposed to come in threes." She wrinkled her nose. "Isn't that the saying?"

"Oh, Brooke. It's trouble that's supposed to come in threes. Not big revelations."

"Yeah, well, this is your life, not a storybook. I think that means you can have whatever you want take place in threes." She opened the door. "We need some retail therapy. Let's go shopping."

Smiling, Addie grabbed her purse and joined Brooke. She wasn't sure if she needed retail therapy, but at the moment she reckoned it couldn't hurt.

Chapter 30

Daniel had always admired Lovina Stutzman. He liked her forthright nature, the way she didn't suffer fools, and how she'd not only taken in Addie and raised her as her own but also had dared the entire Amish community of Apple Creek to say anything about it. People liked to say she was *formidable* but even his mother had said that *tough* was a better descriptor.

Lovina was tough as leather, and not the soft and supple kind, either.

All that meant that he'd respected her but had never been apprehensive about talking to her. He'd even laughed when other people actively tried to avoid private conversations with her. To him, she'd simply been an older lady who had needed a walker in order to get around. How difficult could she be?

He was currently learning that she could be really difficult. He should've given his friends' opinions more credence.

She'd been the one who had answered his knock on the

door. Within seconds, some of his optimism about the evening slid away. It turned out the woman might have recently been hospitalized and might need a bit of help to get around these days—but there wasn't one thing wrong with her tongue.

"Good evening, Lovina. How are you feeling?"

"I'm not sure," she replied, looking him over. "I'm trying to decide how I feel about your taking my granddaughter out tonight."

Trying to decide? "Speaking of Addie, is she ready?" He looked down the hall hopefully.

"I reckon she'll be along in a few." Turning around, she pushed her walker down the hall. "You might as well come on in. Close the door behind ya. You're letting a breeze in."

He calmed his nerves by reminding himself that the woman had always been brusque. Doing as she said, he followed her down the hall, thinking that some things never changed—and that Lovina Stutzman was constant as an evergreen tree.

When they got to the living room, she said, "Sit down if you'd like. Not in my rocker, though."

Taking a seat on the couch, he fought off a smile. Lovina was filled with pepper and sass tonight. She really was as bristly as a hedgehog. Sometimes he couldn't believe that the woman had raised such a sweet girl. "So, ah, did you have a nice day?"

She rolled her eyes. "I'm seventy-two and now have to use a metal walker to get around my own *haus*. It was good enough, I suppose."

"Good enough is good enough, ain't so?"

Though it looked like she was determined to keep him in his place, her lips twitched. "One could say that. Now, where are you taking Addie to supper?"

Daniel realized he was going to be treated to the full brunt of her mood. She was definitely not pleased with him. He was actually starting to sweat.

He really should've brought both her and Addie flowers. Or chocolate. Anything to sweeten her mood.

"Supper?"

She sighed. "*Jah*. I asked where you were going to eat. And so far, you have not given me an answer."

Feeling like a mouse in a barn cat's lair, he shifted uncomfortably. "I'm going to take her to my parents' house for supper."

"You're taking her to their house, did you say?" She narrowed her eyes. "Or your own?"

He was sure his neck was bright red. "We're going to my parents' house." Just to be sure she understood, he added, "I am not going to take Addie to my house for supper."

"So you won't be alone together tonight."

Feeling that this was a trick question, he cleared his throat. "Well, we will be alone in the buggy, but that's it. There will be a lot of people at my parents' place." He was sounding like an idiot.

He glanced upstairs. Where was Addie and why was she running so late?

A line formed between Lovina's thick, gray brows. "Yes. Well, now. That brings up a good question. Why have you never gotten your own buggy?"

"I only recently bought *mei haus*, as I'm sure you know. Also, I work long shifts at a hospital. I have no need for a horse and buggy."

"Except, perhaps, to take my granddaughter out."

"Except then, yes." He swallowed. Did he dare mention the small shelter for Hero at his house?

"Oh, my stars, Mommi, leave poor Daniel alone," Addie called out.

Daniel was so glad to hear her voice, he gave a huge sigh of relief. Looking up, he smiled at the pretty sight she made. She wore a bright green dress, a white cardigan sweater, and white tennis shoes. Her dark blond hair was pinned up neatly as always, and the white kapp on her head looked neat and crisp. As usual, Addie had on her glasses. The tortoise frames set off her pretty green eyes.

And she was smiling down at him.

Even though her grandmother was watching his every move, he smiled up at her. "Hiya, Addie. You look nice."

"You do, too. I'm sorry I was running so late," she said as she started down the stairs. "I hope it won't be a problem at the restaurant?"

"He ain't taking you to a restaurant," Lovina interjected. "Daniel Miller here is taking you to his parents' *haus* instead."

Addie paused on the fifth step. "What did you say, Mommi?"

"You're having supper with his whole family tonight," Lovina fairly yelled.

Addie's pretty smile had just turned upside down. "Daniel, is this true?"

His grand idea of showing Addie off to his family—and demonstrating to Addie how serious he was about her—was failing miserably.

Since there was no way he could change their plans, he said flippantly, "I wouldn't lie to your grandmother." He grinned, hoping she'd appreciate his quip.

She didn't. Addie looked even more worried. "But I didn't make anything for your mother."

"That's *gut,* because I invited you over for supper. *Mei mamm* is cooking." When Addie just stared wide-eyed, he added a little more tentatively, "I bet a couple of my sisters will be cooking, too."

"I really wish you'd told me that we were going to be dinner guests at your parents' house."

"But we're not guests, not really."

"I am."

"Are all ten of ya going to be there?" Lovina blurted.

"Well, um, altogether, there's twelve of us, you know. Ten kids and two parents." He smiled again. As if doing math was something to be proud about.

Her grandmother scowled. "You didn't answer me."

"*Jah*. All, um, twelve of us will be eating there tonight."

"I believe Addie makes thirteen."

So much for his math. "Yes."

Addie still seemed upset. "Daniel, I thought we were going to a restaurant. That it was going to be just the two of us."

"Well, it was, until I stopped back home to get Hero and to help out for a spell. That's when *mei mamm* suggested we come over. Everyone thought it was a fine idea." Since Addie still looked upset, he murmured, "I'm guessing that it weren't."

Thinking quickly, he added, "You know what? Mamm's plans don't matter. We can go to a restaurant after all. Where would you like to go?"

"You're going to change plans just like that?" Addie pressed her hands together. "What will your family say?"

"I don't know. We, ah, we just won't show up."

She looked horrified. "We can't do that. They'll think something happened to us. They'll think we got hurt in a buggy accident."

"Or that you took her to your house instead," Lovina said.

He glared at her grandmother. "I told you, Lovina, I'm not gonna do that."

Lovina folded her arms over her chest. "Are you sure you want Daniel Miller to court ya, Addie? He's not very good at it. I feel sure you could do better."

Suddenly looking amused, Addie walked to his side.

"We'd better get going, Daniel. Otherwise, your very large family is going to wonder where we are. Bye, Mommi."

"What time will you be coming back?" Before Addie could answer, Lovina fired off another question. "What time do you intend to bring Addie back home, Daniel?"

"Well, now, I don't rightly know. . . ."

"Mommi, you know that ain't none of your business," Addie said. "Now stop being so bossy and rude."

"I was only looking out for you."

"*Nee,* you were enjoying making Daniel squirm. Good night. I'll see you in the morning." Looking back up at him, Addie smiled. "I'm ready now."

He opened the door, guided her out, and shut it firmly behind him. At last, they'd escaped. "I didn't think I was going to get out of there alive."

"I'm sorry, Daniel. She was just playing with ya."

"It was excruciating."

Some of the merriment in her expression faded. "She can be a handful at times, I know. Are you sorry you asked me out?"

"Not at all." Reaching for her hand, he led her to the buggy. "Let's get on our way and I'll tell you all about how supper with my family came to take place." He lowered his voice. "I'm sorry I didn't think to ask your opinion. I guess I thought maybe you'd enjoy being around all of them. They're a lively bunch."

"I was surprised and nervous, but I'm better now. I'm looking forward to it."

After he handed her into the buggy and directed Hero on their way, he said, "I promise, everyone in *mei* family is excited that you and I are seeing each other. They might be pesky, and the house will be loud, but they should be on *gut* behavior." *A lot better than her grandmother's,* he silently added.

When Addie only nodded in response, he went on. "I promise it will be all right. I wouldn't bring you over there if I thought you would be miserable."

"I know. I'm just a little *neahfich*—that's all."

"You've got nothing to be nervous about. My parents always say you're the nicest girl in Apple Creek, and I happen to think you're one of the prettiest, too."

"That's so kind of you to say."

"Nothing kind about speaking the truth. I mean it, Addie. I'm the one who is counting my blessings right now."

"Just don't leave me alone for long periods of time with your siblings, okay?"

He smiled as he reached for her hand. "Never more than ten minutes, tops."

By the time Addie sat down next to Daniel at the Millers' enormous dinner table, she wished she'd asked Daniel never to leave her side. Or that she'd taken him up on his suggestion to simply avoid the Miller house altogether.

Simply put, she felt like she was a sparrow in the middle of a flock of mockingbirds. Or perhaps a cat in the middle of an animal shelter for dogs. She felt that out of place, even though no one was being mean.

Just incredibly chatty.

"Are you hanging in there?" Daniel whispered as his two youngest siblings, Brodie and Anna, were sent back to the kitchen to wash their hands more thoroughly.

Addie barely had time to nod before Brodie and Anna returned to the table and Timothy, Daniel's father, cleared his throat.

"Let us all give thanks for the meal we are about to receive."

Grateful for the silent moment of prayer, Addie bowed her head and closed her eyes. She gave thanks for the food, the many hands that had prepared it, and for the presence of Daniel in her life. When the silence lingered, she decided to also give thanks for moments of silence.

When she raised her head, Anna, who was sitting across from her, was staring at her hard. "Are you done yet, Addie?"

They'd all been waiting for her. "*Jah.*"

"We can eat now," Brodie announced.

Almost in unison, serving dishes were picked up, portions taken out and passed on.

"It's best to get what you can and pass quickly," Daniel said. "Food doesn't last long."

"He who lingers misses out," seventeen-year-old Jack explained.

"Gotcha," Addie said. When Daniel passed her a plate of fried chicken, she quickly snatched a chicken breast and then handed the plate to one of his sisters.

Marta, Daniel's mother, smiled at her from the end of the table. "I guess our brood must seem overwhelming to you."

"I canna deny that it is. But I'm enjoying myself." She smiled at thirteen-year-old Emily, whom she'd spied at the stove when Daniel had given her a quick tour of the house. "The meal looks delicious."

"Beth and I made the mashed potatoes and the corn."

"Beth and Emily are twins," Brodie supplied.

"Yes. I know."

"How come we're overwhelming?" Anna asked.

It took Addie a moment to switch gears. "It's a bit overwhelming because I grew up with just my grandmother. Mealtimes at my house are a lot quieter."

"Where were your parents?" Brodie asked.

When Daniel stiffened next to her, she pressed a hand on his arm. "They didn't live with us." Before Brodie could ask about that, she spoke again. "But even though I wasn't blessed like you all to have a big family, the Lord did give me something else."

"What?" Anna asked.

"A pet donkey named Snickers," she said with a smile.

"Is he really a pet?" Beth asked.

"Oh, *jah*. He's also a service donkey."

"What's that?" Brodie asked.

"Snickers helps people in need. Sometimes folks respond better to animals than people."

"I've seen therapy dogs but not donkeys," Beth said.

"There aren't many around. Snickers is special," Addie said.

"He's extraordinary," Daniel said. "Snickers visits all sorts of places and even walks inside."

"Really?" Jack asked.

"Oh, yes. *Mei* donkey has mighty *gut* manners."

When all of Daniel's siblings started chuckling and asking more questions about Snickers and donkeys in general, Marta leaned toward Addie. "I'm glad you've joined us, dear. I think you're going to fit in with this noisy bunch just fine."

Addie smiled. "*Danke.*" Then, when the large bowl of mashed potatoes came her way, she quickly spooned a portion on her plate and passed it on quickly.

"*Gut* job," Daniel teased.

"*Danke,*" she whispered back.

Yes. Everything was going to be just fine.

Chapter 31

It was eight o'clock. After they'd eaten supper, everyone had helped with the dishes. Daniel had tried to encourage Addie to sit in front of the fireplace with him to enjoy a few moments of quiet, but she'd refused.

Instead, he'd rolled up his sleeves and dried dishes next to her.

As usual, they had an assembly line of sorts as they worked together. Two kids were at the sink, two others were in charge of clearing the table, another two were organizing the leftovers and putting the kitchen back to rights. He and Addie helped dry dishes while Jack and his father put them away.

To his surprise, Addie had giggled and chatted the entire time. It was as if she was enjoying the novelty of it all. His mother had noticed it, too.

"You're a good worker, Addie," she said. "You're welcome to come over for a meal anytime you'd like. With or without my son."

"Danke."

"Do you really not mind drying dishes?" Emily asked.

"You forget that it's always just been me and my grandmother. We have fewer plates and forks to clean up, but no one to help me do the rest of it. Kitchen duty usually takes hours."

"I would hate that," Beth said.

"Don't be rude," Daniel said.

"I'm just being honest, Dan."

Smiling softly at him, Addie whispered, "Don't be so worried. I really am having fun."

Now that they were in his buggy, he was at a loss as to what to do next. If her grandmother wasn't such a tyrant, he would've brought Addie home early and lingered with her on the sofa. He surely wasn't ready to face Lovina, however.

Stopping the buggy on the side of the road, he said, "I don't know where to take you."

"I have an idea."

"Great. Where would you like to go?"

"Your house."

"Addie, you know I can't take you there."

"Why not?"

"I promised your grandmother."

She smiled slowly. "Then let's not tell her. She won't know what we do."

His mouth went dry. "Addie, there's nothing I'd love to do more, but I don't want you to be uncomfortable."

"I won't be uncomfortable. I'll be happy because we'll have some privacy for the first time all evening."

Privacy did sound good . . . but was it wrong to want that? "I'm trying to do everything right, you know. To court you properly."

"Daniel, that ship's already sailed. You were my secret admirer, remember?"

"I guess you have a point. Though . . ."

"Come on. I've never seen your *haus*. I think knowing where you live is pretty important. Don't you?"

"All right. But, ah, I don't want you to think that I'm being disrespectful."

She reached out and pressed her hand on his knee. "I trust you, Daniel.

Her trust was wonderful. It made him feel ten feet tall. Maybe even worthy of her.

When Hero pulled them up his driveway, he noticed Addie looking around with interest. The lantern hanging from the back of the buggy, together with the bright moon, illuminated the property.

"This is pretty, Daniel."

After tying Hero to the hitching post at the front of the house, he said, "*Danke*. It's not very big, you see. I bought the *haus* from a retired English couple. Their needs were simple."

He went around and helped her down, then took her hand. "Come on. I'll show you the inside, and then I'll take you home."

She smiled up at him as they walked. Once again, he noticed how soft and smooth her hands were—and how well she fit beside him. "Even though I hadn't intended to take you here, I am glad you're getting to see the place. I'm proud of it."

"I like how you live so close to your family, but you have some space, too."

"I like that, too." He chuckled. "It's funny—I saved all I could from my job. When I heard this house was on the market, I asked my *daed* to go talk to the bank with me. I thought for sure my father was going to give me a long lecture about borrowing money and living on my own at such a young age."

"You were only eighteen, right?"

"Right. Just a little younger than you are now." He

opened the front door. "But my father supported me instead of trying to encourage me to stay at home. The joke is that he and *mei mamm* were looking forward to having nine *kinner* at home instead of ten." Seeing Bob stretch and pad toward them, he released Addie's hand and knelt down to pet the beagle. "I guess you remember Bob?"

She bent down to scratch his ears. "I sure do. Hiya, Bob."

Bob allowed her to pet him for a few seconds before he turned around and walked back to the kitchen. "Bob ain't really a nighttime dog. He likes to sleep."

"I do too." Addie straightened. "Oh, Daniel. Look at everything! Your house is so pretty."

"Thank you, but it would be better if you could see it illuminated. Let me light a lantern. Wait here." Daniel hurried to the kitchen and lit the lantern he usually kept in the center of the table.

When he returned to her side, he held out his arm. "I'll take you around now."

Addie pointed to the small living room to the right. "Let's start there."

"All right. So, um, this is a sitting room. The house has two living spaces. The other space has a fireplace."

Addie ran a hand along a bookshelf. "What do you do in here?"

"Not a lot. Bob likes to sit on the chair in front of the window if it's sunny out."

"I bet it would be a wonderful-*gut* sewing room."

"I bet it would." Daniel could imagine Addie doing all sorts of projects there—and how nice it would be to come home and see her hard at work on some project instead of finding the space empty.

He reached for her hand again. "Back here is the kitchen. I have a new stove."

"It's lovely. You've got lots of cabinets, too."

"I painted them white. Well, Bradly and Roman and I

did." He tried to view the kitchen from a woman's perspective but wasn't sure how someone who actually cooked a lot would like it. "One day I aim to get a new sink," he said, then wished he hadn't. Was he trying to sell her the house . . . or a life with him in it? He wasn't exactly sure anymore.

She walked into the living room. "Here's your fireplace. And Bob."

"*Jah.* He likes being cozy." Feeling more and more awkward, he pointed to the door. "The bedroom and bathroom are down here."

Addie opened the door and went in. "Daniel, look at your bathtub!"

"It's cast iron. We couldn't remove it."

"Whoever would want to? And you have a closet, too! And . . . a big bed."

"*Jah*. It's a queen."

Their eyes met. For the first time since they'd walked inside, Addie started looking as self-conscious as he felt. "We should go back to the living room."

"Yes. Um, I'll go check on Bob."

Of course, his dog was fine. He was lying on his dog bed with one eye open. Watching Daniel and Addie and probably hoping that Daniel wasn't going to make him go outside to do his business.

Daniel knew he should get Addie back in the buggy and take her home. Right now, he was thinking that even being with Lovina was better than being alone with Addie next to his bedroom.

Maybe.

"We should probably go," he said. But instead of leading her toward the door, he set the lantern down on the floor.

Addie stepped toward him. "*Jah*. I guess so."

She smelled so good. He reached for her hands. "What do you think of the house? Is it too small?"

"For you and Bob? Not at all."

"What about for two people?" he whispered.

She smiled softly. "I think two people would be very cozy here. Comfortable."

The lantern that he'd been carrying sent a light glow over the room. There might be a whole lot of reasons he shouldn't be pulling Addie into his arms, but he couldn't think of a single one at the moment.

Especially when she fit against him so well. Her hands were clinging to his shoulders, and she was looking up at him. Her lips were parted.

"The last time I kissed you, I didn't ask if it was okay."

"I didn't need you to ask."

"I didn't tell you how much you mean to me."

Her green eyes twinkled. "Are you going to tell me this time?"

"Oh, yeah." At last, all of his doubts and nervousness dissipated. "I'm falling in love with you, Addie."

"I'm falling in love with you, too, Daniel."

He pressed his lips to her forehead. Glided them to her cheek. When she tilted her head with a sigh, he kissed her jaw. "If I kiss you in my kitchen, are you going to tell your grandmother?"

"Never," she whispered.

He smiled before he claimed her lips. When she relaxed against him, he ran a hand along her back and deepened the kiss. And was sure that no moment had ever been more perfect.

When he lifted his head, Addie was gazing back at him in wonder.

He ran a hand along her cheek. "Are you okay?"

"I'm not sure. I think you might need to kiss me again."

"I'll kiss you as many times as you like, Addie," he murmured as he lowered his head again.

Few moments had ever been so perfect.

Chapter 32

As wonderful-*gut* as supper at the Millers' had been, Addie was very much wishing that she hadn't eaten so much. Now, sitting in the living room about twelve hours after she'd returned home, she was fairly sure she was going to throw up.

For the last thirty minutes, she'd been alternating between looking out the window for her mother's car and walking around the house, looking for flaws. In between, she'd taken a tour of the kitchen to make sure that her cake hadn't fallen and stopped by the bathroom mirror—just in case there was something on her face that hadn't been there five minutes before.

"You're gonna wear yourself out with all this fretting and fussing, Addie," Mommi warned. "Kate won't care about anything besides you."

At the moment, that didn't exactly make her feel any better. What if her mother found her wanting? What if she didn't end up liking Addie? What then?

Or, what if *she* didn't end up liking Kate Stutzman? There was a chance of that, she reckoned. Kate was an Englischer, worked in a factory, and had had a hard and difficult life. How could someone like Addie compare? Her life had been very sheltered and boring in comparison. What would they even have to say to each other? The farthest she'd ever been from home was Lehman's Store in Kidron.

Peeking out the window again but seeing no sign of a vehicle approaching, she asked, "Do you think she might have changed her mind?"

"*Nee.*"

"But she might have. What do you think we should do then?" Addie hated how insecure and negative she was sounding, but she couldn't help herself. She was a nervous wreck.

With a groan of effort, her grandmother got to her feet and shuffled closer behind her walker. "Addie Holmes, you've got to settle down," she said in the same tone she used to use when Addie had been so excited about an upcoming birthday that she didn't want to go to bed. "Take a deep breath. Or better yet, come sit down."

"I can't. I'm too antsy. If she doesn't come, do I try calling her?" She bit her lip. "Or do I just accept it?"

A little bit of the vinegar that had seasoned her grandmother's voice left. "If she doesn't come, I'm sure you could call. If she doesn't show up, it likely means that something happened or she got sick . . . *jah*? But Kate is going to be here. I know she is. She's been waiting for this day for years."

"But still. Things happen—oh! Here's her car."

"And here she is." Shuffling closer, Mommi reached out one veined hand and placed it on Addie's cheek. "You are forgetting two things, child. One, you are special and worth knowing. If you've learned anything these past few months, it should be that."

"And the second?"

"That the Lord is in charge. Not you. Not me. Not even Kate. He's already determined that you two should meet, and He already knows what is going to happen."

"You're right." How could she have forgotten that?

"Of course I am."

"I love you, Mommi."

"I love you back." She released a ragged sigh. "Now go get the door. Kate's about to knock."

Addie turned, ran her hands down her light blue dress, rearranged the ties on her *kapp*, and opened the door.

"Addie."

There she was. Her mother. The woman who had been through so much and had given her up out of desperation. She didn't look anything like Addie had expected. She had on a long skirt and a plain white T-shirt. A patterned sweater filled with bright colors was on top of it. On her feet were plain black flats. She didn't have on a *kapp* or covering, of course. Her hair was red and cut short. It fluttered about her face. But her eyes? Her eyes were Addie's.

"*Jah,*" Addie responded at last.

"Addie, you're gonna let flies in if you ain't careful. Let Kate in and shut the door."

"Sorry. Please come in."

Kate walked through and shut the door behind her. When she turned around, she was smiling. "You are exactly the way I imagined. No, prettier. You're perfect."

"You don't look anything at all like I thought."

Kate blinked, then chuckled. "I reckon that is probably true."

Mommi cleared her throat. "Addie, please take Kate into the living room and offer her a chair."

"Please come in." Addie paused. Had she already said that? "I mean—"

"I know what you meant. Yes. Let's go sit down." She

walked ahead of Addie and greeted her mother with a whisper and a kiss on the cheek. "Let me help you, Mamm."

"I don't need anyone's help, you know."

"Of course not." Kate shared a smile with Addie.

A tiny bit of the apprehension that she'd been feeling began to ease. Yes, they were still strangers, but maybe there was more of a connection between them than she'd thought would be possible.

"I'm going to get the refreshments from the kitchen."

"Would you like some help?" Kate asked.

"No, I've got it. *Danke*." Addie hurried to the kitchen and pressed her hands on her cheeks. Kate had showed up and didn't seem scary.

There wasn't much to prepare. An hour before, she'd set out the tray, covering the cookies and scones she'd made with a clean linen dishcloth. Carefully, she poured coffee into three cups, arranged the sugar and creamer on the tray, and then carried it into the living room.

"*Danke,* Addie," Mommi said.

After putting the tray on the table, she turned to Kate. "Would you care for coffee or a scone?"

"Yes, please. Did you make these?"

"Addie does all the cooking here. She does a *gut* job."

Kate picked up the cup and sipped. "Tell me about you, Addie. Mamm says that you help all sorts of people around town. And that you have a donkey?"

"I have a couple of small jobs, yes. But I mainly visit places with Snickers. He's a service and therapy donkey. He and I call on people, and he seems to make people feel better."

"I'd like to meet him. Would you take me out to the barn?"

"Of course. Snickers likes meeting new people."

"I hope he'll like me."

Addie heard the same tone of wistfulness that she herself had used when she'd been staring out the window. Maybe they weren't so different after all? "I'm sure he will. He's a gentle, friendly sort."

Mommi chuckled. "You'll be amazed when you are around him, Kate. I was not happy when Addie brought him home, but that little donkey needed her and she needed it. Now he's something of a celebrity around the county. I've even had folks come here to visit. They don't want to go home before they get to say hello to him."

"That's wonderful, Addie," Kate said.

Snickers was wonderful, but Addie had been going on and on about him as if she had something to do with his attributes. It was far too prideful. She refilled everyone's cups. "So, Kate, you work in a factory?"

Her mother blinked as if she needed a moment to catch up to the quick change in topic. After sipping from her cup again, she nodded. "Yes. I work on an assembly line just outside Wooster. Do you know where that is?"

"I know it ain't far, but I've never been there."

"Oh, you would like it. There's a college there. So there are always a lot of kids your age in the coffee shops and restaurants and such. As for my job, I spend most of my time fastening three pieces of plastic together."

"You do that all day long?"

"Yep. For eight hours, though we get three breaks, one of which is lunch. I enjoy it. My coworkers are nice, and we laugh and joke sometimes." Glancing at Mommi, she added, "Like I told you on the phone, Addie, I'm grateful for the opportunity. Not everyone is willing to overlook a person's past."

"You had to prove yourself, Kate, that's all," Mommi said. "And wait patiently for change and accept the Lord's will."

"And grace."

"Ah yes. There's always His grace."

Addie felt as if Mommi was speaking to her instead of her mother. Or maybe she was at last realizing that she wasn't the only vulnerable person in that room. Her mother was as anxious for acceptance as she was. Addie could either give her the peace she'd been looking for or withhold it out of a need to hurt.

But while Addie's life hadn't been all that easy, neither had her mother's. Yet their trials hadn't broken them down. Instead of wallowing in self-pity, each of them was standing on her own two feet. Strong, because they'd come out on the other side.

"Kate, would you like to walk to the barn and meet Snickers?"

She stood up. "I'd like that very much."

Leaving Mommi, who was looking very pleased that they were doing something together, Addie led Kate to the mudroom and put on a shawl. Kate slipped on her jacket.

"Living here in this old place seems to suit you, Addie."

Addie looked around, noticing that the house could use a fresh coat of paint and some repair to a few pieces of the trim around the windows. The gravel drive was pocked with puddles and the henhouse seemed a little saggy. The barn, too, was old and a far cry from the beautiful new metal barns that some of the Amish around town were erecting.

"I guess it does," she said at last. "To be honest, I never even think about living someplace else. I never noticed any of its faults. All I saw was home."

"That's the difference between the two of us, I guess. You see home, and I saw a place that I couldn't wait to leave."

"You were really that unhappy here? Was it because you didn't want to be Amish or because of Mommi and Dawdi?"

"Oh, boy. Maybe it was a little bit of both." Kate shrugged. "Back then I was unhappy with everything. I realize now that I was unhappy with myself most of all. That, in the end, was why I left. I was searching for another side of myself. Searching for a part of me that I could love as much as the dream of what I wanted . . ." Her voice drifted off. "Boy, I'm not making a lick of sense, am I?"

"No, I think you are. When Daniel and I first started talking and getting to know each other, I wasn't very happy with myself, either. For some reason, I had started looking at the blessings in my life as liabilities."

"Did Daniel change your mind?"

"Yes, but it wasn't just him. It was a lot of things. It was realizing that I might not have had parents, but I had a wonderful grandmother. That I might not have had a lot of friends, but I did have a lot of people in my life who cared about me. I might have an unusual pet, but he is a really good one. That the Lord hadn't given me obstacles to overcome; He had given me opportunities to appreciate."

"I'm so sorry that you suffered so much because of my faults."

Addie had experienced some difficult times, but she couldn't neatly place all the blame on a missing mother. Some of her low self-esteem had come from her mother leaving her at her grandmother's house, but some of it was simply part of her makeup. She was, by nature, a person who liked to please and help others. When that didn't seem to matter to young people her own age, she'd dwelt on the negatives instead of the positives. She'd been that way as long as she could remember.

Addie turned to face her mother. "I don't think we should apologize to each other for things we can't change."

"We certainly can't change the past, can we?"

"I don't want to anymore, either."

"Me neither." Addie smiled. "Are you ready to meet Snickers now?"

"I am."

Snickers perked up when Addie opened the door and walked over to the edge of his stall. Eager to see him, she opened the gate. "Are you afraid of horses, Kate?"

"No. Not at all." She lowered her voice and held out her hand. "Hiya, Snickers. I'm Kate."

Snickers whickered, took a few steps forward, then nudged her hand with his nose. Kate gently rubbed his nose, then ran a hand along the side of the donkey's head.

"You're a sweetheart, ain't so?"

When Snickers brayed his agreement, Kate laughed.

Addie smiled at her. "I think he's just given you his approval."

"I'm glad. One day I hope to be able to be in your life, too. That's my dream. It's been my secret dream for years now."

At last, she let go of the hurt she'd been carrying. "You are welcome to be in my life, Kate."

Her mother shook her head. "I know you are a sweetheart, but you're letting me off too easy. Addie, I'm going to prove myself. I'm going to become someone you can trust and depend on. Even if it takes years, I'm going to do whatever it takes for you to want to know me."

Kate's words were incredible. They were also humbling. But they weren't needed. Addie didn't want or need her mother to jump through hoops to be worthy of her.

She shook her head. "I don't need any of that. I just need you to want to be in my life."

"Do you really think it can be that simple?"

"I think it must be. I've learned lately that making something as wonderful as love into something that's complicated and difficult is wrong. After all, love should be freely given, right?"

Her mother nodded. "Addie, could I . . . could I give you a hug?"

"I would like that."

Her mother gently enfolded her in a sweet embrace. She curved her arms around Addie, held her close. And in those few seconds, everything fell into place again.

Addie felt loved and cared for and wanted.

Closing her eyes, she gave thanks.

Chapter 33

Six months later

"A note came for you, Addie," Kate said as she walked into Addie's bedroom carrying a breakfast tray.

Still groggy from sleep, Addie sat up and brushed her hair away from her face. She saw her mother wearing tan slacks, a pretty navy oxford cloth shirt, and tan flats. Her hair—so like Addie's—was pulled up into a high ponytail. It made her look as young as she was—a thirty-six-year-old woman who'd had a baby when she was still a teenager.

Blinking again, Addie became aware of the loaded tray in Kate's hands—and the delicious aroma that was filling her bedroom. "Oh, my word. Is that coffee?"

Kate approached her bed and set the tray on Addie's bedside table. "It's about time you noticed," she teased. "I've brought you coffee, chocolate muffins, raspberries, and orange juice."

"It looks amazing. Thank you!"

"You're very welcome, though I doubt the coffee and

muffins will compare to what else is on this tray." She held up a white envelope. "You received a letter from your bridegroom this morning."

"Daniel was here?"

"Indeed he was." She winked. "He was looking very bright-eyed, too."

"I hope you and Mommi didn't tell him I was still in bed."

"Of course we did! Your grandmother thought Daniel might need to be prepared for the fact that his future wife sometimes needs a lazy morning."

Addie covered her face. "I can't believe she told him that."

"Don't worry. Daniel said he came over early so you wouldn't see him. Seeing each other before the ceremony is bad luck, you know."

Addie sat up straighter and arranged her sheets and quilt around herself. Then she held out her hands for the cup of coffee her mother had just poured for her. "*Danke*. There was no need to go to so much trouble, though."

"Of course there is. It's your wedding day and every bride-to-be needs to be pampered a bit. Or have you forgotten that already?"

"I haven't forgotten, but you didn't need to go to so much trouble."

"I told Mamm that every girl needs to be served breakfast in bed at least once in her life."

Addie winced. "I bet she had something to say about that." Lovina Stutzman most definitely did not believe in lazing about sipping coffee while other people waited on her.

"Oh, she did, but Mamm did unbend enough to say that I might have a point."

"You might, hmm?"

"Of course, your grandmother was determined to give you fried eggs and toast."

Addie shuddered. "I couldn't imagine sitting in bed eating

fried eggs. I can barely eat them at the table. How did you win that point?"

"Easily . . . I reminded her that you served her all kinds of wonderful-*gut* meals during her recovery. And that I just happen to make really good chocolate muffins." She set the tray down on the bed beside her. "So, how are you doing, Miss Addie-Bride-To-Be? Are you nervous? Happy? Excited?"

"I think I'm everything." Honestly, she was overwhelmed with joy. Not only did she now have her mother in her life and she was about to marry Daniel, but practically everyone in Apple Creek was attending their wedding. So many people had called on her to offer their best wishes and support. Some people had even wanted to see Snickers. The Lord had been so good.

But she was still a little nervous about the upcoming ceremony.

"Do you think it's normal to feel so many things at one time?"

Her mother nodded. "I know it is. I've always thought that big days demand big feelings."

"I do have those. I love Daniel so much." She covered her mouth, embarrassed that she'd just gushed about her future husband like that. "Sorry."

But instead of smirking, Kate's expression softened. "Oh, honey, don't you be embarrassed about that. I wish every bride sounded so giddy on her wedding day." Bending down, she lightly kissed Addie's brow. "Enjoy your breakfast—and your letter."

"Thank you, Mamm." It was the very first time she'd called Kate that—well, since she'd been just four years old. It felt like the right moment, though.

Kate froze. "Oh . . . now you're going to make me cry. I'm getting out of here before I make a mess of myself." She paused. "But please, you linger in bed for a while, okay? You're going to have only one wedding day. Enjoy it."

Addie felt her heart swell as her mother went out the door, taking the time to close it despite her hurry.

It was little things like that that had made Addie appreciate having Kate in her life so much. She was younger and saw life in a brighter light than her grandmother. That luminosity had been transferred to Addie—helping her look at things the same way.

After taking a sip of coffee and a bite of the still-warm muffin, Addie picked up her letter. It was in the same plain white business envelope as the others had arrived in. On the front of the envelope was written her name.

She couldn't help but smile at it. She didn't know if she'd ever be able to see her name on an envelope again without thinking about all those letters she and Daniel had exchanged.

After another bite of muffin, she opened the envelope and pulled out the note.

> *Dear Addie,*
>
> *Happy Wedding Day. Tonight, when I close my eyes, you will be my wife. I know when I say my prayers, I will wonder what I have done for the Lord to give me such a tremendous gift.*
>
> *That is what you are, Addie. A gift.*
>
> *When I started writing you, I wanted to help you see how much you were valued. I wanted you to realize how much I valued how unique you were. But now I understand that you always were those things—I just had to catch up.*
>
> *Even more humbling was the way you made me feel special and valued, too. Your honest*

words and fresh way of seeing the world encouraged me to be that way, too. Your selfless spirit made me want to do more for other people. And your bravery during the past tumultuous weeks inspired me to be braver. You, Adelaide, are beautiful inside. Don't ever forget that.

I promise to do my best for you. I'll always put you first. I'll always appreciate you. I'll always love you, Addie.

See you soon.

Daniel

Tears pricked her eyes as she neatly folded his letter and carefully set it under her pillow. She'd pack it in her bag and eventually add it to the stack of other letters Daniel had sent. Thinking about the future, she imagined telling her children about their parents' courtship. She could only guess how they would respond to hearing the tale! It really did sound like a fairy tale-where else would one read about a courting couple exchanging letters in a hollowed-out tree trunk? It was fanciful, indeed.

Still imagining the conversation, she finished the muffin and washed it down with her cup of coffee. Wondered if, perhaps, such things were better left as a secret.

But then she realized how much good had come out of the courtship. Not just their relationship, but also the personal growth they'd both experienced.

Maybe their future children needed to know that sometimes things happen that one can't predict. That were beyond one's wildest dreams.

Maybe one of them was going to need to hear a fairy-tale romance to believe that good things still happened to good people. Maybe one of their daughters was going to need to know that knights in shining armor and romantic princes didn't always wear crowns or ride fancy, white, high-stepping horses. Sometimes they were Amish and drove a buggy.

She wanted to be sure to give her future children—her daughters, especially—hope that even if one was Old Order Amish and lived in a tiny town like Apple Creek, it was okay to dream about living happily ever after.

Addie giggled. They would just be happily ever Amish.

It was silly, she knew. But maybe that was what wedding days were for. Fanciful thoughts and romance and love.

After all, this moment in time would never come again.